CAT STEP

Alison Irvine

dead ink

First published in Great Britain in 2020 by Dead Ink, an imprint of
Cinder House Publishing Limited.
ISBN 978-1-911585-62-6

Cover design by Luke Bird
lukebird.co.uk
Cover photgraphy by Tal Heres at Unsplash

Printed and bound in Great Britain by Clays Ltd, Elcograf S.p.A.

www.deadinkbooks.com

CAT STEP

Alison Irvine

dead ink

For Jan and Vic

Part One

I.

Emily will ask me one day about Lennoxtown. She may discover that she and I lived there briefly when she was on the cusp of four and five and I'll need to have answers when she asks me why we didn't stay. I'll tell her something of the story. She'll believe me because I'm her mum. By then I may have made sense of her dad.

The truth is Emily and I danced a *demi-detourné*. We stepped up to Lennoxtown then turned away from it, a half turn, even changing feet so that a new foot was in front. Yet there was no ballerina's precision or elegance; it was ugly.

Lennoxtown is hard to turn away from, I'll give it that. Those hills. You catch them as you come round a bend, half submerged in cloud or crossed with sun and shadow or shining with the gold that comes off the grass you get up there. I imagined us climbing them, the Campsie Fells, picnicking, exploring, lying out in good air. But we came in March and winter wasn't over and it rained and rained and my plans didn't work out.

There was one thing I could have done differently. My mum said I should leave Emily with her and go alone – have a break, live a little, earn some money if there was any to be earned – and I nearly accepted, I nearly thought it the most sensible of all the options I had. I paused – *en l'air* – *extension* – and then took her with me.

I use ballet terms but I was never a ballerina. I did the training and I almost had the technique, but not the physique or that extra porcelain quality. I was a dancer, a very good dancer: a tapper, a hoofer, a high-kicker. I wore feathers and sequins and American Tan tights and travelled the world on cruise ships. I will tell Emily that.

This is what I won't tell her: she had been awake between the hours of two and three the night before, crying and thrashing with a temperature and a sore head. I gave her paracetamol and put a cold flannel on her forehead and thought if we ever got back to sleep it would do us good to lie long into the morning. But she woke at six and although she was calmer she was weak and didn't want anything other than television. In the end she didn't even want that. I tried to curl up with her on my bed and help her get back to sleep but she wouldn't settle.

We had nothing in. The bread was gone, the milk was off. She liked fish fingers, and I knew if we drove to the Co-op I could buy some fish fingers and more milk and bread and she would fall asleep on the way home. I knew it would work for her. It always had.

I told her she could wear her dressing gown over her nightie and I'd buy her a treat. I brushed her hair but I didn't wash her face or clean her teeth. I found her wellies because they were easy to put on and I tied her dressing gown. See how I'm telling it? I had to tell it in this detail many times to many people.

I'd forgotten about the roadworks and the temporary traffic lights and of course by the time the lights turned green Emily was asleep. I wondered if I should drive straight home but I had a queue of cars behind me so I had to go on and once I was through the roadworks I was two minutes from the Co-op and we did need fish fingers and milk and bread and other things I'd remembered like toilet roll and toothpaste. So I made the decision to go on.

I couldn't get a space close to the entrance so we parked at the back of the car park under the fir trees where the crows had their nests. When I cut the engine I thought the sudden lack of noise might wake her as it often did, but it didn't. I turned in my seat and checked her. Her lips were parted. Her cheeks were red. She'd kicked off her wellies and peeled her socks from her feet and I could see black hairs on her shins. I thought about carrying her in, but it would have woken her and, God, to wake a sleeping child – an ill child at that – and then drive for hours afterwards trying to get her back to sleep was not an option. I have driven around with her fighting sleep as if it was death closing down on her.

I opened a window to give her an inch of air. I locked the car. I ran to the Co-op. Perhaps I was longer than the few minutes I thought I'd taken. How long does it take to pick up milk, bread, fish fingers and toilet roll? And a slab of chocolate. And cheese and toothpaste. And a Freddo for her treat. I told the woman at the checkout that I didn't need a bag – and then I changed my mind, so I watched her pack my bag, gave her my Co-op card, paid for my shopping and ran from the shop.

When I came out of the Co-op I saw there were people standing by my car looking towards a running boy. Cap, jeans, red top, that's all I saw: the sprinting back of him and the flailing soles of his trainers. Something had happened.

'There was a thief,' a woman said. 'He's run off. We know who he is. Greg's talking to the police.' She pointed to a man who was on his phone, pacing. The man looked at me as he spoke and then turned away towards the traffic on Main Street.

I needed to check Emily.

'He's a menace,' the man said, off his phone and making me listen. He pushed his hair back with both hands, shoved his phone into his pocket, adrenalin, urgency all over him.

'But the car's not even fancy,' I said.

'You left something on your front seat.'

I'd left my phone. I'd put it on the passenger seat to save me carrying it in. The window was smashed but not shattered. Emily was asleep. Fast asleep. She'd slept through it.

'You can't leave anything in your car round here,' the man said. 'There's a ring of them. They'll steal it and sell it on.'

'At this time of the morning?' I said, which struck me as an odd thing to say but it was too early to have my car broken into, surely? The sky was weak, the crows were barely awake and the clock on the sandstone church behind us showed only half past eight.

I looked at the people around me. The man and two women, one with a dog on a lead. I checked on Emily again. She was unhurt. My phone was still on the seat, the window could be fixed. These people had stepped in to help me.

'Thank you,' I said.

Nothing. They looked at Emily and then at me.

'You left her in the car by herself,' one of the women said. Her dog pulled on its lead and barked at another dog across the car park. She told it to sit and in the same tone of voice said to me, 'Anything could have happened.'

'She was asleep,' I said.

'That's even worse.'

I sensed the fullness of her judgement, in increments, like the gradual lightening of the morning.

The other woman spoke. 'My niece is a social worker. She tells me this is a problem with some parents. You know it's against the law?'

I unlocked the car and opened the boot and put my shopping down.

'Please don't make me feel guilty. She's not well. She's been up all night. I know my daughter.'

'And look at her legs. Look at what you can see. Does she even have underwear on?' The woman peered through the window at Emily.

I got angry then and when I turned my head I felt the shooting stars I'd been having for days. I told them to get away from the window and of course she had underwear on but when I checked at home, she didn't. She wasn't indecent, she was covered, even though her dressing gown had ridden up to her thighs, but they will have used that against me too, that her legs were exposed.

'I'm taking my daughter home now,' I said and went to open my door. 'She's ill. I know what's best.'

'Don't touch the door!' the man shouted. 'That's the police here now.' He raised a hand and beckoned the police car to where we stood. 'You'll have to stay. They'll want statements from us. They might be able to get the little shite if they have enough evidence.'

The woman with the dog nodded and told her dog to stay.

The police, one man and one woman, asked whose car it was. I said it was mine which was almost true. They didn't need to know it was my mum's. They must have seen Emily asleep but they made no comment. The policewoman took a notebook and pen from her pocket and wrote. Voices crackled through their radios.

The man gave a description of a kid aged eighteen or nineteen. 'I know who he is, I know his name.' He seemed desperate to get him arrested.

'Did anyone else see him?'

They nodded.

'You?' the policewoman asked me.

'The back of him.'

She made me describe what I saw then asked if anything was stolen.

'No,' I said.

'I got to him before he could take anything,' the man said.

They asked for our names and addresses, they took phone numbers. I told the police more than I'd told anyone in the whole time we'd been in Lennoxtown; that I was living in one of the houses at the foot of the Campsies, Audrey Watt's old flat; that I was there for a month or two to clear it and sell it on behalf of her family who were dead or far flung.

Emily slept on. I noticed people in the car park looking at us. I put my hand in my pocket and felt for my keys.

'I'd like to go now,' I said.

'We're just finishing up,' the policeman said.

The policewoman pressed her fingers to the crack in the glass. 'She can't drive with the window like that.'

'I'll get it fixed.'

'It's not safe to drive.'

'But I need to go. She's not well.'

The police looked at Emily asleep in the car.

'I'll get it fixed. I won't touch it.'

The woman's dog barked again and strained against its lead.

'She could wind the window all the way down,' the policeman said to his colleague.

They looked at Emily.

'Do that,' the policewoman said. 'And get it seen to right away.'

I was climbing into the car when one of the women said, 'I want to report something else.' She looked at me and then turned her body away from me.

I sat down and listened for the sound of Emily's breath. I heard her soft snores. I heard a bus coming down Main Street and crows cawing from high branches. I felt the tingling stars in my head again. And then I knew I was being looked at so I stepped out of the car and faced them.

'Is this true?' the policewoman said.

'That I left Emily in the car? Yes,' I said.

'I'm not saying this to get her in trouble but anything could have happened, it was a dangerous situation.' The woman was agitated and tears were in her eyes. She squeezed her fingers as she told the police that they had watched the car for five, ten minutes, with Emily alone in it. It wasn't ten minutes.

'Is this true?' the policewoman said again.

'It wasn't ten minutes.'

The policewoman turned to a fresh page in her notebook.

'I'll pop in and get the paper,' the man said to the woman with the dog. He said goodbye to the police and walked backwards a few steps, pointing his finger at me. 'They'll catch him. Mind you don't leave anything in your car.' I think he was talking about my phone.

Emily was still asleep.

'She was sick,' I said to the policewoman. I hated how feeble my voice sounded.

'It is an offence to leave a child unattended in a car.'

'I've never done it before.' That was a lie. A straight lie.

'What if he'd stolen the car?' said the woman.

'Why are you still here?' I said and I hated her. I hated Lennoxtown, the rain that accompanied the blustery wind, the stupid kid in trainers who'd tried to steal my phone so early in the morning, and I hated my stupid self. I watched the policewoman's pen as she made notes. I watched her eyes, saw her turn to her colleague to talk privately.

The woman's dog yapped.

'Give us a few minutes please,' the policewoman said to the two women. 'Then we'll take your statements.'

She turned to me and I was no longer the victim of a crime, I was the perpetrator. I saw the cold switch in her eyes and no matter what I said – *she needed to stay asleep, I was gone for all of three minutes* – I felt loathed by her.

'We could prosecute you,' she said.

'Why?'

'Because you've committed an offence.'

'But there was no harm done. Look at her.'

'You committed an offence all the same.'

She studied me, then consulted with her colleague, then studied me again. It was quiet in the car park with the crows in the tree tops and the church looming on the high hill and the bystanders waiting their turn to talk.

'Expect a call from social services,' she said. 'And we'll be in touch about the attempted theft. You can go.'

It felt like a punch. I closed the car door and wished for consolation from someone who knew me – my mum, Robbie, someone, anybody – but there was only Emily and she was

9

asleep. As soon as I started the engine Emily woke and said in her straightforward way, as if she'd never slept, 'Mummy, there's a taxi.' She was right. Driving along Main Street was a Glasgow taxi, a black cab, like they have in London, and I thought someone must have paid a fortune to come all the way from the city to Lennoxtown in that.

While I waited to turn out of the car park, I glanced into my rear-view mirror and saw the police talking to the two women. The man was standing next to them holding a newspaper. I stretched my left hand behind me, felt for Emily's leg and gave it a squeeze.

'You didn't see any of that did you? You didn't hear anything in the car park?' I noticed the hardness in my voice.

'Any of what?' she said. 'I'm hungry, Mummy, is there something for me to eat?'

2.

The doctor checked Emily's ears, her lungs and her heart and as soon as she checked her throat she diagnosed tonsillitis and gave her penicillin. I was pleased her heart was okay. We had to register as new patients in the surgery above the library. From the waiting room I saw the Co-op and the parking bay where the bystanders and police had surrounded my car. I saw the steep sides of the Campsies and the main road that lay like a line drawn from east to west at the foot of the hills. Our flat was off this main road, on one of a cluster of streets that curled into dead ends or abutted fences and farmland. Ours was a street of cream coloured houses and flats on whose external walls the windows seemed strangely small, as if built intentionally to shut out the glare of the sweeping sky. From our living room window, because we were a floor up, we had a good view of all that sky and looked down on hedges and paved driveways.

Later that day I let Emily lie on the sofa with the television on and I stood outside, cold without a jacket, while a glazier fixed my car window. Was it wise of me to leave Emily in the flat while I was on the pavement below – I don't know – but there was only one of me and I didn't leave her long anyway. I left the front door open. She could have come down the stairs and found me.

'It's a safe area, really. You were unlucky,' the man said. Then he turned to look at the Campsies. 'You can almost feel them breathe from here.' The cloud was high and grey and the muted burgundies and browns of the hillside gave the afternoon a peaceful feel. I told him of Emily's frustration at the fenced-off field at the end of a cul de sac around the corner.

'Take the Crow Road out of Lennoxtown,' he said. 'You'll get a good run up there.'

I said I would.

He told me his office would call to take payment from my card. I tried not to think about money.

After he drove away I stood on Audrey's doorstep, our temporary home, and looked into the windows of surrounding houses. I saw no one, only curtains or blinds or reflections of clouds. I liked living this close to the Campsies. I liked the way the hills reared up from the backs of gardens and almost smothered us with green, so unlike the bricks and cluttered rooftops of our old street in London. I liked the fir trees that lined the foot of the fells too, and thought the cool air under their branches would be good to smell.

I didn't expect the utter isolation. Not a person spoke to me. People must have known Audrey. She'd lived in the same flat for decades, yet her neighbours didn't seem curious about us, not even the man who lived below. I thought someone would want to poke around the rooms, asking to keep items of hers that perhaps she'd promised them or taken loan of and never returned. But no. This is what we came for – it's what I wanted, I reminded myself and climbed the stairs from the front door to Emily.

She was sleeping. Strands of her hair were caught in the corner of her mouth so I picked them free and put the backs of my fingers to her hot cheeks. I squeezed myself next to her on the sofa and pulled her towards me so her head lay in my lap. Her fringe needed a cut. I wished I had scissors – I knew where they were, they were in the kitchen drawer – but I didn't have them or a pen or a book or anything useful so I watched CBeebies, the sound from the television so low I could barely catch the words. It was a rest.

Then Emily lifted a hot hand and touched my chin.

'You're awake. Hello.'

'My throat is sore.'

'Poor Emily. Can you eat anything?'

She shook her head. I helped her sit so her body was curled into my side and her head was on my shoulder. We stayed that way, watching the near-silent television. I stroked her thin arm and she rested her hand against my chest. Her cuddles were soft when she was sick and I felt a little guilty at preferring them. Usually, she fidgeted or elbowed me accidentally or pulled at my ear lobes. For a shy child she was demanding.

The doctor had told me to keep her hydrated even if she wouldn't eat anything, so I helped her sip from a cup of water. It wasn't nice to see her grimace. Her fingers touched her throat and I felt bad for her.

'Shall I put you in my bed on my cold sheets?' I said.

'Will you lie with me?'

If I lay down I'd fall asleep. 'I will for a bit,' I said.

I carried her to my bed in Audrey's room and lay close to her. Not so close that I would heat her up but close enough to cradle her head in the crook of my arm.

Then I remembered. She might wet the bed.

'Do you need a wee?'

'No, Mummy.'

'Can you try?'

'I don't need to.'

'Please. Please. I'll carry you.' All the rooms in Audrey's flat led off the one corridor so nothing was far.

'No.' She curled her body into a ball and because she was in the middle of the bed she was hard to move. I tugged on her arm and she yanked it away.

'Please, Emily, just get up now and then that's it, you can sleep.'

'I'm tired.'

'I know, but come on, Emily.'

You mustn't tell them they'll wet the bed, you mustn't mention bed-wetting ever, but she would have, she would have. I got my hands around her body, under her legs and her back and pulled her to the edge of the bed. I don't think I was rough. I was firm. She kicked me and tried to wriggle out of my arms but I managed to pick her up and carry her to the toilet. She cried and pushed against my chest. 'I don't want to do this either,' I said. Ludicrous, to fight with an ill child. Finally, I got her on the toilet seat.

'What a lot of fuss.'

We waited. I kneeled on Audrey's pink bath mat and noticed the dirt at the back of the cistern.

'I miss my old bedroom.' Emily's chin dipped to her chest.

I don't know why I was surprised. 'Why?' I said.

'I miss my toys.'

'They'll be there when we get back.'

'And I miss my granny.'

She missed my mum. Of course she did. She cried the sad tears of an ill girl and I told her everything I could conjure about why we were better in Lennoxtown. 'This is a holiday. There's a road called Crow Road; we'll see what's at the top. There might be crows. Mummy and Emily are having a break.' I didn't tell her that I knew my mum needed a break from us. She blew her nose on the toilet paper I gave her then she closed her eyes and rested her head on my shoulder. Perhaps I should never have put her on the toilet. I should have let her fall asleep on my bed and lifted her like I did when she was a toddler.

'Nothing coming.'

'We're here now. Can you have another try?'

'I don't need one.'

'Count to twenty.'

While she was counting and I was kneeling with my hands on her knees the doorbell rang. Nobody had rung the doorbell before.

'Who's that?' I said.

'Is it Granny?'

'No, it won't be Granny.'

'Is it a tiger?'

'Probably not.'

The doorbell rang again and I heard the letter box open.

I put my finger to my lips. 'Shush, Emily.'

There was a woman's voice. 'Is anybody home? I'm looking for Liz Morley.'

'Can I get off the toilet?' Emily whispered.

'Wait. Shush.'

'Why aren't we answering the door?'

Her eyes were excited. I pretended it was a game. I couldn't explain why we weren't answering the door. I heard my mobile phone ringing and hoped the woman at the door didn't hear it too. There were three hard raps, then there was silence. The trickle of Emily's wee came soon after.

'Good girl! Good girl!' I passed her some toilet paper and we washed her hands.

I carried her into my bed and pulled the duvet to her waist.

'Mummy, can you cuddle me?'

'Wait a second.' I'm selfish, I know. I picked up my phone.

There was a message from a social worker called Sara. 'I came round to talk about the incident in the car park this morning. The police have passed me your details. I just need a wee check-in with you and your daughter.' She left a number. I turned my phone off. Fuck. A social worker. My first phone call, my first knock at the door, from a social worker.

'You'll feel better tomorrow,' I told Emily and kissed her forehead.

I'm angry at the social worker even now for spoiling that sleep of Emily's, for getting in the way of me and her on what was a peaceful, docile afternoon, because the whole time I was patting Emily's shoulder and singing her a lullaby I wasn't really concentrating on her or the words I sang. I was thinking about the police and the bystanders and the social worker and I was frightened. Emily fell asleep with her mummy hardly aware of her, and I can't say that was the first time either.

3.

Within days she was better and hurling herself onto the sofa or bumping down the stairs to Audrey's front door. She rolled herself up in the living room rug then yelled to be let out. I found it funny the first time. She made a mess in the rooms, trying on shoes and scarves, attempting to help while not helping at all, you know what children are like.

Our time in Lennoxtown was always supposed to have been brief: two months, no more. We should have cleared the flat and got it ready to sell and we should have done other things too. Spotted daffodils. Hunted for tadpoles. Explored the forests and fells. But it was still howling winter when we got there and I was worried about all the time I would spend on my own with Emily. She wasn't an easy girl. We were in a dead lady's house with three built-in wardrobes and a floor-to-ceiling cupboard full of possessions to clear. Each day I looked at her jumble of stuff and didn't know where to start. Honestly, I couldn't think straight with Emily around me all the time. So that's why I did what I did. I cut her fringe, enrolled her in the local nursery and began to look for work. Robbie would have called me an eejit. Robbie was Audrey Watt's grandson and Emily's dad. He's the real reason we came to Lennoxtown.

Emily didn't want to go to nursery despite the trays of sand and water and the play-dough that the children made fresh each morning. She didn't like the noise. My mum said nursery would be good for Emily's shyness and I agreed, although she wasn't shy in the house, that's for sure. I didn't tell my mum about the police and the social worker's knock at the door.

The nursery staff told me they'd had girls like Emily before and picked her up and walked away with her. Go, they told me. I waited in the parents' room, listening for her cries, wondering if it was worth it – I could have cleared a kitchen cupboard in the time I spent waiting. So I made calls about my benefits, calls to the Salvation Army to offer them Audrey's furniture and calls to dancing schools and care homes to see if they wanted a temporary dance teacher.

When I came into the playroom at the end of each morning's settling in, Emily clung to my legs and cried. The women told me she cried frequently if they moved away from her to wipe a spill or fix another child's apron. 'She's a sensitive wee soul,' they said. 'She has a wee voice that's hard to hear.' I didn't recognise this child. 'She watched some children playing in the house corner. She didn't join in but observing other children is a good start.' I should have taken her out there and then, not only because she hated it but because as well as observing Emily, they were observing me.

I didn't take her out of the nursery. She stayed in the playroom for longer periods. I went home for an hour, emptied a set of drawers, loaded black sacks into the car and sorted through Audrey's stuff for relics to keep or sell.

During one of those hours I let the estate agent in to knock his knuckles on the walls and assess the decor. He took the stairs two at a time and ignored the piles of magazines and cardboard boxes I'd put on each step.

'Campsie view,' he said with his head out of Audrey's bedroom window. 'That will help.' He closed the window and told me there were things I could do to make the flat sell quickly or at a higher price, like clear the front garden, paint the walls, perhaps even re-plaster if I was inclined. 'Put a bed in here or get a table and show it off as a dining room,' he said of Audrey's spare room. The Salvation Army had lifted her table and chairs only the day before. 'Spend a couple of hundred to make a couple of thousand,' he said. I saw the flat as he saw it: forlorn and dated with worn-down floors and cracks in the walls. The living room was nice, he told us. We liked that room too. And the kitchen. It had a view of the neighbouring gardens and the fenced-off fellside.

I could clean cupboards but I had no money to spend on redecorating. Audrey's grandson and Robbie's brother Aidan lived in Australia. He told me to go ahead with the work – the plastering and painting.

'How do I to pay for it?' I asked.

'Get bank details and I'll pay them from here. I'll try and find someone who can do the lot.'

I forgot Aidan was still connected in Lennoxtown, that there were people he'd been to school with living in the village still, who knew them all, the whole family.

'I'll put some extra money into your account too,' he said. 'You're doing me a favour.'

I was cheaper than an air fare, he'd said, right in the first phone call, when he'd told me their granny had died and he didn't want to come back. He would rather it happened without him stepping foot in Scotland.

'Only if you can handle it, mind,' he'd said to me.

'We'll be fine.'

I sorted Audrey's belongings into piles for the charity shop and piles for Gumtree. I kept her jewellery and some photographs to send to Australia. Any cash I made from the Gumtree sales I put in a vase and used for expenses. I told Aidan I would give him what was left. The Salvation Army returned to pick up two chests of drawers and a cabinet.

My mum phoned. 'Have you got anything to sit on? Tell me you kept some furniture back?'

I told her we had a small sofa and a matching armchair.

'What's her house like?'

'It's cold, Mum. I keep the heating on.' I looked around me at the rectangles of clean wallpaper I'd exposed when I took her picture frames down. Emily had a few toys and I'd stuck some of her nursery drawings to the walls, but it didn't feel like our home, because nothing was ours and the bulky things of the house, the big units that stopped the echoes, were gone.

'How long will you be?'

'A few more weeks.'

'I could take some holiday?'

'No. Don't waste your leave.'

She said no more. I knew she wanted to go to Spain to stay in her partner's timeshare.

'How is Alan?'

'He's well, thank you.'

'I've been trying to get some classes,' I said.

'Teaching? I thought you weren't staying long.'

'I'm not. But it's something I can do so I might as well do it.'

'Does it pay well?'

'Probably not.'

'Make sure you eat. Tell me if you get unstuck.' I heard her breathe. 'This is bold, what you're doing, Liz. And brave.'

'It is.'

'But you've made it difficult for yourself.'

'I had nothing to lose.' I think I offended her. I think I was wrong.

She asked about Audrey. 'Did anyone go to her funeral?'

'Friends from her luncheon club, I think. Aidan didn't go. I should visit her grave.'

'Only if it won't upset you. How's Emily? Where's Emily?'

I looked at Emily's pyjamas on the floor and her scattered crayons.

'At nursery. She misses you.'

'Of course she misses me.'

'Do you miss us?'

'Of course I do.'

'There's nothing of him, Mum, no pictures, nothing.'

'Some people are like that,' my mum said.

She was at work. She had to get off the phone because her boss wanted a word.

Twice I avoided the doorbell and heard the social worker's calm voice calling me through the letter box. I convinced myself it would end soon; denial is a trait of mine. I didn't need a social worker. If I ignored her for long enough she would move to a more pressing case; there were plenty of them. So I kept the curtains closed. One sunny afternoon, in the way a cat would, Emily stuck her head and then her whole body behind the curtains and sat on the window sill looking down at the street. I called her back. That's how we lived.

After a week, I chanced it. I asked the nursery staff how long I had. 'We'll try the full morning this time,' they said and although Emily cried when I kissed her goodbye and her keyworker had to lift her up and carry her away to the play-dough table with her arms stretched towards me, I left her. I ignored the shooting stars in my head. They would pass, like everything.

4.

The sheltered housing was a five-minute drive from Lennoxtown past farmland and a Lidl. I told myself I could do my shopping before the class so I would achieve something even if the dancing didn't go well. The Campsie Fells were in sight the whole time, or at least they were at the back of me, which felt promising because they were the only thing I liked about Lennoxtown.

'Let's see if there are any tenants around,' the manager said. Her name was Ruth. She worked in an office with her back to the window and looked after the upkeep of the concrete blocks and the letting of the one and two-bedroom flats. She took me along a plain corridor to the lounge. I've never seen so many sideboards in one room. There were framed photographs on the walls and vases of fabric flowers on the tables. A radio played a song I knew Emily liked. The room was okay – better than the corridor. In a kitchenette off the lounge two women unloaded a dishwasher.

'Your timing is perfect. They were talking about setting up some kind of exercise class,' Ruth said. 'Zumba. Although I think that's a bit energetic.' She looked over at the two women in the kitchenette who passed the sunlit doorway holding crockery and tea towels.

'My class would be ballet-based,' I said. 'And I'd drop in a bit of contemporary too.' They didn't need to know my body was the wrong shape and my technique not quite sharp enough for ballet. I could teach a class.

'It'll come down to how we sell it to them. Don't say contemporary, they won't understand.'

I looked around and worked out that I would need to move the tables to the sides of the room and make a line of chairs to form a barre.

Ruth called the women over to us. They came with their tea towels in their hands and I noticed that one of the women walked with turned out feet.

'June, Eve,' the manager said. 'This is Liz. She's a dancer. If I book her in, will you come to her class?'

'Not me,' one of the women said. 'I don't do dancing.' She folded her tea towel.

The other one, the one with turned out feet said, 'I never took to dancing.'

'Are you sure?' I said and I pointed at her feet. 'Because your toes are turned out, look, and your posture is good.'

She stared at me as if I'd told her a lie.

Ruth shook her head. 'I have a note on my desk to book an exercise class and here we are with a real-life dancer in front of us.'

I smiled.

The woman with the folded tea towel said, 'It wasn't me. I wanted to do painting.'

'I can't paint,' I said. 'So it's dancing or nothing.'

'Nothing then.'

Ruth said, 'Okay, Eve,' and then she turned to the other woman and said, 'June, can you remember who it was who wanted an exercise class?'

'It might have been Senga.' June looked straight at me. 'What kind of dancing?'

'Ballet, mostly.'

'Is that what you are, a ballerina?' Her chin tilted up when she spoke.

I shook my head. 'I used to work on cruise ships. Show dances. Tap and jazz, that kind of thing.'

That interested them. They asked questions about where I'd been so I told them some places: Miami, Dominica, Barbados. The woman, Eve, had a daughter in Toronto. 'Have you been there?' she asked and seemed disappointed when I told her I hadn't.

'But I've been to New York,' I said.

'What are you doing here then?' June surprised me with her forthrightness. I looked at Ruth, unsure of what to say.

'I could do with the money,' I said. 'And I like dancing.'

'Why don't you audition for the pantos and that?'

'It's March. The panto season is over.'

June nodded and I stood there, waiting for someone to speak.

'I have a daughter,' I said. 'So I can't travel far or do evening jobs like pantos.'

That softened their mouths. We shared details of our children. 'I have two children and four grandchildren, two girls and two boys,' Eve said, 'and not one lives in Scotland.'

'I have two grandchildren, a girl and a boy,' June said and blinked.

There were footsteps from outside in the corridor. Ruth beckoned some people into the lounge and introduced me. They stared, all of them, two men and a woman, studying me. I stood straighter. I was taller than most of them, even the men.

'Are we doing it now?' the woman asked. 'I've got a taxi waiting. I can't do it now.'

'What kind of dancing?' a man said. They were so sceptical, so buttoned-up.

I put my handbag on the floor and stepped away from them. I lifted my right leg and grabbed hold of my foot. Then I stretched my leg so that I was doing the standing splits and raised my left hand for balance. 'Ta-da!' I said.

That rattled them. That made them laugh. 'Bravo,' a man said. The woman who was waiting for a taxi said, 'You'll have us all at Stobhill.'

'What's Stobhill?'

'Infirmary.'

'You're not from here, are you?' June asked.

'No.' I bent to pick up my handbag. 'Right, a fiver a class. You'd lose that on a lottery ticket. Try it once and see if you like it.'

'I'm not a gambler,' one of the men said.

'What day?' June asked.

Ruth told them she would speak to me then put up a sign.

'As long as it's not too hard, I'll come along,' June said, looking at me. 'Although I've never been one for dancing.'

The others said they might come.

'Wear comfortable clothes. Tie your hair back. Don't wear your pearls. Bring water.'

That was it. We left the lounge with its photographs and sideboards, and the radio still playing, and I went with Ruth to her office to choose a day. I told her I could finish no later than quarter to twelve because I had to be back in Lennoxtown to pick up Emily. When I left I saw between a gap in the buildings the Campsie Fells. The view went straight through and in the sunlit sky between me and the hills seagulls darted about. I could have leaped into that space and flown I felt so good. Joy returned like a downpour of fresh rain, clearing the shooting stars from my head. Dancing was my rightful thing. I should never have stopped.

5.

I will tell Emily this: never look down on a dancer, classically trained, who doesn't make the *corps de ballet*. Never criticise a girl who tries but fails to get the West End chorus jobs she's recalled for, who dances on the Palladium stage but looks out at empty seats until she's told to pack up and go home. Never sneer at the cruise ship girls doing the West End routines in ships' carpeted theatres. Dancing is dancing. It is strength and passion and energy. It's a corporeal freedom that nothing except sex will match. It's a sense of belonging. A total release. You're born to it and you're lucky to do it.

At the start of my training they told me I'd never be a ballerina. No, before I even began my training they told me to come back a year later when I'd lost weight and improved my technique. When I finally started college, they told me I'd never dance classically. It's hard to hear something that disappointing, even when you're expecting it. I worked hard in the ballet classes all the same, believing that a pin-head *pirouette* or a seamless *développé* would be helpful whatever style of dance I performed. I was right.

In my other classes – my tap and jazz classes – it was different. They said: You're a performer. You make us watch you. Girls, come to the side and look at Liz. This is the drive we want to see. This is the energy. See her commitment to every step? This is what we want.

So, although they told me many times to lose weight, to sharpen up, to work on my core, they also praised some inner spark in me, my flair I suppose, and I came through college confident. I knew what I wanted. West End shows. Number One tours. The Lido. The Moulin Rouge. And if that eluded me: cruise ships bigger than hotels, can-cans, grand finales, sunny ports, money, glamour, stories to tell my grandchildren and to make my parents proud.

I nearly walked out of the audition that started everything. Some momentary collapse of confidence after a run of rejections. I saw all the girls in their make-up, packed into a hot waiting room, warming up or texting or discussing past jobs, and thought I could never do it, I could never stand out.

They taught us a dance combination – something from *Chicago*, I think – step tap shoulder roll, step tap shoulder roll – and we danced in lines in the studio. They stopped us and divided us into two groups and we danced again. They told certain girls to go and certain girls to stay. I stayed. Then they told all of us to go away and return at two o'clock. I sat in Soho Square and phoned my mum who was working in her open-plan office a tube ride away. 'I'm so close. I can't bear it,' I said.

'Bear it,' she said. 'You can do this.' I hear now the sorrow in her voice, knowing she might lose me as well as my dad, but at the time I only heard my own happiness reflected back.

The afternoon audition was as tough as the morning. Tougher. I stayed in the room until there were only four lines of girls left, then only two lines. Then there were just eight of us. They wanted six. We danced as a group, we danced in pairs, we stood alone in front of the panel and sang. When I walked out of the studio and the pigeons flew up from the pavement I knew I couldn't have tried any harder.

They telephoned the next day and offered me the job. A nine-month tour leaving out of Tampa, Florida. A month of rehearsals on ship throughout the night, midnight to seven. I cried. And accepted, of course. No ties, no partner to leave behind, no rent, no bills, no commitment. I danced on the cruise ships for nearly five years. I literally travelled the world. That's where I met Robbie, on the ocean, somewhere between Miami and San Juan, under the glare of the ship's fluorescent lights, five floors below sea level.

6.

We tried one of those sing-a-longs in the library. We sat on coloured cushions next to parents or grandparents whose toddlers pulled books from shelves and clutched crayons. Emily sat on my lap, turned her body into mine and refused to sing. My voice was the loudest so I sang more quietly. Come on you people, I thought. 'Come on, Emily,' I said. She pulled at my ear lobes. Afterwards, she wanted to sit on the cushions and read books and that was fine by me. I felt relaxed enough. A woman smiled at me and I grabbed at her smile in a fierce way. We shared the ages of our children and she told me Emily seemed small for four but hers were giants because her husband was six foot three so perhaps she was just used to giants. A baby boy slept in a sling against her chest. Her daughter climbed into her lap. The woman's hair swung at her chin as she told me she was waiting in the library because she had another one to collect at three and it would be pointless to go home for only ten minutes. Undressing them then dressing them again, sticking their arms in coat holes, putting their gloves back on.

'I thought work was hard, but children…' She widened her eyes.

I liked her.

'Have you lived in Campsie long?' she said.

'Where?'

'Here. Campsie.'

'Lennoxtown?'

'You clearly haven't. We call it Campsie.'

Emily used her thumb to turn a page of her book. I stroked her head and twirled a piece of hair around my finger. 'Can you read it, Mummy?' she said, and I should have read the book but the woman spoke again.

'Do you know anyone here?'

'You're my first...' I was going to say friend.

'I'll give you my number. I'm Caroline.'

I didn't expect tears to spring.

'Where do you go? What do you do?' I gestured at our children. Emily tugged my arm and asked me again to read the book.

'There's a playgroup in one of the church halls. That's about all. Or I come here. It's warm. There's a toilet. You get a good view of the street.'

We looked out of the windows at the main road with the garage and the Co-op opposite. Something must have resonated because she asked me, 'Did you hear about the woman who left her baby in the car?'

'No,' I said, and my cheeks must have flushed, they must have.

She told me a story about a woman whose car got broken into while she was in the Co-op buying wine and fish fingers. She'd left her daughter in the car crying her eyes out and the police were after her. She was in awful trouble. I listened to this story and when Caroline said, looking at me with her tired eyes and her hair swinging at her chin, 'I feel a bit sorry for her actually. I think she was a bit unlucky. What are you supposed to do?' I almost whispered, 'It was me, it was me,' but I didn't.

Emily pressed her heel into her bum.

'You can't take any chances though,' Caroline said and checked her phone.

'You need a wee,' I said to Emily.

'I don't. I want to read the book.'

'Yes, you do, I can tell. I have to make her go. She won't go unless I make her.'

'Oh yes, we've been there,' Caroline said.

I took Emily's wrist and pulled her up. Away we went. *Soubresaut*: a sudden leap.

After she'd peed, a great swift gush, we left the library. I waved through the glass at Caroline sitting with her phone and her children. I wish I'd gone back to her but shame shut that down. In the car I asked Emily to give me five minutes' peace while I made a phone call. I left a message for the social worker. I've been busy which is why there's been a delay, I said. My phone stopped working, it cut people off as soon as they rang. The social worker will have been familiar with excuses like that from people like me.

A man stood on Audrey's doorstep. He took his hands from his pockets and walked down the path towards us. I thought he might have been a policeman. It's true that fear can make your stomach flip.

'You told me half two,' he said as I unplugged Emily from her car seat.

'What?'

'I'm here for the clock.'

Gumtree! I'd forgotten. So many texts from so many people saying they'd come at this time or that time, and some came and some didn't. Emily got out of the car and I moved her away from a bottle she wanted to kick.

'I was just about to leave,' he said.

'Sorry.' I took my keys from my bag.

'I want honey on my toast,' Emily said to me.

'Honey it is.' We walked up the path. Emily stood with her hands and nose pressed against the front door. I asked her to step back so I could get my key in.

'I've got a vase to view at three fifteen in Stirling and I'm late now,' the man said.

I ignored him.

'Some scenery you've got here. The shadows on those hills. Looks menacing.' He wouldn't be ignored.

But neither could the fells be ignored. The clouds were full and high and between them there was blue. Pushed by some barely felt wind their shadows covered the ground in slow-moving patches. The man rubbed his hands and blew on them.

'It changes every minute,' I said and I showed him inside, to Robbie's gran's things.

The clock had a picture of a bird at every hour and at every hour a bird's call chimed. I'd put a battery in to make sure it worked and the first time it chimed Emily and I had looked at each other, startled, then listened after that for other bird calls. We liked to mimic them.

'I'm a little disappointed in the quality,' he said.

Fuck the quality, I wanted to make my daughter her toast. I accepted his four pounds, bartered down from the five I'd suggested and had to search for coins to make up his change. I flicked on the heating. The flat was cold.

He asked if I was having a clear-out and I showed him other things I'd put aside: some ornaments and lamps and books. It seemed a betrayal, laying out a life like that for a stranger to pick over. He took two lamps with matching shades and gave me a tenner to go with the four pounds.

As he walked through the hall carrying Audrey's things Emily shrieked and grabbed hold of my jumper pulling on it so hard she nearly toppled me.

'I don't want him to take the clock,' she said.

'He's bought the clock.'

'I want the clock. I like the clock. I want to keep the clock.'

'You can't keep it. We've sold it to the man.'

She pulled at me harder and I tried to prise her hands off my jumper. 'Just go,' I said to the man and followed him down Audrey's stairs. When I closed the door Emily threw herself onto the floor, put her forehead to the carpet and cried. She turned on her side and kicked the wall.

'Stop crying! Stop kicking!' I said but she wouldn't stop.

'I want the clock, I want to keep the clock. I like the birdies.' She kicked the wall again.

I knew she was hungry. 'I'll make your toast.'

'No!' Her cries were desperate.

When I knelt to comfort her she kicked me. I hated it when she kicked me. It was wrong and it hurt and it made me sad. There was so much rage between us and I didn't understand how it had happened. I'd only had her in the door for five minutes.

I noticed the brown envelope on the doormat and because distraction had worked before I said, 'The postman's been. We have a letter.'

That made no difference. She continued to kick so I caught one of her legs and held it as she kicked. Sometimes she would laugh at me trapping her this way but she didn't that day.

'Look! Exciting! A letter in a brown envelope. Who is it for Emily? Is it for me? Is it for you?'

She stopped kicking and lay still. I noticed the lines on her leg from the elastic hem of her sock and I wanted to kiss her calf but was afraid she'd kick my face.

'Will you open my letter for me?' I squeezed her ankle.

She pushed herself onto her hands and reached for the brown letter. Anger gone, face calm, lips wet. I leaned against Audrey's door and was glad of the cold at my back. I don't know you. That's what I was thinking. I don't understand you. I don't even know how to be your mum.

But I tried. 'Open it. Who's it to?'

She liked that. She sat down and struggled with the envelope. I knew better than to offer to help. She picked out the pink piece of paper with delicate fingers.

'Is it for you, Mummy?' She handed it to me.

It was.

'What does it say?'

I laughed.

'Why are you laughing?'

And then I sighed.

'What's wrong, Mummy?'

We have made several attempts to contact you…As a matter of urgency, please call the social work office…the welfare of your child…we will be forced to involve the police.

'I just called her.'

'What does it say, Mummy?'

'I just called her.'

'Is it for you, Mummy?'

I inhaled as if preparing for a double *pirouette*. 'To Emily and her mummy. This is a ticket for the playground near to Emily's nursery. You must use it on a sunny day. Bring a Fruit Shoot and a Freddo.'

She took the letter from me and read it upside down. I turned it round and pointed out her name, Emily, typed on the page. She blinked and I saw from her eyes when she looked at me that I'd deceived her completely.

'Can we go, Mummy?'

'Of course we can.'

I just wanted her to be happy, I really did.

And then the doorbell rang and we stood up, dishevelled, Emily with the blotches on her cheeks that came out when she cried, standing with the letter in her hand. I thought it might have been the man who bought the clock, back to complain about the shit bird calls. What time was it? Three o'clock. He would have heard the wood pigeon. I shouldn't have sold it to him. Emily liked it and I did too.

But it wasn't the man who bought the clock.

'Sara from social services,' the woman said. A motorbike's roar kept me from hearing what she said next. She leaned in. 'We sent a letter. You can ignore it now.'

The noise of the motorbike faded. 'I just called you,' I said.

'I know. I jumped in the car when I got your voicemail. Ignore the letter. It's form. We have to do it if we can't get through to someone.' She held out her hand. I didn't know if she wanted me to shake it. 'You can leave it with me.' Her face looked mild but she stood as straight as me, I'll give her that. 'Or throw it away. The letter. We're here now.'

I took the letter from Emily and gave it to the social worker but Emily screamed as if she was dying and shouted, 'No!'

I realised. 'We need the letter back. It's our ticket to the playground.' I winked and held out my hand. The social worker stared at me. I thought they were supposed to read signals, social workers, be perceptive, be good with people. She didn't read any signals until Emily screamed again and lay on the floor.

'Please give her the letter,' I said.

She bent down and handed Emily the letter. 'You must be Emily.' I noticed the red streaks in Sara's hair and looked over the top of her head to the street outside, saw my car and considered grabbing Emily and fleeing all the way back to London.

'Can I come in?' She looked up at me.

I let her in. I wondered what she would think of the way we lived.

'Where do you want to inspect first?' I said. It was difficult to climb the stairs because Emily was tight at my legs tilting me off-balance.

'Let's just sit.'

'Do you want a cup of tea?'

'No, thank you.'

'I've never known a health visitor or midwife to accept a cup of tea. You must think we keep dirty houses.'

I lifted Emily up and carried her on my hip like I did when she was small. The social worker said nothing. I took her through the flat, passing the rooms either side of the hallway, to the living room at the back. She removed her coat and pulled a folder from her bag. I put Emily down, opened the curtains and sat on the armchair, waiting for it to start. Emily's pyjamas, her dressing gown, some books, dolls and a mug lay on the floor. We both watched Emily for a few seconds until Emily became self conscious and threw a plastic cup at the TV.

'Emily, don't do that,' I said, and to the social worker, 'What's going to happen?'

'I'm really glad I've met you at last.'

She looked at Emily and reached out a hand. 'Are you better now? I hear you were poorly. My wee boy is the same age as you. He had a bug last week. I hope you're much better.'

Emily moved closer to me.

'The purpose of this visit is to check the family unit is doing okay. To follow up from the incident in the car park. The police always pass these cases to us. It's a matter of course.'

'The family unit is fine thanks.' And then I said, 'People do it all the time but they don't get caught.'

'Just let me go over these first few things. You've not long moved here, have you? Who's at home? Is it just you and Emily?'

'Yes.'

'Are you in contact with her dad?'

'No.'

She made a note.

'Do you have any family?'

'I have a mother in London.'

'So you're completely alone here.'

'Yes.'

She made another note.

I didn't need to tell the social worker it was my intention to be alone, that I was giving my mum a break after nearly five years, that I thought she had compassion fatigue and longed for an empty house so she and Alan could eat steak and he could stay over without being woken at six in the morning.

'Emily is four, five in April. Did she go to school in England?' the social worker asked.

'No.'

'Oh. Why not? How does she feel about starting school here in August?'

'We won't be here in August.'

'Oh. Where are you moving to? You'll need to enrol her wherever you go. She should be at school or registered for school at her age.'

'I know.'

I said no more and the social worker said, 'We'll revisit that.'

The question irritated me. Starting school was something my mum and I had argued over. I'd deferred Emily for a year citing exceptional circumstances. One of the dancers on the ship had talked about home-schooling her children and until I moved to Lennoxtown I'd liked that idea. I wasn't going to think about schools until we'd cleared Audrey's flat, had our holiday in the hills and moved on.

Emily found my phone and asked to look at photographs. I let her.

'I know you're registered with a doctor, that's good.'

'It was tonsillitis Emily had. She got antibiotics.'

We both looked at Emily who swiped her finger across my phone.

'Which is why I left her in the car. I made a judgement. She was sick. Are they going to prosecute me?'

'I'm not the police. I can't speak for them.'

'But they said they'd be in touch and they haven't.'

She might have shaken her head, I couldn't tell. 'Technically the police could prosecute if they felt there was good reason. It's called "Abandonment". But I don't have anything to do with that. My job is to look after Emily. And you, obviously.' I could tell she was trying to reassure me, to keep me away from subjects that might make me troubled. She must have seen women like me before.

'I didn't abandon her.'

'A child could be in danger of overheating, she could be left for an extremely long time, she could be particularly distressed.'

'She was none of those things. She was asleep.'

Sara leaned towards me, resting her elbows on her thighs. Conspiratorial. 'Sometimes the car is hit by another car. Sometimes, and one of my colleagues has had this, the car is stolen with the child in it. Remember, your child is a minor. Whatever you do and wherever you go, you are responsible for her. What if that thief had taken Emily? What if the glass had cut her?'

I nodded. 'I didn't mean for anything like that to happen.' Obviously. The glass didn't smash properly anyway.

'I know. I'm telling you some of the consequences of leaving a child in a car. It really is always best to take them with you.' She sat straight then pulled a diary from her bag. A sheet of folded paper fell to the floor.

'They were horrible, those people in the car park. They had no right to treat me like they did. Emily pass up that piece of paper.'

Emily ignored me, absorbed with the photos on my phone, so I reached for the paper and handed it to Sara. We were quiet. I'd seen the way she looked at me when I spoke and I think she believed me, I think she did.

Emily said, 'Mummy look at that one,' and showed me a picture I'd taken of her outside her nursery. 'Look at that one, look at that one.' I had to look.

'I can tell you care about your daughter.'

'I do.'

She had a skill, that social worker, to calm me down without appearing to try. I began to relax as we talked about the ongoing winter. Sara told me she couldn't ever count on March because as well as daffodils, it brought hailstones and hurricanes and snow. She talked about her son's love of snow.

'Will he be starting school in August?'

'Yes.'

'Would you leave him alone in the car?' The question seemed to surprise us both.

I could tell Sara was a woman who thought before she spoke, unlike me.

'Before I worked in child protection, I possibly would have, but not now,' she said.

The room became darker. I stood up to switch on a light and saw thick clouds over rooftops.

The doorbell rang again. We'd never had so many visitors. Emily looked up from the phone. 'Hide! Shush!' she said and put her finger to her lips.

'We don't need to hide,' I said, pretending to laugh, but Emily climbed onto the armchair and curled up with her hands over her face. She leaped off when the doorbell went again and froze with her arms outstretched and her eyes moving comically.

There was a shout through the letter box: 'Anybody home? Hello. It's Paul. The plasterer. Aidan Watt sent me. You want me to look at your walls.'

'I need to get this,' I said to Sara and I nodded at Emily who unfroze, ran down the hall and slid on her bum down the stairs. In poured the bleak daylight as she opened the door.

Paul wore white overalls and carried his phone in his hand. I saw the weariness in his face change to surprise as he clocked me, tall, in front of him. I notice these things.

I let him in and he put a hand to the walls. His fingers were pink with dried plaster.

'Are these the ones?'

'Yes, it's these and the bedrooms. Aidan wants you to give him a quote to get rid of the Artex and fix up the holes. There are some big chunks missing from some of the walls.'

'I can skim the Artex for you, aye. I can do your painting for you too, not a problem.'

In the living room, he nodded to the social worker who sat where I'd left her, on the sofa. He touched the walls and looked at the ceiling. 'Not a problem,' he said again. He half smiled at the rectangles of clean wallpaper and said, 'I'll paint over this, will I?' and I said, 'Yes.' I showed him the kitchen that needed painting and then we walked to the door. Emily told me I'd forgotten about her toast. I had.

'How long will this work take?' I asked. 'Because I don't want to be here for much longer.'

'I could come over at the end of next week.'

'No sooner?'

'I'm fully booked.'

His phone rang and he answered it, turning away to speak. 'I'll phone you back,' he said and he looked at Emily when he'd finished.

'How old are you?'

'Four.'

'My wee girl's seven. Do you go to the nursery? Holly goes to the primary school next door.'

Emily wouldn't answer so I said, 'Yes.'

'I haven't seen you up there.'

'We're new.'

'Mummy, you said you'd make me toast.'

He smiled at me. 'I'll leave you to it. Tell Aidan I'll email him a quote.' He had a carefree end of the day energy about him as if he liked the sound of a can's opening. I liked that. He took another look at the walls and the ceiling in the hall and I observed the blackness of his lashes, heard him feel for his keys in his pocket.

When he'd gone I went straight to Audrey's bread bin and put a slice of bread in the toaster, calling out to the social worker that I wouldn't be two minutes. As I was buttering the toast, she came into the kitchen. 'I won't keep you much longer.'

'Here, Emily. Go and sit on the sofa. What do you say?'

'Thank you.' She held the plate in front of her like a gift.

'Are you managing financially?' the social worker asked.

'Yes,' I said. I wasn't. I had my child benefit and my tax credits and no rent to pay. I'd lived like this for nearly five years in London, staying with my mum, earning bits of money from bits of teaching, but my mum paid most of the bills and Aidan was doing the same here. If I was left on my own I would sink.

She'd put on her coat and I walked her to the door. 'I am going to need to come back and have a chat with Emily when it's convenient for you,' she said as she stepped outside, holding her diary.

'Why?'

'It's something we must do.'

'How did you know she was registered with a doctor?' It occurred to me, just then.

'It's a check we make.'

She put her hood up because rain was falling softly now. On another day I might have looked for a rainbow.

'Why?' I said.

'To see if they have any concerns about Emily.'

'Like what? I left her in the car for five minutes.'

Her assertive voice, the calm, straight-talking manner. 'When somebody avoids contact with social work, as you did – the unanswered phone calls, nobody at home – I have to do a bit of digging to see if any other services have concerns.'

I heard rain on her coat and car roofs.

'And the GP gave us no cause for concern.'

'Good!'

'But I will be speaking with the nursery.'

'Oh my God! Why?'

'It's all part of our procedures. I'm concerned that you have no family here to support you. Do you have friends? Are you getting regular breaks from Emily?'

Was I? She went to nursery. Most people had less time apart.

'No, but I'm fine. Emily was sick. She had a temperature. We had nothing to eat so we went to the shop and she fell asleep in the car. I did it as fast as I could but there was a man in front of me with five hundred lottery tickets and when they finally put someone else on the tills I realised I'd forgotten the milk so I asked her to wait and I raced to the back of the shop to get it because they always put the milk at the back for some fucking reason. And I paid the money and she took ages to pack my bag then I ran out of the shop and there they were crowded around my car. She was asleep for God's sake. There was no harm done. Absolutely no harm done. I would have driven home and lifted her out of the car and put her in her bed and she might have slept on if those interfering bastards hadn't held me up and summoned the police.'

See. I told the story again and again. And I put in swear words too.

'And while I'm on the subject, the police treated me like I was a piece of shit. Utter contempt they had for me.'

She nodded her head.

'Who else?' I said. 'Who else have you spoken to?'

She tried to hand me her business card. 'Liz, if you need support from anyone – me, your GP, the nursery staff – it's all there for you.'

'I don't.' Did I? Did I? I was managing. I was coming off my tablets. That was a good thing, despite the shooting stars.

'I'll contact the police and tell them we're monitoring things. Prosecution is highly unlikely.'

'Prosecution!'

'Please don't get yourself worked up. I'm trying to help.' Her fingers hovering near my arm. My eyes hissing at her open face.

'I don't need help.' Did I? 'Off you go and investigate someone who actually abandons their child.' *Frappé*. A fast action with the leg. Never before had I needed a social worker. Never before.

I shut the door and walked into the kitchen to stare out of the window at the washing line and wet paving slabs in Audrey's garden. The thought occurred to me then that I should call my mum and get her to take her leave up here with us in this cold-walled house. If I accepted help I'd take it from my mum, not a social worker.

I checked on Emily. She had crumbs and honey on her face. There was a knock at the door and Paul's voice shouted through the letter box. 'I forgot to leave you my number. Probably best not to call Australia each time you want to get hold of me!'

'Just post it through please!' I shouted. 'We're naked!'

Fuck them all.

Emily laughed and began to strip.

It snowed, like the social worker said it would. In the third week of March. The blizzard came early one morning and drove snow and sleet onto the tops of frenzied trees. The wind subsided but snow continued to fall and by mid-morning roads and pavements and the great sides of the Campsies were white. The place ached with white. We discovered soon after that we liked to throw sticks and stones onto the frozen lake by the old hospital. I loved the unearthly sound they made, clattering across the ice. I loved the force of my throws. Yet the stark snow made me feel more exposed than ever, as if I was being watched from all over Lennoxtown, by people who never left their children in cars, by happy families who did activities or baked.

7.

I think teaching ballet to people who've grafted or birthed or buried and lived long lives is a good thing, no matter how much or how little their bodies can dance, so I'm glad I started my classes at the sheltered housing. I was tempted to cancel them after the social worker came to my house. I didn't want to be the woman that people talked about, the upstart from London with the slack parenting who thought she could barge into Lennoxtown and presume to teach dance. It was misguided, this jaunt of ours. Perhaps if his gran hadn't died and Aidan hadn't asked, I would have continued with my life in London, getting through each day and going some way towards recovery. But I was still at the stage where the mention of Robbie's name triggered too many feelings, so of course I came to Lennoxtown, the place of his birth. It's done now. I taught the classes.

Before I dropped her at nursery Emily saw me take my make-up bag from a drawer. She asked me where I was going and demanded she wear make-up too. I told her to smile and brushed blusher onto the apples of her cheeks. There was toothpaste around her mouth. I licked my finger and wiped it off. I held her under her arms and lifted her up so she could see into the mirror. She weighed nothing. We looked into each other's eyes and then she turned her face to inspect her cheeks.

'You have your cruise face on,' I told her. 'I have my cruise face on too. Except I left off the glitter.'

'Can I have some glitter?'

I put a dab on her cheekbones and lifted her up again.

'Mummy, you have a line here, between your eyes.' She touched my wrinkles then stroked soft fingers across my forehead and down my face.

'Yes, but look at my smile!'

Emily smiled too.

'Wish me luck,' I said.

'Good luck, Mum.'

She'd never called me Mum before. I think that was her way of acting grown up. So I had to act grown up too.

There they were, in the pink-carpeted lounge, waiting for me. I noticed the women I'd met the previous week. June with the turned out feet sat at a table with keys bunched in her fist and Eve, the woman who wanted an art class, was next to her, talking to a man in a dressing gown. A woman sat with her hands clasped on the table in front of her and two more women with the curved backs of age or osteoporosis folded paper napkins and put them in a handbag. A man placed his newspaper on the table, stood up when he saw me and said, 'We're here to audition for *A Chorus Line*,' and there was laughter.

I laughed too and sang 'One Singular Sensation' a little too loudly.

June put down her keys and coughed.

'I thought it might have been too early in the morning for you all,' I said.

'It's better than sitting in our houses,' Eve said.

June said, 'It's too early for Margaret. She won't come.'

I put my bag on the floor, pushed some tables to the sides of the room and they helped me by catching the vases of flowers before they fell. I asked someone to turn off the radio and I made a barre out of a line of chairs. The chairs were sturdy with strong backs and I had to lean into them to push.

'Have you done any dancing before?' I said.

'I used to jive,' said the man with the newspaper.

'Two left feet, me,' June said.

'That's where my parents met, at the dancing,' the younger of the two women folding napkins said. 'Didn't you, Mum?' We stopped to look at her mother who smiled with coral lips.

'Where?' the man with the newspaper asked.

'Dennistoun Palais.'

'I will have asked you to dance then, Agnes.'

'You will have been in nappies. She's ninety-six.'

'I've always fancied myself as a toy-boy.'

'I'm eighty-nine,' said the man in the dressing gown.

'And not in nappies yet,' June said.

That's what I remember about them: their loose talk and their great age.

'What about you?' I asked the woman who sat with her hands in her lap, the only one not to speak.

'She doesn't say much,' said Eve.

'Did you go to the dancing, Alice?' June spoke loudly. Alice nodded her head. 'Oh, aye.'

'I haven't seen her in months,' June said and I understood then that it was a rare thing for them to meet on purpose in the lounge with the pictures of past residents smiling at them from their frames on the walls.

I asked them to come to the centre of the room and stand by a chair. As the daughter helped her mother and the man in the dressing gown pushed his frame I rubbed my arms, looked at their serious faces and wondered how I would get them to dance without falling or hurting themselves.

'It's freezing in here,' I said.

'The heater's on,' said June.

'This room's like us. Takes a while to get going,' the man with the paper said.

I realised they were as nervous as me. I looked at them all, facing me, their fragile hands resting on the backs of their chairs, the man's dressing gown tied tight around his waist, June's chin tilted. The beat before curtain up. *Five, six, seven, eight*.

'We'll do some *pliés* with *port de bras*,' I said. 'That's leg bends and arms.'

I put some music on.

'But first we'll sort out your feet.'

I showed them how to stand in first position, keeping their heels together and turning out their toes. 'Heads up, chins up, tuck your tummies in, tuck your bums in. My teacher used to call your bum a tail. She was more polite than me.'

'Nobody's polite here,' June said.

I checked on June's feet and I was right, she was as turned out as any eager eleven-year-old. All of them were taller than they'd been before, even the women with willowed spines.

'One hand on your chair, the other hand here, in *bras bas*,' I told them. I shaped my arm into a curve and held it low, my hand just in front of my thighs.

'Keep your shoulders down, pull them away from your ears, don't think about your stresses and strains. John, is it John? Don't grip the chair, relax that hand.' The man with the newspaper told me he would fall over if he didn't grip the chair so I told him to grip it less.

'My mum is not allowed to fall,' the daughter, Senga, told me.

'She won't fall, will you Agnes? That's us in *bras bas*. Now we'll take the arm up to first position, and down again.' I showed them how to move their arms from first to second position and from first to fifth, how to move with grace from fifth, through second and back to *bras bas*.

It was the most soothing thing I'd done in months. They went with it. I recalled the phrases and instructions my teachers had said to me. I lightly touched their shoulders and elbows and wrists, pulled gently on fingers to shape hands and remembered gentle fingers on my own hands and the way, in class, I would try to alter my balance and my body in the tiny directions the teacher had prompted. If I was strict, I couldn't help it, it was the only way I knew to teach.

When I told them to go with the music, to stretch their fingers to the very edges of the phrasing, I did the same myself. I was eighteen again, striving for perfection, besotted with the smell of leather shoes and Lycra. I don't know where they were, my class, but I saw a fineness in their faces that hadn't been there before. I know we all see what we want to see, but it was there.

I walked down the row of chairs and told them to change direction and face me at the other end of the room. The man in the dressing gown was slow to turn, and so was Agnes the elderly mother.

'You can dance by sitting on a chair,' I said, but they stayed standing and after *demi-pliés* and *port de bras* using the other arm, we worked on forward and back bends and *relevés*. They struggled for balance but managed it, rising from first position onto their tiptoes and back down again.

'Pull in, pull in,' I said. 'Smile, you're dancing!'

John untied his laces and threw his shoes to the side of the room. So did June. So did Eve.

'Are you all right, Mum?' Senga said.

'Wheesht! I'm dancing!' Agnes shouted.

I turned up the volume on my music player and Camille Saint-Saëns's 'The Swan' soared between us as we stretched a leg from first position to the front and from first to the side and then made gentle quarter-circles through the positions. 'Slide your toes along the floor, and close and pull in.'

'What is this we're doing?' Eve asked.

'Ballet dancing,' June said.

'It's preparation for *rond de jambe*,' I said. 'Round the leg.'

'Round the bend.'

'Rond de John,' John said, and I saw his pointed toes in his green socks.

'I mind when this lounge was filled with dancing couples,' Eve said. 'Now everyone stays in their rooms.'

I let them talk because it didn't stop them dancing and their voices were soft and affable. When the music came to an end I told them to shake their arms and legs but some found that hard to do so I told them to stop.

'What's your name?' I said to the man in the dressing gown.

'Charlie Hughes,' he said to me.

'Are you hot? Do you want to take your dressing gown off?'

He winked and shook his head. I couldn't see his mouth because his beard was so thick. The woman who rarely spoke, Alice, held her hands out. When I took them she said, 'I have warm hands. My hands are never warm.' And they were. The dancing had warmed her up.

I should have checked they were comfortable to stand without support but I didn't. Nobody said they couldn't. Charlie used his frame. For the last part of the class I cleared the chairs and asked two lines of dancers to travel towards each other and meet lightly at their fingertips then travel away. *Promenade*.

'Walk softly, feel your weight transfer from one foot to the other,' I said. 'Touch your fingertips when you meet. What does it feel like?'

Nobody answered, but they went with it. I chose some music we warmed up to on one of the ships. 'Ah, Debussy,' said Charlie. A dance captain had made me a playlist and I was grateful for it.

'Travel towards each other as if you're happy to see each other,' I said. 'How do you move? Where are your hands? Are you light? Are you heavy? What are you doing with your eyes? Now come back to your starting positions and *promenade* as if you're brave. Change your movement slightly,' I said. 'Change the intention.' I saw their footsteps become bolder and their chests puff. Eve came to Charlie while he stood still, narrowed his eyes and gripped his frame, his elbows at angles.

'Now travel as if you're lonely.' Their movements changed again. I was June's partner because she was on the end of the line and had no partner. We held eye contact, as I'd insisted we do, and when she walked towards me, lonely, I saw a glimmer of sadness that I was sure caught the mirror of mine.

They asked me to stay for tea so I did. Eve put the radio back on. John took his newspaper, excused himself and sat away from us. June offered me a biscuit.

'Was that all right?' I asked her when the others were talking.

'Aye, it was fine. It was different,' she said. 'Agnes there.' She gestured towards the mother whose daughter was breaking a biscuit in half for her. 'She's been so, so low. I never thought she'd join in. But aye, it was different, it was good.'

I've always liked praise. I took another biscuit and watched Charlie in his dressing gown say something to Alice. Their heads were bent towards one another, his yellow-white, hers grey.

'How long have you lived here?' I asked June.

'Five years,' she said. 'They were threatening to build another block between me and my view and that would have finished me off, but they're not now. I can sit by my window and do my crossword knowing that nothing will change. Well, the view changes every minute, that's the beauty of it.'

'I love the Campsie Fells,' I said.

She picked up her keys and looked at me. 'Why are you here?' she asked.

She confused me.

'I'm teaching dance.'

'I'm not asking why you're here teaching dance. Why are you here in Campsie, on your own? Don't you have anyone? No family?'

I knew what she meant now. I said, 'I'm here to house sit,' and we left it at that. I felt my answer disappointed her a little, as if her question had reached to the edge of the musical phrasing and touched me and I'd slammed it back. But it felt too complicated to say that I had wanted to take us out of our lives for a bit, to snuffle around, to search the village for something I could hardly name and if I could name it at all it would be one all-consuming word: Robbie.

'You're charging a fiver, are you?' June said.

'I was going to make this a trial class. For free.'

'Nonsense. A fiver's not enough,' she said.

'I can't charge any more. Old people are poor.'

They all heard that. Charlie laughed and Alice laughed.

'You've got another mouth to feed. I think it should be pay what you can,' June said.

'Okay, pay what you can,' I said. 'Thank you.' I knew they didn't have much money.

She took a pint glass from the kitchen and held it in front of each dancer, collecting my money. I finished my cup of tea and gathered up my speaker and bag. June tipped the glass of notes and coins into my hand.

'And how's your wee girl?' she asked, in a straight-out way.

'She's fine, she's well. She's at nursery. I'd better go and get her,' I said, looking at the time on my phone and realising that I had only eleven minutes before I needed to pick her up.

'I used to clean the primary school next door,' June said. 'I knew all the weans in Campsie.'

After I left, I wondered how long they would sit in their socks in the lounge. I remember Senga telling her mother that they were going to Stobhill later for an appointment. I was saddened to think of Agnes being so, so low, and it struck me how plainly June had spoken about it, in a voice that wasn't hushed, that they could all hear, as if they recognised that being so, so low could happen and did happen to them all. Sadness is a quiet thing, surely.

8.

Because the ships sailed their long voyages at night and often by the morning we were docked in a port, it was rare to stand on deck in daylight and see nothing but sea. We had no windows in our cabins anyway, no way of knowing if it was dark or light outside or if land was close by. Tiny cabins they were with tiny bunk beds. Two dancers to a cabin. We shared a wardrobe and a chest of drawers and we had a drawer each under the bunk beds. We slept with many partners in many beds. Everyone did. When our shows were done we drank the subsidised drinks in the crew bar and returned to our tiny cabins in the tiny hours of the morning. It was usual for me to see a new naked arm thrown from beneath my roommate's covers. It was common to see girls and boys in pants and T-shirts walking barefoot down sleeping corridors.

I loved the costumes we wore – the bikinis and headdresses and backpacks that held huge feathers. I loved the magicians, the husband-and-wife acts, the flamenco troupes who danced with their black shoes and black eyeliner and pulled-back hair, the tribute groups, and my solo – 'Big Spender' – that I performed under a spotlight while the dancers in my troupe changed costume and grabbed a breath.

Those years sang. They still sing for me. I expected to have more. To think I was worried about the size of my body, if I would fit my costumes, determined to be the one the audience couldn't take their eyes off, to kick higher, turn more sweetly than anyone else and make my movements look as effortless and easy as breathing. To miss my parents in London, and fret occasionally about my dad's health, to be insecure about that vague wave of future I had to face when I got off the ship, to make sure I got another contract as soon as I could was all I had to worry about or all I chose to worry about. I didn't know that those days and hours and moments could sustain a life.

Robbie was a fitness instructor in the gym. I went to him because I'd heard that a girl could be disembarked for being overweight or underweight. If she didn't fit her costume she didn't look good and oh no they didn't make the costumes for the girls, they got girls to fit the costumes. Those glittering bikinis and corsets made far more journeys on the sea and saw far more dark and spotlit nights than we did. One of the girls I danced with was eating tissues. Another wasn't eating at all. I like my food. Always have.

Robbie wore his uniform T-shirt and told me, as he was inducting a husband and wife, to come back at seven-thirty the next morning when the gym would be quiet. I did.

He was mouthy, like me. Some would say cocky. I'd seen him in the crew bar. He liked to talk and joke. Never still. But he explained each piece of gym equipment with professional patience and watched me work it myself to make sure I'd understood his instructions. I slowed myself down in order to listen to him. I knew how to work gym equipment but I let him talk.

'Do you run?' he said.

'No.'

'You should try it for stamina. We have a running club in here. At midnight. We run 10K together.'

'You run at midnight?'

'We have to do it when the guests are asleep.'

He wiped the handles of a spinning bike and threw the paper towel into a bin. 'I've seen you dance,' he said. 'You could handle 10K.' He pronounced K like key. I had to listen carefully to his accent, watch his face, keep an eye on his lips.

After our final show one night, when I'd showered and attended to the blisters on my feet, I went to the gym with my roommate. We looked through the door and saw them; men and women in shorts and T-shirts, running hard, music blaring, hands in fists, muscles spreading as their feet set down on the treadmills. I watched Robbie run, watched his cheeks hollow as he breathed, saw how fast he ran, how alive his face was, saw him raise his head and look straight into my eyes through the glass door. That was the moment. That was when I knew we were each other's. I know it's unbelievable but it's true. I'll tell Emily that. She'll like that.

I had to go inside.

'Are you running with us?'

'I'm just looking for...' I didn't know what else to say.

He continued to run. The other runners ran too, feet pounding on. He kept eye contact and nodded.

We found a way to be together and, because of his ebullience around other people, I was surprised by his stillness. I expected his hands to be as busy as his chat. I expected speed. But no.

'You're kind,' I said.

It was as if he'd uncovered himself for me and I knew, despite my youth, to be kind back. We were brave and stupid, taking risks with our hearts that we shouldn't have. No. We were absolutely right to.

Of course, after we'd slept together he showed off around me. But despite his self-assurance, he approached everything with a kind of formality and gentleness and a softness that I understood quite quickly to be love. I suppose you have to be in the right place to catch it, but I caught it and loved him back.

'I stayed in London,' he said, when I told him where I was from.

'Where were you born?'

'A village near Glasgow.'

'Would you live in London again?'

'With you I would.' He was serious about me. I was in no doubt.

I came to know the exquisite tenderness that a *pas de deux* demands when I was with Robbie, much more so than when I was going through the steps in class, so much so that I wished I could dance with a partner again and feel it this time. Aren't all of us better at everything after a grand passion? The presenting of one body to another: a woman's arched back – *cambré* – lifted to stop bare and plain before her partner's open chest. Eyes that fix, lips that brush, a hand that catches a thigh, the heat where the tops of the legs meet, the cradling of a body, the celebration of a body, the embrace and love. A *pas de deux* was sex with love. As I said, I'd love to dance with a partner again.

'Do you get homesick?' I asked him. 'Do you miss anyone?'

'My brother,' he said. 'My parents passed away.'

'That's too young, surely?'

'That's how it goes,' he said, and told me that his brother was working in Australia. He'd gone when Robbie took off on the ships.

'Do you miss anyone?' he asked me.

'I feel a little guilty,' I said. 'My mum's at home looking after my dad. I miss them both.'

'It's a long time away if you're missing what you've left,' Robbie said.

'It's easier now I've met you.'

So we were in love quickly. That's the truth. I said they were the best days and they were. I wish I'd known it at the time. I just presumed there would be more. To think, my body could dance for hours at a time, my back could bend, I could triple *pirouette* and not get dizzy, and I could fall in love so easily.

9.

The police came to my door to frighten me, I presume. It was the same policewoman from the car park and a different policeman.

'We've identified the thief,' the woman said.

'Who?'

'A local man. He's done other break-ins. We're gathering evidence.'

'And we have witnesses,' the policeman said.

'What will happen?'

'We'll arrest and prosecute,' the policewoman said. 'If he pleads guilty you might not need to go to court.'

'If he doesn't?'

'We could prosecute you for Abandonment.'

I don't think one should have followed the other. I think the policeman spoke too soon because there was a pause after which his colleague corrected him. 'If he doesn't plead guilty you'll need to go to court to testify,' she said.

Then they should have said their piece to frighten me. I did feel the threat of them with their uniforms and radios and hard boots and pocket books in front of me on Audrey's doorstep.

'Why would you think that was a good idea, to prosecute me?' I said.

'If we think it's in the public's interest or the child's interest it would be a good idea.'

'And do you?'

'You technically committed a crime,' the policeman said. 'You broke the law. You put your child in danger.'

'We'll be in touch,' said the policewoman.

'If I'm to be prosecuted?'

'Yes. And when it goes to court. Which it probably will.'

'When what goes to court?'

There was a beat before they spoke which I'm sure they enjoyed. 'The attempted robbery from your car.'

I thought that I would leave Lennoxtown before they came back. We would be gone, me and Emily, and they wouldn't be able to drag me to court for anyone or anything.

The policeman looked past me into the flat.

'Is she in?'

'Who?'

'The old lady who lives here.'

'She's dead.'

'Oh.' He seemed a little struck.

His colleague frowned. 'Did you fix your car window?'

'Yes.'

'Good.'

The policeman half smiled at me before the pair of them walked away and got into their marked car. The gold on the hills above the white-walled houses mocked me. Too beautiful. Even the sheep shone with gold.

The social worker returned, as she promised she would, on the day Paul came to plaster the walls and ceilings.

'A brief word with Emily. And a brief word with you,' Sara said.

'Come on Emily,' I said, 'let's get this done,' and I opened the door wide to let the rain and the wind and the social worker enter the flat.

She stepped on the plastic floor covering Paul had put down. The hall walls were plastered salmon pink and a bare bulb hung above us. The lounge was messy. Emily sat on the sofa, too close to the edge, but she often sat that way and never fell off.

'Do you want to speak to both of us or just Emily this time?'

I reached for the remote control to turn off the television.

'No, Mummy!' Emily said.

'We need to talk to the social worker,' I said.

'No!' Emily flung her body backwards and slid off the sofa. Tears came.

Paul opened the door, on stilts. He dipped his head under the frame. Emily screamed. 'Should have said, I'll be on these for a while. Easier to reach the ceiling. I'll keep this door shut in case your wee one comes out.' His metal stilts were splattered with plaster.

Emily resumed her crying. 'Can we pause the telly?' she said.

'We can't pause this telly.'

'We can pause Granny's.'

'I know.'

Our voices were getting louder. I stood up.

The social worker asked for five minutes with Emily so I left them and went to the kitchen to fill the kettle with water.

Paul ducked under the doorway. 'Can I show you something,' he said.

'Do you want a drink?'

'I'll take a coffee.'

I let the kettle boil and followed him into the room with no bed, the one I took the table from. High on his stilts Paul showed me the damp pink walls and lighter patches where the plaster had begun to dry. 'You'll need to keep the heating off while this dries. Sometimes it cracks and there's nothing you can do about it. If it cracks, I'll come back. But if you keep the heating off it should be okay.'

The room's coldness was unpleasant. It was a bleak room now. Nothing of Robbie's gran left and nothing of us.

'What colour do you want me to paint it?' he asked.

'I haven't really thought about that. Cream, I suppose. Magnolia. Whatever colour sells houses.'

I stood in the doorway and watched him stretch above his head, holding a board in one hand and a trowel in the other which he used to skim plaster across the ceiling. He was steady on his stilts, taking wide solid steps. I leaned into the hallway, listening for sounds of Emily and the social worker.

'You're better off just putting some music on,' he said. 'You won't hear anything through the door.' Paul didn't say any more but he was a smart man, he knew something was going on.

'She's my pal's missus,' he said and I thought, of course, they all know each other here.

'It's nothing serious,' I said. 'Well, I don't think it is. I left her in the car for two minutes and someone called the police.'

He stopped working. 'My girlfriend told me about that. Well, my ex-girlfriend now. My daughter's mum.'

'How long's she been in with her? Five minutes?'

'You'd think they'd go after the real child abuse cases. Waste of everybody's time.'

His stilts looked like metal bones, plaster-splattered tibia and fibula. I studied anatomy at dance college and knew that I was prone to a lateral ankle sprain and Achilles tendinitis.

'Don't you have to be careful on those things? Don't your arms ache?' I said.

'I get used to it.'

'Can't you use a ladder?'

'I could. But it would take longer and cost you more.' There was a slight strain in his voice as he stretched to the ceiling.

'But if you fall, that's dangerous isn't it?'

'You need to remember to throw the trowel if you fall, just get out of the way of the trowel.'

'Throw in the trowel.'

I laughed at myself.

'I haven't heard that before.' He smiled and rubbed his forehead. 'I've only fallen twice. Once I stepped backwards onto something a spark left lying around, and once I tripped on a dust sheet. It's why I use the plastic instead.' He pointed his trowel to the floor. 'You're not allowed stilts on building sites anymore. It's frowned upon. Health and Safety. But it's okay just me doing a homer.'

It occurred to me that everyone broke the law in their own small way.

He stretched to spread plaster over the ceiling. His balance was impeccable, his movements no more and no less than was required.

'You'd make a good dancer,' I said. 'You must have a good core.'

He laughed and rested his arms. 'I don't know about that. This flat is going to look lovely once you've finished with it,' he said. 'You won't want to leave.'

'I don't know about that.'

I left him to his work and stood at the window in my bedroom. The rain had stopped and flashes of blue sky showed behind the clouds. A woman pulling a shopping trolley walked slowly on the other side of the street. Two older boys from a house with a swing in the garden kicked a football. From inside our flat I heard the scrape of Paul's trowel and the low murmur of the social worker's voice but I couldn't hear Emily. Perhaps Sara was showing her pictures of sad faces and happy faces and asking her to say how she was feeling. I hated the thought of Emily's finger hovering over a sad face, of her giving simple answers to loaded questions and incriminating me in God knows what. My left eyelid trembled, a twitch I couldn't control. No wonder. Robbie used to help with that kind of thing.

We visited Robbie's gran when I was pregnant with Emily. So I'd been to Lennoxtown before on a wet winter's day. We drove from Glasgow airport in a hire car and I felt sick as we chugged through the rain. I remember winding down my window and not caring that rain was coming into the car and falling on me. When we got to Lennoxtown the cloud was so low the hills were completely hidden. I couldn't see them at all and it was a surprise when the cloud finally lifted and there they were, full as a face in front of me.

So Lennoxtown was a village in the falling rain. And his gran was a lady who kept a cold house. It was freezing. We were back from Florida. We told her I was pregnant. A girl, she said, looking hard at my stomach, There's a girl in there for sure. I was only fourteen weeks. My stomach was flat, the muscles well worked from the dancing and the gym on the ship. How could she know?

I couldn't see any of Robbie in her face. She was a small woman whose roll neck jumper hung off her bony shoulders. Her body had been operated on too many times with cancers taken out from her lungs and lymph nodes. She said she'd never smoked a cigarette in her life but Robbie remembered that his grandad always had a pipe in his hand, so maybe she'd picked up her cancer from his smoke. She liked to take her tea on a tray and watch the game shows. That's what she told me on the day we visited her anyway.

She had a weep over Robbie's dad, her son, who she said she missed every minute of every day. Robbie put his youthful arms around her shoulders and she cried into his neck.

'We'll put some flowers down,' he said. 'Do you want to come with us?'

She said she couldn't because they were calling the raffle at her luncheon club and she'd promised she'd be there, but she asked if we'd put some flowers on Robbie's grandad's grave too, and his mum's. She told us exactly where they were, which rows, which gravestones were either side, but Robbie knew. Once, she called Robbie by his brother's name, Aidan, and we wondered if she understood who she was talking to. I saw a flicker of distress on Robbie's face.

The man from the luncheon club knocked on the door, his minibus parked outside, and she told us it was time for her to go. She smartened herself with a woollen scarf and told us to find something to eat in the kitchen. 'Leave me a couple of crackers. That's all I'll eat when I get in.' We said we would be back to see her at the end of our trip. 'Let yourselves out,' she called. 'Just pull the door shut. I have keys.' We helped her down her stairs and watched the man close the minibus door. She waved and he tooted.

'Do you want to say hello to anyone?' I asked Robbie. 'Show me anything?'

He said no, there was nobody he wanted to see. Only his gran and he'd seen her and found her resilient. Her breadbin was empty. Her fridge contained a couple of yoghurts and not much else. I grabbed a banana and a custard cream and we shut the door behind us. Robbie drove in silence and didn't want to answer any of my questions about his village. He gave no comment on the handsome church at the top of the hill or the stone buildings on Main Street. We drove along the looping streets to the graveyard and we stooped through the rain to find the graves.

We got the flowers from the Co-op. We bought food there too. So I'd been to the Co-op before, with Emily barely formed in my womb, safe from the worst her mother could do, not yet abandoned.

'Mummy!' Emily's hands were round my legs. I turned from the window and walked with her into the cool salmon hall with the bare bulb and the clicking sound of Paul's stilts coming from the plastic floor cover in the spare room.

'Are you all done?' I hugged Emily as she hung on to my legs.

'Liz?' The social worker. She asked for a final few minutes with me, so it was my turn in the lounge on the sofa. Emily came too. She grabbed at the remote control.

'I've had a chat with Emily and there is some further action needed.' Sara looked at me without blinking.

I shook my head. 'What kind of action?'

'The nursery is a wee bit concerned about Emily.'

'In what way?'

'She's showing signs of detachment. She's painfully shy. Lacking in confidence. Her behaviour can be erratic.'

Emily was listening. I beckoned for her to come and sit on my lap. She did so and lifted my top, putting her hands on my belly. I pulled my top down. She put her hands back on my belly.

'Stress and isolation can make things spiral.'

'Who's stressed? Is Emily stressed? I don't think she is.' It seemed to me futile for her to continue. 'We're not going to be here long. Honestly, we're only staying a couple more weeks.'

Emily put her hands down the V of my top. I removed her hands. She put her head to my chest and asked for milk. She liked to pretend she was a baby.

'Well, while you are here, perhaps we could get our heads together at the nursery to see how we can support you.'

'No.'

'Please, Mummy.'

'No.'

'Can you tell me a little about your relationship with Emily's dad?'

'No.'

'Can you give me an idea of how you're coping with things?'

'No.'

And Emily said 'No' too, copying me, pulling up my top and pressing her hands onto my belly again.

The social worker stood up and Emily threw her arms around her legs. It was a relief to have my body to myself. I watched Sara bend to pat Emily's back. Emily took her hand. 'I'm going to arrange a meeting with you, me, the nursery and a specialist family worker,' she said to me. 'It'll take place at the nursery. I'll make a dash while the rain is off.'

We walked through the cool hallway.

'I'll send a wee note to your health visitor.'

'Put a sign up on the nursery notice board too,' I said.

I thought I heard Paul laugh.

And then she was gone. And Emily clamoured for the attention she'd lost while Sara had been in the house so she jumped and pulled and chattered while I went straight to the kitchen to sort out her tea. The trouble with visits from social workers was that they put everything out. The tea was late, the bath was late, Emily was hungry, I was hungry. I made Paul his coffee and drank one myself. I think his company did us good. He spoke to Emily as well as me which stopped her from seeking my attention. He showed her a scar on his elbow from when he fell off his bike as a boy. He told me his asthma flared from time to time. He liked to take his bike out to Fintry and beyond.

'I can't ride a bike,' Emily said, and I thought, There's another thing I need to do.

When the eating was done Emily and I watched Paul on his stilts. He was finishing up. Patches of plaster were lighter looking than others. The room was cool already with the windows open. He stood on his high legs looking down at us.

'How long before you'll paint the walls?' I asked.

'I can fit you in next week.' He sat on the window ledge and unbuckled his stilts.

'Good.'

'Can I come back and check my work?'

I knew what he meant and welcomed the thought of an adult at my body rather than a child. 'Anytime,' I said. I surprised myself.

We liked a bath: Emily because she relaxed in the warm water and bubbles, me because I could do things knowing that the water was entertaining her. I could gather up wet or dirty washing, I could clean, I could fold, I could make phone calls. Perhaps I should have considered, because of the trouble I was in, whether or not I should be leaving her unattended in the bath but I had to do stuff, I had to, otherwise we would drown in undone chores and when she went to bed, that was it, my body caved, cracked, submitted to a great punch of tiredness. I couldn't be tidying up then. That's how it felt to me anyway.

I always sat with her for a bit though.

'What did Sara the lady say to you?'

'I can't remember.'

It fascinated me, what she chose to respond to, and what she didn't.

'Did she ask you any questions?'

'I can't remember.'

'I bet she said, And how is your mummy? Is she the best mummy in the world? Does she make the best baths, the nicest dinners, does she give the best cuddles?'

'Yes!'

'You do love me, you do!'

I liked her. We played while she sat in the bath and water filled the tub. Something felt held between us, like the tiny popping bubbles. I did most of the talking, unable to stop the chat or the singing, feeling a touch too high. I knew why.

'Head back. Flannel.'

I poured water from a jug over Emily's head. Her tipped-back head was smooth. Her narrow shoulders glistened with the fallen water.

'Mummy?'

'Yes.'

'When I grow up I'm going to be a dancer like you.'

I kissed her forehead. 'You can put your head back to normal now. That's lovely, Emily.'

'I can dance already.'

'I know you can.'

I rubbed shampoo into her hair. Emily held the flannel to her eyes and I rinsed the shampoo. 'Last time. There. What did she ask you, Emily?'

'Will you get in with me?'

I remembered the time the three of us squashed into our London bathtub, me and Robbie passing Emily between us until I felt afraid that she was too small and too fragile to be in a big bath, her parents' balance not quite secure, our confidence not quite formed.

'Will you get in?'

'I could...'

'Please, Mummy. You can have these bubbles here.' She pushed a handful of bubbles towards the other end of the bath.

I sat on the toilet seat and pulled off my socks. Emily squealed in happiness and drew her knees to her chest then pushed her heels along the bottom of the bath. She made waves.

My phone rang. It was Australia. Robbie's brother.

'Emily, hold on, I have to get this.'

It would be early in the morning in Australia. Aidan would be calling before leaving for work. I had to answer or I would need to phone him back and it cost too much. I answered.

Emily called out for me.

'Emily, shush, I'm trying to concentrate. Say that again?'

He wanted to know about Paul. Did I get his bank details? Was he going to paint the flat too? Take this number of a painter just in case Paul falls through.

'Mummy, are you coming in the bath?'

'In a minute.'

'Mummy, come now.'

'I didn't hear the number, Aidan. Wait. I'm not ready. Can you tell me again? What's his name?'

I had to leave the bathroom to get a pen and paper. Aidan wanted to chat. Had I seen this friend of his, had I remembered him to the owners of the garage? No, I hadn't. Through the bathroom door I heard Emily's shouts getting angrier. I heard crashes and smashes.

When I returned to the bathroom, the floor was soaked with water and bubbles. The bath mat was in the bath with Emily. Her toys were on the floor. She threw water from the jug at me when I approached her. Then flung the jug at me too.

Knowing what I know now, I suppose I should have given her a warning. Then, it seemed essential to pick her up and haul her out of the bath. But she fought. She kicked and splashed and lashed out. I had her in my grip, but she fought so hard we both slipped. I hurt my back. She said I hurt her leg and I might have done because I fell on her by accident. 'There'll be no telly, no sweeties, no treats,' I shouted at her, but she roared all the same and hit and kicked me and she hit herself too which frightened me.

'That's it!' I lifted her up and yanked her to the top of the stairs.

'Sit there and calm down. You're in trouble. You're in time out.'

Emily screamed that she didn't want to be in time out. Her hair was flat against her head. I threw a towel at her and when she pushed it away I put it round her shoulders.

'I'm cold!'

'You stay in time out.'

Emily cried some more and then breathed hard through her nose, purposefully blowing out snot so that it dribbled into her mouth.

'I need a tissue.'

'You did that on purpose.'

'I need a tissue.'

I went to the bathroom for toilet paper and when I returned Emily had gone. She was hiding on my bed so I retrieved her and set her back down into time out. The shouting started again.

'You could have been out of time out by now.'

Emily cried and I shouted and it seemed as if the world was ruined. Everything was desperate, nuts, crazy, horrific. My daughter wouldn't stop crying. The social worker wanted to see me again. My mum was far away and she didn't want us anyway. My head was filled with rage and sparks from tablets I never wanted to be on in the first place.

The doorbell sounded. I couldn't be sure because of all the noise, but when the doorbell rang again and I saw the shape of a man through the rectangle of glass I left Emily and went to open the door. Paul stood with his hands in his pockets. Emily's cries continued.

'Is everything okay?' I asked.

'Yeah.'

'Mummy!'

'Did you want something?'

'No. Yes.'

Pale and naked, Emily appeared next to me, her arms by her sides, her face mangled with anger and upset.

'Emily, get back in time out.'

'No.'

'This isn't a good time is it? I came to see if—'

'You hurt me, Mummy.'

'No, I didn't.'

'You did, you hurt me.'

I turned to Emily and pointed up the stairs towards time out.

'It doesn't matter,' he said. 'Keep your heating off until the plaster's dried.'

When I shut the door the crying stopped. Everything was quiet. I heard a car door shut and then an engine start up. I presumed it was Paul turning in the road and then driving away.

I sat with my naked girl. She had snot on her face. I wiped it on my sleeve. The ends of her hair leaked water over her neck and shoulders and down her chest. Blue veins stood out on her daddy's white skin. Her eyes were red. I expected to be kicked or hit or for Emily to wriggle free from my arms but I put her on my lap anyway and we hugged and I felt her cold hair on my face and neck and my clothes getting wet. We were of the same, me and Emily, remorse taking us over so that we couldn't do anything but sit with our cheeks touching, saying nothing.

'What was all that about?' I asked.

'You didn't come in the bath with me,' Emily said.

'You shouldn't have thrown the jug at me.'

It seemed that was all there was to say. I dried Emily, putting cream on the backs of her legs and on her arms which helped with the eczema she'd had since a baby. She asked for a cuddle and we held each other tight, me kneeling, Emily standing in her nightdress, for so long, the longest hug, until I suggested we get a hairdryer and see what we could do with her curls.

In former days, I would have poured wine and sipped from the glass while I read Emily a story in bed. I would have refilled the glass once she was asleep and I wanted to, so desperately, so I poured the rest of a pack of Revels into my palm and pushed them into my mouth. I checked that Emily was sleeping, pulled her covers up to her chin and kissed her cheek. Then I went to the bathroom, put my foot on a towel and slid it over the wet floor, wiping up as much of the water as I could.

It was only when I sat down that I realised with the heating off, the house was freezing. I hoped Emily hadn't got too cold sitting in time out with only her towel. I felt a bit ashamed that things had escalated so quickly when I should have been trying really hard to be a good mum.

10.

All women. At the multi-agency meeting. They were waiting for me in the parents' room at the nursery: Sara, my social worker; the nursery head who wore green glasses and high heels; and a woman I'd never met before from the council's family department. I think that's what she called it.

Sara pointed to a chair next to her. I sat.

'Where's Emily?' I said.

'She's having some lunch in the playroom. We won't keep either of you long.'

The nursery head stood to open a window. 'It gets quite stuffy in here,' she said. I heard shouts from the school playground next door.

I didn't mind that I wasn't good enough for ballet, I didn't mind that I got down to the last two lines but no further for *Chicago*, for *42nd Street*, for *Sunset Boulevard* because all along I expected my life not to be like this. However average a dancer I was, I expected not to be sitting on the wrong side of the table in a roomful of professionals about to pick apart my parenting.

'Now, this isn't all doom and gloom,' the nursery head said. She pushed her glasses further up the bridge of her nose, a purposeful push with two closed fingers.

'Not at all. Not at all,' Sara said.

The shame was intense. I couldn't find my toughness. I was meek. My shoulders were hunched so I straightened them and wondered how it would feel to sit at that table when you'd never in your life been called confident, when you'd never high-kicked in front of a crowd or danced barefoot under a spotlight. I suppose those women brought sisters or mothers with them to sit by their sides. That made me think about my own mum. She wasn't meek. I should probably call her.

'Do you want a cup of tea, Liz?' Sara said.

So she did drink tea. 'No thanks,' I said.

I waited.

The others refilled their cups. The nursery head dropped two sugar cubes into her black coffee and stirred.

Sara opened a hardback book and clicked the top of her pen onto its pages.

I took a deep breath and said, 'You know, if you were to pull me up on my parenting, it would have been back in London, not here. You might have had a point back then, but to do this here, it's senseless.'

I wasn't going to tell them that I cried every day in London, that it hurt to stay alive. Emily would pass me tissues and sleep next to me while I watched television. I neglected her then, I know that. My mum took her for me whenever I wanted, which was all the time. My doctor gave me antidepressants. She told me to take lots of photos of Emily so that when I was better I'd see that I did in fact dress her nicely and look after her well. I don't think I did either. The photos are still on my phone.

Sara said, 'I've updated the room with your experience with social work thus far. We'll not focus on the incident in the car park. That's a police matter.'

The shame, the shame.

'We're here today to see how we can support you and Emily.'

As if she'd seen my shame the nursery head spoke: 'I do want to say that you're not the first parent who's been referred to social services. We see all sorts in the nursery. Without breaking confidences, I just want to say that it would surprise you, some of the things we deal with. We'll get to the bottom of this.'

'Shall we start with you then, Moira?' Sara said to the nursery head.

But I said, 'This is a waste of your time. Sorry to be rude, but we're not staying in Lennoxtown. You don't need to do this for me.'

'We're doing this for Emily,' Sara said. 'And we will contact social work wherever you go. It doesn't stop here.' She could bite, Sara.

The nursery head leaned forwards. 'We've observed Emily in nursery. She gets awfully upset at times. She displays some behaviours that we're a little concerned about.'

'What behaviours?'

Sara looked down at her hardback notebook. The other woman sat back in her seat to listen to the head.

'She gets distressed if her keyworker leaves the room. She's hard to console when she's upset.'

'She's always been like that. That's her way, I think.' I'm her mum, I should know. Then I said, 'Where is her keyworker?'

'I'm afraid we were short-staffed. I couldn't take her out of the playroom.'

'Do you find Emily hard to manage at home?' Sara said to me.

As I was about to speak, a woman opened the door, poked her head into the room, saw us and said, 'Sorry.' She withdrew and closed the door. I wanted to say sorry and leave, like her.

'At times, yes,' I said.

The women nodded.

'But I don't abuse her. I'm not abusive.'

'No one's saying you are,' said Sara.

'But you're saying I'm damaging Emily.'

'We have markers,' the nursery head said, 'as to how a child is developing. We want her to be going along up here –' she raised a freckled arm, 'but she's still here at the moment.' She flattened her arm. 'And we don't want her going down here.' She raised her elbow a little which made her fingers point down to the table. 'It's often the relationship with their significant carer that we check on first – it's mostly the mother but that's not always the case.'

'It's the mother in this case,' I said.

The nursery head smiled and pushed her glasses back up her nose.

'Can you tell us a bit about Emily's dad?' Sara said.

'I'd prefer not to.'

'Why not?'

I sighed. 'Really, I don't want to start on that.'

'He's not around?'

'No.'

'What about your mum? Emily mentioned she has a granny,' the nursery head said.

'Yes, she has a granny. My mum.'

It occurred to me then that I was self indulgent, that the escape I sought was of little use to Emily, who liked the cushions on her gran's sofa, who liked the comfort of a familiar body. My own mother had only an address for me and hadn't seen her granddaughter in weeks. I'd thought the hitting and tantrums and relentless bad behaviour, every hour of every day, was normal, was what being a four-year-old was like, but maybe Emily was missing home.

'That's a lot of pressure on your shoulders,' Sara said.

'What do I have to do?'

The women seemed to exhale collectively. Sara closed her notebook. 'You could come once a week to a family support session,' she said. 'It's very informal. Little tips on dealing with the difficult things. A bit of support.'

'I don't want you observing my parenting.'

'Not at all,' the family worker said. It was the first time she'd spoken. 'It's just reminders of things you probably do anyway, but maybe should do a little more of. Playing together. Listening to her. Time when you switch off your mobile phone.'

'She only wants the television,' I said.

'We know it's not easy. We've all been in situations with our own children where we've been tearing our hair out, beside ourselves with frustration, haven't we?'

The women around the table nodded sympathetically and energetically.

'You've got a lot going on in your life,' the family worker said. 'It's understandable to want to take the easy option or to lose your patience.'

She was wrong. There wasn't enough in my life. There was only a dead woman's house and me and my daughter without plans or even inclinations. I should call the woman from the library who gave me her number. I should invite Paul over. I wanted to get back to the dancers in the sheltered housing.

'Your mental well-being is a priority too,' said Sara. 'I don't know if you feel you're a bit low.'

Were they right? Were they on to me?

'We've got a quick questionnaire we could do right now. You just say if you agree, strongly agree, disagree—'

'I don't want to do a questionnaire, thank you.'

From the playground I heard a bell ring and then shouts and running feet and the raising of a teacher's voice. I looked towards the window but saw only the rough stone that they built the houses with in Lennoxtown.

Sara spoke again. 'Look, we don't believe Emily is at risk in your care. But we want to meet with you regularly in order to support you and to check that all is well. We want to set Emily up for a good and happy life. We need to get you two working as a wee team, help you get her confident and ready for school. Just stick with us for a bit, yes?'

'What if I don't want to meet with you?'

They flinched at that. Sara spun her pen on top of her hardback book.

The family worker held her hands around her mug as she spoke. 'Nobody's forcing you to, but we're recommending it. Go on, Liz, eh? It'll just be me and some other mums in a room like this. It might even be this room.' She kept her gaze on me until I nodded my head.

They brought Emily in wearing her coat and outdoor shoes, all changed and ready for me like a parcel. I sensed them watching me and it made me embarrassed to kiss her. That must be a thing, being embarrassed to kiss your own child. But Emily was as she always was. She pulled hard at my handbag, tugging at the zip, stuffing her hands inside.

'What have you got for me?' she asked.

'Don't tug.'

'I'm hungry.'

'Haven't you just had lunch?'

'I didn't like it.'

She tugged at my bag again, pulling it off my shoulder. I looked over at the women who were watching me.

'Don't pull, Emily,' I said again and then, 'can we just leave please, and we'll talk about this outside.'

The women stood and smiled and rearranged the chairs. Emily ignored them when they called goodbye. I was glad to hear the door close.

Life-changing. Heart-stopping. What would Robbie say? He would say, Oh Liz, what have you got yourself into? What were you doing, coming to Lennoxtown in the first place? Run, away, Lizzie, run away.

II.

One morning on our way to nursery, with the Campsie Fells cast gold by early sunlight, we saw Paul. He was leaning against the metal fence around the primary school, holding on to the railings. His body was flat against the fence and he looked like a lover. As we came closer, I saw he was talking to a child. A girl. His girl. Her hands held the railings too and she stood on her tiptoes and their faces were close. I had a sudden flash of envy even though that intimate scene was not for me, it was nothing to do with me. I'm not even sure what I was envious about other than it had something to do with love.

And then a woman stood next to Paul and passed a lunchbox through the railings to the girl. Her mother, I presumed. She put her hand to the girl's cheek. As Paul and the woman turned around to leave, I thought, God, they're as pretty as each other, a pair of beauties. It was hard not to stare. Then she snarled something at him and he snarled back at her and they stopped on the street and spoke words that I couldn't hear. I was fascinated by them. Paul caught me staring and smiled. I turned my stare to a smile and held tight to Emily. I hadn't forgotten about him coming to my door, washed and shaven in his clean clothes. I thought it was time he called again.

We began to see each other. It was never to take the place of Robbie, just a way of bringing me company. Even Robbie would have said, Take what's there, don't be lonely. He would also have said, Mind you're straight up with him. I think I was.

I made a list of barre exercises I thought my students could manage. *Battement tendu, battement glissé* – closed beat, gliding beat – stretches of the leg to the front and the side and the back that required a hand on the barre so a ninety-six-year-old's balance could be held. Agnes and Charlie could stay at the barre for the whole class if they wished. I thought I would try my more agile dancers – Eve, June, John – with a jump – a *sauté*. It would challenge their hearts and hips and knees, but they could try it, why not. When they were finished I would demonstrate an *échappé sauté* – an escaped jump – from fifth into second; they could progress to that, I was sure. And to give them a show I would dance a couple of *sauté fouettés,* whipping my leg in the air from the side to the back as I landed in *arabesque*. Beautiful. I would look like a ballerina doing that. Seeing Paul had emboldened me.

I went to the meeting for children and parents and carers. It took place in the parents' room as they'd said it might, after Emily's morning nursery session. What those women didn't understand was that I forgot about Emily's tantrums almost as soon as they happened. We were like that. We would wake up the next morning and cuddle and she would hold my hand and inspect it and comment on my fingernails and veins or ask to press her warm hands onto my belly fat, the belly that she grew in. I think that's normal, isn't it, that switch from despair to harmony? Apparently not.

I accepted a cup of tea and sat in an armchair. The family worker led Emily to a low-down table, poured water into a plastic cup and offered her cut-up apple and banana and satsuma segments. She wouldn't stay at the table and instead took her plate to me and stood at my knee. 'She'll become more independent when she gets used to us,' the family worker said as Emily ate her fruit. She was a good fruit eater. That's luck, I know, because she doesn't like vegetables.

There was nothing formal about the meeting. In fact it was so informal I wondered if the social worker and the nursery head knew that this was all that went on: the kids got fed and the parents got a seat. I thought perhaps I could throw out a question or two about the shouting and the hitting: did anybody else's kids still do it at four nearly five? Or I could make a casual remark about my rage and see if anyone else felt it. No, I would keep my rage to myself.

I looked around me and spotted Caroline, the woman from the library with the swinging hair and the many children. She held her teacup in one hand and waved with the other. She must have clocked my surprise. Maybe she was as surprised to see me, but she can't have been. Surely I was perfect for this kind of group.

'I didn't know your wee one went to the nursery. What's her name?' She held her baby now instead of her tea and was opening her maternity top as she sat down next to me. 'I'm trying to wean him off but he's refusing.' The baby's face was reddening and his mouth formed a cry. She put him to her breast and took a deep breath.

'Her name's Emily.'

'Hello Emily.' Emily said nothing. 'That's Carmel over there. You met her in the library.'

Emily looked but didn't speak.

'I had to rush off. At the library.'

Caroline scratched her cheek and pushed her hair from her face. 'It's hot in here. Don't worry. Sometimes you just have to go.'

I expected we would be called together to listen to a lesson or demonstration, to share experiences publicly, but the clock on the wall showed the minutes passing and nothing formal was said. The family worker spent time with some of the women but she didn't approach me. Perhaps I was more like Emily than I thought and she was giving me space. The only thing she offered me apart from the cup of tea was the leftover fruit. 'Eat it up,' she said to us.

'I haven't had any lunch,' Caroline said.

'Me neither.'

We ate the leftover fruit piece after piece. The family worker passed us crackers and we ate them too. I think it was on purpose, feeding the parents in case there was nothing to eat at home. We were close to that. Not quite, but close.

'I was surprised to see you here,' I said to Caroline. 'You seem so together.'

'You must be joking.'

I wondered if she was on antidepressants too. Now that I was coming off mine I looked at other people and couldn't believe that their serenity came from anything other than medication.

'Carmel's speech is slow,' Caroline said. Her daughter was helping the family worker stack cups. 'And they thought she would benefit from this.'

I nodded. Caroline seemed happy with the intervention. She sat her baby on her lap and leaned back into her chair.

'What about you? Can I ask?'

I told Emily to give her cup to the family worker. Then I said, 'She's not settling in very well at nursery. We're new here, I think I told you that.' Then, 'I'm the one that left her in the car.'

Caroline sat up and turned to face me. Her baby smiled. I looked from face to face and thought how similar they were. 'Oh my God, that was you?' Caroline said. 'You poor thing.'

'Yes,' I said.

'Are you…? Are they going to…?'

'I don't think so. But social services are keeping an eye.'

'Ugh. And I brought it up with you. I'm so embarrassed.' Caroline lifted her baby so he was high above her head. 'Fuck them,' she said to her baby as the family worker came round to remind us that the session was on again next week. We got our children in their coats and left.

Robbie liked to watch me dance in the same way I liked to watch him run. It was rare that he wasn't needed in the gym, but if he could, he stood in the technician's box, kept out of the way of the sound and lighting engineer, and watched me, telling me afterwards how the audience reacted to this or that routine. He liked my strong thighs. I liked them too. He said I had flair. I knew I did. I'd never felt more proud of my body and what it could do. I was supple, I was fit, I was strong. I was a thing of beauty and grace. That, I appreciated. The sunrises and sunsets, I rarely saw them, so I appreciated them too. The ample wages I appreciated. The calm seas I appreciated when we caught the tail end of a hurricane and the ship rocked and water slapped out of the deck pool and we had to grab the handrails wherever we walked. The excursions when we docked at ports, I appreciated. The four-wheel drives, the beaches and sand and scuba dives, I appreciated. The meals cooked and presented to me, I didn't appreciate. The cut-price drinks in the bar, I didn't appreciate. The time out from life's realities, not that either. We stood aside while drugs dogs sniffed our cabins, knowing we were untouchable because that wasn't our life; nothing to do with us. Being with Robbie on a cruise ship on the pitch black ocean, under silver constellations, while whole continents got on with the business of trade and politics and war, I cared for nothing of that. Hedonistic me.

Then my dad deteriorated and I heard over long-distance phone calls that he was becoming quite frail which was a surprise because we'd been told only six months earlier that the medication had stabilised him.

'Do you want to fly home?' Robbie said.

'Am I allowed to just leave?' We had one day off a week. I had solos and positions in dances that no one else could fill.

We sat together in the crew bar, quiet with our drinks and my dilemma.

'What would you do?' I asked Robbie.

'I would go home,' Robbie said. I knew he would say that.

He held me close that night. He couldn't avoid it, the bunks were so small, but I felt calmed and was glad of him.

'Don't be ridiculous!' my mum said when I told her of my plans. 'The man's not dead, he's got leukaemia and it's stabilising. You stay out there until you're on a longer break. Send me some photos and I'll show them to him. Go and have a nice time and I'll see you in a couple of months.'

I did what my mum said and stayed on the ship with Robbie.

We used to leave our cabin doors open which is how Robbie got into trouble. All the staff cabins were on the same stretch of corridor and it was understood that if you wanted company you would leave your door open or go into someone else's room. So I was never lonely, even before I met Robbie. If I wanted solitude I could simply close my door. It seems astonishing to me now that I could muster up the hours of casual conversations I had on the ship and that I could sit comfortably among people who took chat for granted.

Robbie was berthed with the beauty therapists and the life guards. I was berthed with the dancers and singers and musicians, but our cabins weren't far from each other's. We slept, generally, in my room. Robbie's roommate had a girlfriend who slept in their shared cabin most of the time and my roommate was seeing a musician so she spent her nights in his cabin. But even if she wasn't sleeping with him at night, Robbie slept with us. We all did it. There was an intimate acceptance.

Robbie went back to his cabin one day, the one his roommate slept in with his girlfriend, and took a change of clothes, a book and two paracetamols from his drawer. He didn't take any money from his roommate's girlfriend's bag but that is what she accused him of.

'My money's missing,' she said as she tore into my cabin. He had to go back to the gym in ten minutes.

'Where did you leave it?' we asked.

'In my bag. In your cabin,' she said to Robbie.

'Are you sure it's gone?' I said. 'Did you spend it?'

'I didn't spend sixty dollars.'

She stood in my doorway with her hands on her hips. 'Robbie, you and I get along all right but you're the only one who's been in the cabin all morning.'

'Are you joking?'

'Can you just return it and we'll go back to normal?'

They never went back to normal. I never doubted him. He was honest. More honest than me. And we didn't need money. We had more money than we'd ever had in our lives. But something like fear came over him. It was the only time I'd seen him angry. He was loud. Perhaps it was stress his heart didn't like. With minutes before he was due to start in the gym we followed him to his cabin and watched him lift pillows, shake duvets, tilt mattresses and tumble the contents of drawers in his hands. The space was tiny. There was no money. He left us to go back to the gym. I called in to see him an hour later and he was talking patiently to a woman who wanted a go on the rowing machine. Compared with their age – so many on the ship were of an age we could only aspire to, not comprehend ever being – he looked like a boy, wearing the shorts he'd returned to the cabin to get.

The girl told her supervisor and Robbie was taken into his office for questioning. I waited for him and he came out looking grim.

'He wants to search your cabin,' Robbie said to me.

The supervisor found nothing of course but threatened to bring police on board at the next port. He said he would withhold Robbie's passport, all our passports, until the money was found. We'd just left Miami. We stood on the deck and there was nothing around us but sea and the first stars in the deepening sky.

'I want to get off,' Robbie said. 'I have to get off.'

'But you didn't do it.'

'No. They think I did, they think I did. Again and again.'

'It's all right.'

'It's not all right.'

Two passengers came close to us and because he was a professional and because he was able to do it, I watched him change his posture and loosen his shoulders and shake the tension from his body.

'Good evening,' the male passenger said.

'Good evening.' We raised our heads and I saw the last of the purple in the black.

'Don't ever leave me,' Robbie said.

'Never.'

The next day Robbie's roommate told him she'd found her money. It wasn't in her handbag; it was in a zipped pocket in her backpack. She never apologised to Robbie and he never spoke to her again.

My dad timed his death for a break in our contracts. We flew home for his funeral and I introduced Robbie to my mum who was frayed with grief and tiredness.

After the funeral, seeped in sherry, her face hot, she put an arm round me and held me close. 'Oh, Liz, what am I going to do?'

'Don't do anything yet. You'll be okay, Mum.'

Her breath smelled sweet. Her fringe was wet. 'You should have come home,' she whispered, her lips touching my cheek.

'Mum?'

'I was wrong. You should have come home.'

She was right.

We stayed for three weeks, me at my mum's house and Robbie on the floor of his old flatmate's house. He spent some nights with us and some nights away. By the time we were ready to fly back to Tampa for nine months we wanted nothing more than each other.

'Next time we leave the ship, we stay together, we don't separate,' he said to me and I said, 'That suits me.'

My mum met Alan soon after my dad died, which I found strange but it made me feel less guilty about leaving her, because essentially I had failed her twice: once by not coming back and a second time by not staying.

12.

John stood outside the sheltered housing, a cigarette dying in his fingers. 'You again,' he said, 'I'll get my tap shoes and cane,' and I touched him on the arm as I passed. He stubbed out his cigarette and rubbed his hands together as he followed me in. I presumed they would all be pleased to see me. But nobody appeared willing to start the class. Charlie stood by his frame, dressing gown snug around his body, hair combed back from his forehead, his jaw moving, as if chewing on something. June stood next to him holding a pint glass, Eve and Alice sat side by side not speaking and Senga and Agnes picked coins from a purse. Rita, the cleaner, was in the far corner of the room and the vacuum cleaner cord rippled along the floor as she worked. The radio played.

'We'll wait for the hoovering to finish,' I said and sat on the floor to take off my trainers and put on my ballet shoes. They watched me in silence. It made me feel like a child.

'Have you warmed up?' I raised my head to look at them. Nobody spoke. Perhaps they couldn't hear me over the noise of the vacuum cleaner. I stood and stretched my arms above my head, then I let my body fall forwards and I hung, head first, legs wide apart and stretched the backs of my legs and my back too. They were still watching me when I straightened up. So I did a single *pirouette*, landing neatly in fifth. Nothing.

Senga spoke, finally. She told me that she and her mother had a taxi booked five minutes after the class finished and would need to leave promptly. 'It's her eyes this time,' she said. 'Look, she can barely see through those cataracts.' Agnes smiled. Her irises were pearls. The skin on her nose and cheekbones was patched with age.

'Come on,' I said once Rita was turning the handle of the vacuum cleaner and winding in the cord. I grabbed chairs and lined them up, plugged in my speaker and phone. Nobody moved. Eve dabbed at her eyes with the sides of her fingers and Senga gave her a folded napkin from her handbag.

John came into the room, smelling of smoke. He put down his paper. 'That's Ellen away, I'm presuming,' he said.

They all nodded.

'You should have said goodbye,' June said.

'Of course I said goodbye. I went to see her last night.' John put his hand in his pocket and put a five-pound note and a pound coin into June's pint glass. June glanced at me, as if to say there you go, he can afford it.

'Thank you,' I said. 'Who's away?'

'Ellen.'

'Who's Ellen?'

'She lived next door to Eve,' June said.

Eve folded her napkin and put it up her sleeve. Her fingers shook a little.

Rita stopped by us and said, 'Where is it she's gone?'

'Barrhead,' June said.

'Not Barrhead,' Eve said.

'Bellahouston?'

'Bellahouston's where the Pope came. I was there. Twice,' June said. 'Wherever she's gone, it's two minutes away from her daughter. They wanted her close by.'

Ellen, their friend, had fallen, weeks ago, and fractured a bone in her hip. The family had decided on a care home.

'Premature,' John said. 'That woman had a lot of life in her. They'll realise they made a mistake when they have to pay her fees week on week.'

'Bellshill,' Charlie said.

'That's it, Bellshill,' said June. 'I knew it was a B. I was thinking Barrhead, Bridgeton, Bellahouston. Bellshill.'

'She'll not come out of there. She thinks it's temporary. But she won't leave,' Eve said.

'Eve was very good friends with her,' Charlie said.

'So was I,' said John.

Rita pulled her vacuum cleaner out of the lounge and said she would be back to make a cup of tea. Two men looked through the doorway and feigned fear when I waved them in.

'They won't come,' June said. 'They go to the bookies.'

So I turned off the radio and stood in the centre of the room. I did another *pirouette*, a double this time, which was met with applause – I enjoyed the praise – and I said, 'Right, it's dance class time. Ladies, gents, get to the barre.' It seemed all I could do. I wasn't a therapist, I wasn't a care worker, I was a dancer, and they were there to dance.

We began with *pliés* and *port de bras* as before. I walked between them and lifted elbows so arms curved gracefully and I shaped fingers and wrists. I watched them tilt tender chins to the ceiling as they raised arms heavenwards, stretching their necks.

'Keep your mouths soft and your necks long,' I said. 'Drop your shoulders. Pull in. You look beautiful.' They were.

They were better than the previous week at their *pliés* and *relevés*, their forward and back bends, their *rond de Johns*, and they coped with the *battements tendus* and *glissés*. We danced to 'Spiegel im Spiegel'. Perhaps the music was sad but I think it helped them achieve a delicacy to their movements. It pierces you, that music, and you might as well use pain if it's there. Watched by the faces in the photographs on the walls, they were a careful graceful troupe.

Next I taught them how to slide the toe up the calf to the knee and hold it there, balanced. It was then I saw how difficult this was for them. Charlie wobbled. So did Alice and Agnes. I thought they would fall.

'Stop,' I said, my urgency in contrast with the peace we'd created. 'Don't lift your toe to your knees. Just point your toe to your ankle. Keep the tip of your toe on the floor.'

This felt safer. 'Raise your eyes now. Look up and over my head. Fly. Soar. Look at that photo on the wall behind me. Who's that? Who is she?'

'That's Ellen,' Alice said and I was pleased to hear her voice so loud and confident.

'What's the medal for?'

'Nursing. She was a matron. She won a prize.'

I was sad to make them turn away from her and work on their other sides.

Afterwards, we took a *demi-plié* in third position and slid our legs along the floor to *demi-plié* in second, transferring our weight, and finishing with a strong standing leg and a pointed toe and closing into third. *Chassé*. To slide. Side to side. Then we *chasséd* to the front – *en avant* – keeping our back legs stretched. Here we scooped an arm from *bras bas* to first, elongating at the wrist and stretching to the front, our back arm following the line of the back leg or holding on to the barre. *Arabesque*. My beautiful dancers. Stretch. Hold that position. Balance. Stretch some more – *allonger* – to stretch out, to make longer. But to not fall.

'Are you still with me?' I called to them. 'Raise your back leg if you can. If you can't, keep your toe on the floor and your arm stretched in front. It's still an *arabesque*. Good. And relax your shoulders. Relax your mouths. Who can give me a smile? Ya dancer!' That's what Robbie said when he was pleased with something. Ya dancer. I always thought it apt.

They smiled, all of them, Eve under duress, but I saw the sides of her mouth nip up briefly. June winked. She was good. The best. I think she knew it.

Near the end of our session, I said, 'Did the lady who's gone, your friend, did she have a favourite song?' and thank God I had Elvis and Ella Fitzgerald, and they were happy to stand in the middle of the room and clap and sway. John took

Eve's hands and they shuffled a jive on the carpet tiles and I told them if I'd known they could dance like that I'd have pushed them harder in class.

'Let's see if Rita has left some water in the kettle,' June said at the end of the song and I thought, yes, that's enough dancing for today.

We drank tea. John took a cup. He sat at a separate table turning the pages of his paper, but closer to us, this time. Agnes and Senga bustled away to their taxi and Alice took her cardigan from the back of a chair and waved goodbye, but Eve, June and Charlie stayed.

'I'll collect your money for you each week,' June said, tapping the nails of one hand against the pint glass, full of coins and a couple of notes. 'I know who squirrels their money away and can afford to pay a bit more.'

'That's kind of you.'

'It's nothing to do with kindness.'

Her tone was stroppy. I liked it.

'Well, thank you then, but go easy please. I'm not up for fleecing old people.'

She told me to get my purse. I held it open like before and she poured in the coins and handed me the notes. It seemed to me that the departure of Ellen had thrown them into all kinds of anxiety. Eve was sad that her friend and neighbour had gone but more sad that her daughter in Toronto and son in Adelaide had made no such offer to take her away too.

She said it must be a reflection on their relationship; why else would they live on different continents, and if that was all there was, what had been the point? I didn't know how to comfort her and nobody else tried.

'I'm happy as I am,' John said, and folded his newspaper.

Charlie said he had five sons and fifteen grandchildren. They shared him out for Christmas. He knew he was, what's the word, cumbersome.

'June?' I asked.

June shook her head. 'My son writes every now and again and says he wants to move me closer. I think my daughter-in-law puts him up to it. But it would be the end of me.'

She said she would miss her view. She didn't scramble up the sides of those fells as a child to leave them behind when the only thing that kept her going of a day was to see them from her window, or to take a bus, occasionally, and stand on them, looking out at all the gold and grass. She stood up and gathered the teacups.

Eve took a photo album from the sideboard and showed it to me. 'Ellen started this off,' she said. 'When somebody died she put their picture in here so they wouldn't be forgotten. The Book of Names she called it. That's Agnes's husband. They lived together. After he died, Senga moved in.' Eve had oval fingernails and a gold wedding ring. She pointed to her friend's slanted handwriting next to pictures of people with wrinkled faces, shining eyes and good dentures.

'Have you got a nice picture of Ellen to go in the book?'
I asked.

'She's not dead yet.'

'Sorry.' I glanced at June, returning from the kitchenette,
who shook her head at me, but in a mocking way, as if I was
daft not mean.

'I'm away to the laundry to do those sheets,' June said.

Eve showed me photographs of parties and dinners and
groups of residents wearing Christmas hats, an occasional child
sitting on a knee. I saw Ruth the manager in some pictures, and
Rita the cleaner. 'We used to look after each other here. We
were enough for each other. Now there's too many single men
who keep themselves to themselves and nobody gets together.'

'Present company excepted,' John said.

'Ruth can only do so much.'

'Does she check on you if she doesn't see you for a while?'

'She chaps the door.'

'Do many people die here?' I asked, and regretted it. They
were quite silent.

'Sometimes,' Charlie said, 'but we tend to go before we
get too sick. To hospital. Or if we've had a stroke or if we can't
look after ourselves we get moved to care homes. There aren't
too many surprises here.'

Eve put the photo album back onto the shelf.

I told them about Audrey, Robbie's gran. Hearing them
talk had made me wonder if Audrey had been lonely. 'I'm in
her house just now with my daughter and it's never quiet,

it's a riot, because children, you know, and I hate the quiet, I hate to think of her hearing her clock tick and having no one to talk to.' You could be lonely with a child, I knew that too.

'Get rid of ticking clocks,' John said. 'And put the talking radio on.'

'Endeavour to leave the house each day,' Charlie said. 'Have a full head of hair and a beard. I let the lassies at the hairdresser's practise on me.'

'Is that why Alice comes here and rarely speaks?' I asked. 'For the company.'

'Alice knows her memory's going so she's afraid to speak,' Eve said. 'Some days she's awful confused.'

I stood up. It was nearly time to get Emily. I would call into Lidl on the way to the nursery to buy fruit. Eve took a book from her bag and said she was going to read by the natural light at the window. John and Charlie left. June met me in the corridor.

'Can I borrow you for a second?' she said.

She asked me to help her pull her neighbour's wet sheets from the washing machine and put them in the dryer. Her arthritis was bad and there was little she could do on days like this. I didn't know she had arthritis. I wondered if the ballet helped her joints or whether she was in pain for the whole class.

'I've been duped. Harry next to me took sick so I helped with his washing while he was recovering. I washed his dirty sheets and put clean ones on his bed. Now he's better and I'm still doing his sheets. Just put them straight in the dryer,' she said.

The wet sheets were heavy. I bent to shove them into the dryer.

'Just switch it on, hen, put it to forty-five.'

I started the machine and the room filled with noise and heat.

'What if you can't do your washing? What if you can't get out to do your shopping?'

'There are girls from the council who come. Charlie has one. Harry has one too. You manage. Most of us have family. Some poor souls don't.'

'What about you?'

'My son's in Essex. He doesn't visit.'

'You're not a poor soul.'

'Thank you. At last someone sees me for who I am.'

She shut the door on the laundry and as if it had just occurred to her she said, 'Come and I'll show you my view.'

I checked my watch and that small gesture of mine seemed to make her self-conscious.

'You've got to get on.'

'No, no, I've just got time. Come on, let's go.' If she felt she was being humoured, she didn't show it.

She walked alongside me down the carpeted corridor, looking up to speak to me because I was so much taller. She kept her back straight and her feet turned out as she walked. We climbed a set of stairs slowly. We passed many doors.

'There,' she said as she pushed open the door to her flat. 'Come through.'

She had a bedroom and a bathroom and an open plan living room with a kitchen at one end and a window at the other. There was a chair by the window and on it a blanket and a book of crosswords.

But oh, her view. The morning sun was on the Campsies. Every tree, hedge and boulder was yellow lit. The fir trees at the Campsies' base smouldered in their deep green.

'June, this is stunning.'

'I feel like a bit of a show off now. But I wanted someone to see what I see. I've had no one in here since I moved in.'

'No one's been in to see it? I wouldn't want to move from this view if it was mine.'

'I can sit for hours. I watch the weather. It's always changing. This view is worth being old for isn't it?'

She seemed defiant.

'Yes,' I said.

'I appreciate it, don't you worry. When we lived in Campsie, my son used to run away into those hills and when he wasn't home by evening I'd be forced to go and look for him.'

'Where did he go?'

'He'd find a hut to hide in or he'd sit in trees for hours. I was searching for him once, walking along, calling his name. I must have had a second sense he was there, a mother's instinct, because suddenly sticks rained down on me from one of the trees. He was a good aim.'

'Is that him?'

On the sideboard there was a photograph in a frame of June sitting on a sofa, next to a man much bigger than her, but with the same chin and the same coloured hair – June's hair was grey, but in the picture it was sandy blonde and the man's was sandy blonde too. Healthy strong heads of hair.

'That's him,' she said.

'What's his name?'

'Michael.'

I looked around her spacious flat and thought of my dad's room in the hospice. My mum had told me it was adequate.

'Shall I put the kettle on? You've not got time, have you?'

'Sorry June.'

'Take the pity out of your voice.'

I laughed.

'I don't have biscuits anyway.'

I looked out of the window and had a sudden vision of myself in a life I hadn't planned. No Robbie, Emily grown up and gone, my mum long gone. Would I cling to a view like this? Probably. Would Emily visit me or would she go away like I had? What would become of us?

June was looking at me when I turned to face her. She pursed her lips and gave my arm a pat but said nothing other than 'goodbye' and I did the same.

Back in the corridor I heard the rumble of the tumble dryer and stood aside to let men carrying a chest of drawers pass. Outside a woman with two black bags stood near a hire van, its back doors open to the sun. I presumed they were Ellen's black bags and would go with her to the care home. The woman threw them in the van with force.

13.

Paul brought a bottle of wine when he came one night to check his work and I had to tell him I didn't drink. He left the wine by the front door and I watched in silence as he ran his palms across his newly painted walls and rubbed a thumb over a tiny bubble of paint he'd spotted by the floor.

Divertissement as they say in ballet. An enjoyable diversion. I said to him – a whispered confession, just as he bowed his head to my chest and his hands were on my waist and then my hips, as if in preparation for a lift – that it had been years since anyone: I'd never wanted to, had no desire to. Yet I was surprised to feel so flush so quickly and it was a strong pleasure to wrap a leg round his leg and feel the slick muscles in his back. We fitted.

Robbie became more alive after sex, more boyish, more talkative, full of energy, jokes, caresses, stories. Paul was more as I'd remembered men. He wanted to sleep where we lay on Audrey's sofa. 'It's best if you don't stay,' I said when we had dozed and woken. 'Mornings. Emily.'

He understood. 'Can I come back though? I'm at my mum's now and I can't invite you over there.'

'And I can't leave her here, so yes, come back.'

He put on his trousers and searched around for his T-shirt, jacket, keys.

'Thank you,' he said to me.

'It was good, wasn't it?'

'Aye, it was.'

He took his wine with him when he left.

I climbed into bed. Emily was there, lying as she did when she was a baby, on her back with her arms half-raised and her fists clenched into a cheer. I curled into one of her fists and it took me no time to sleep, no time at all. In the night I woke with a fear that I'd betrayed Robbie. Is that why I'd come to Lennoxtown, I thought, to sleep with someone from Robbie's home if I could no longer have him? I did betray Robbie, there is no doubt. I also used Paul's body as if it was Robbie's, there is no doubt about that. But I liked it. I liked Paul. Even Robbie would have said it was a good thing for me. *Divertissement.*

14.

Could we tire of the waves and the ports and the crew bar and the nights squeezed into my single cabin bed? Yes, it seemed. A dancer I knew messaged me to say she was performing at the Lido in Paris and they were holding auditions. 'You would get in with your figure,' she said, 'and your dancing. You get to live in Paris. They treat you like royalty.'

I told Robbie about it. He said I should audition. He was ready to go to university in London and take up his place on the physiotherapy degree he'd deferred year after year. London was close enough to Paris.

He had a feel for what would make us happy. Don't do it, Lizzie, he would say about something I felt compelled or pressured to do. Not that there was much in those days. He helped me with my mum. He pointed out her good points, of which there were many, and told me to banish the memory of her leaning into me at my dad's funeral telling me with her sherry breath that I should have come home, she'd borne too much on her own.

He was ambitious and so was I. We were a good match.

'We'll live in London, if I get my place, won't we?' he asked. 'Or, if you get Paris, I could shoot over on the Eurostar at weekends. You'll keep auditioning, won't you? We'll stay together.'

'Without a doubt,' I said.

That's a lie. There were a few doubts but they were shared doubts like where we would live and how we would afford it but I dismissed them because we had a few thousand pounds saved each and that seemed like a lot of money then, seems even more now. So at the end of our contracts we kept our new ones unsigned, disembarked at Tampa and flew home.

The audition routines were tap and jazz and the kind of show dancing that I'd done on the ship. I had the height. Even before we danced they sent some girls home because they weren't tall enough. I was the right size for once and was pleased that I'd run on the treadmill with Robbie and was fit. He'd kept on with his 10K nights with other crew and staff. He did them once a week and each week they tried to beat their previous times. I've heard it said that your body has only so many heartbeats. It's preordained. Your heart ticks until it's done. I wish Robbie hadn't run so much.

They let more girls go before lunch but they kept me on. In the afternoon, they pulled me out of the line and told the other girls to come to the side. They made me do the routine on my own and told the girls to watch me. That's what they wanted to see, that level of performance. I felt the envy but I took it, just pretended I was Robbie with his big mouth and big head and didn't let myself be intimidated. A few minutes later they pulled another girl out and we had to watch her too.

At the end of the afternoon they let more girls go and there were only four of us left. I thought that was it. I thought

I was in. Then they told us we'd made it to the finals and we would be called back the following week when we would do it all again with the other finalists.

In my tap shoes I practised wing after wing after double wing into double break that whole week, on the same laminate floor I'd practised on as a teenager. We were staying with my mum in London. The tubes were down on the morning of the finals and I eventually gave up at Kings Cross, running through Bloomsbury and Oxford Street to Soho, my tap shoes and jazz shoes and water bottle crashing around my dance bag. I barely had time to warm up, but I got there, pinned my number to my leotard and gave them what they wanted.

I got it. Paris. A Lido girl. Robbie bought Cava. He'd regained his place at university. He would start in September. We drank the whole bottle and he raced to the corner shop to buy more. My mum said all those dancing lessons she'd paid for had paid off. We had a celebration in her living room.

I sank so much booze that night I do wonder if Emily was affected. She'd been there the whole time, burrowed into my womb, stuck in while I barrel-turned and *jetéd* and wing-changed, and made herself known when my period didn't come, after I'd signed the Lido contract, after Robbie had accepted his university place and we'd both told the cruise we weren't coming back and we'd decided that on my salary he could come over on the Eurostar on weekends and on holidays but let's get things started for us, shall we, let's get living.

He didn't persuade me to keep her although it was me who considered an abortion. He viewed my pregnancy through the eyes of a man who sees his future and is happy with what he finds. He was in love with me and a baby made sense. I capitulated, I guess, in the way that women do. Certainly if he'd questioned the timing of my pregnancy I might have spent longer toying with thoughts of abortion. Maybe I'd have decided entirely by myself that Emily was ours to keep. I don't know now. I'll never know. I miss Robbie's lack of ambivalence because ambivalence runs through everything I do. I wasn't ambivalent about losing Paris and the Lido though: I was gutted, heartbroken, my ambition stopped.

15.

The young policeman knocked on our door at lunchtime. He seemed unintimidating as he took his hands from his pockets. I thought if I was being arrested there would be two of them so I relaxed.

He looked beyond me into Audrey's painted flat.

'Do you want to see inside?' I said.

'Better not.' He had another peek over my shoulder and said, 'It's a courtesy call. They've arrested someone in connection with the attempted robbery from your vehicle.'

'Oh.'

'They've kept him in custody.'

'Why?'

'He tends to go walkabout on the day of his trial.'

'Okay.'

'You'll be required to attend the trial as a witness. You might not be needed to testify depending on what he pleads but you must attend court all the same.'

'When?'

'You'll get a letter. It will be within two weeks.'

He looked up at Audrey's windows.

I took a breath. 'Can I bring my daughter?'

'Children aren't allowed in the courts.'

'Is there a crèche?'

'No.'

Funny, the thoughts that come. My first worry was for Emily and who would look after her. My second was for me. 'This is nothing to do with me is it?'

'You're called as a witness.'

'No. The caution. The car park. My daughter.'

I caught distaste in his face. 'No. This is the case against Aaron Long. But stay out of trouble because you're on file.' He spoke as if he was doing me a favour.

'Will they mention it in court?'

He softened and a little of his mildness returned. 'You know what lawyers are like. They might ask. Be prepared.'

He stepped away from me, down the path towards the gate, glancing at the violas I'd bought from Lidl and put in pots on the drive looking all sweet and pretty.

Of course. The man's lawyer would want to portray me as the unreliable witness, the irresponsible woman. I'd watched films. I knew how these things went. I didn't even care about the boy or the break-in.

The policeman said, 'So, the Sheriff Court in Glasgow, expect a letter.'

'Where's that?'

'By the river. Google it.'

He walked further down the path then stopped. 'You've done a good job on the weeds.'

'Yes.'

'She kept it beautifully.'

'Who? Audrey?'

'Aye. Until she couldn't manage it. Then it got a wee bit overgrown.'

The policeman must have been ten years younger than me and Robbie. He was unlined, unruffled, a boy policeman.

'You grew up around here,' I said.

'Her grandson was the reason I joined the force.'

'Robbie? Or Aidan?'

'Robbie, aye.'

Wind rustled leaves and I was rushed with pride. I wished Robbie could have heard that. The fitness, the discipline, the morality, if you believed that police possessed it, and this young policeman just about seemed to: it didn't surprise me that Robbie would inspire other people because he inspired me.

'I've wanted to ask if people here knew him but I've been afraid to—'

'I can see why—'

'—in case they didn't know him.'

'Yes.' He frowned slightly and closed the gate behind him. 'You'll get a letter. Glasgow Sheriff Court.'

I watched the tree branches, their new leaves shaking, and I thought again about Emily. I could put her into nursery at eight-thirty but I would have to leave the court at eleven to pick her up by twelve. If it went on for longer I didn't know what I would do. Of course it would go on for longer than eleven. I'd have to bring her with me. But I couldn't leave her on a seat outside with some pens and a colouring book. Maybe I could ask Caroline to come with me. But she had children too. I thought about asking Paul and I thought about asking June. I felt less ashamed at asking June. She didn't get visitors. She might appreciate a day out to court.

16.

I picked up Emily from nursery and promised her a Freddo and lunch in the back seat of the car if she would walk on the Campsies with me. This spring day needed us in it. Our bodies needed to be tousled by the first breeze that wasn't freezing. She agreed.

I knew where we'd go. As the Crow Road climbs the Campsies it passes a car park opposite a path up the fellside. We stopped there and weren't the only ones eating our lunch in our car. I noticed several vehicles with couples or lone men inside, parked with their windscreens taking on the wide open fells. We watched people emerge from their front seats, hair blown about as they shut their doors and zipped their coats. As they passed they looked in at us and then they were gone, up the hill on the other side of the Crow Road.

I climbed from the front to the back seat and ate next to Emily which she loved, handing her sausage rolls and a boiled egg from a plastic pot we'd bought at the Co-op. We watched the clouds shifting and moving, breaking up to let the sun stream through for a few seconds. Shadows slipped fast across the grass.

Emily got boiled egg down her front but who cared about that when you were trying to bond with your child. 'Mummy, I've had an accident,' she said, egg yolk on her lips and chin.

'It will come out in the wash,' I said, but she wasn't talking about the egg.

I lifted her out of her car seat and inspected her. Her bum was wet so I told her to stand outside the car while I looked for some spare clothes. I found a pair of leggings and a pack of wipes. Sweet victory. See, why couldn't those women at the nursery witness this? There were no pants in the car so I said she could go knickerless under her leggings and she didn't seem to mind.

The path up the hillside was well worn and I felt the jagged corners of stones through the soles of my trainers. There were tufts of grass either side of the path and patches of mud that I had to walk around. Emily trod straight through them.

'Tell me if you need a wee,' I said to her.

'I don't.' She let go of my hand and squatted to pick a dandelion. Robbie called dandelions pee-the-beds. I held back from telling Emily that. See, I did try to be a good parent.

'Tell me something you did at nursery today.'

'Um,' Emily said. She dropped the dandelion, put her finger up her nose then into her mouth.

'Stop that.'

'I like the taste of it.'

'It's dirty.'

She touched her palm to the tips of some wild grass.

'I told a joke.'

'What joke?'

'Why did the banana cross the road?'

'I don't know. Why did the banana cross the road?'

'Because it needed a poo.'

I pretended to roar with laughter and Emily roared too.

'Do you need a poo?'

'No, Mummy, it was a joke.'

We threw stones and snapped sticks and ran and balanced on clumps of grass. I liked the kick of the hills and the wind churning my hair. I loved the billowing tree tops and the soft moss that covered the rocks. I wondered if I would ever tell anyone else about Emily and the car park and the court case and the social workers or if I would keep it between me and these hills. If I told my mum she would come racing here, using up her leave and telling me she'd tried to warn me this might happen. What would Robbie say? He would call me the unluckiest girl in the universe.

This was a start, though, our hillside climb, and although Emily was happy to sit in the dirt by a hut and scrape sticks into the earth whereas I wanted to scramble higher, I sat down with her and watched her play. This was a childhood, surely? Wasn't I doing something right? I leaned back onto my hands, lifted my face to the sky and felt a small warmth on my cheeks.

When I opened my eyes I saw a woman tramping towards us. She was coming down the hill with turned out feet and swinging arms as if intent on giving someone a telling off. I stood up.

'Don't look so frightened, Liz, they do let me out sometimes,' June said when she came close by.

I called Emily out of the hut and said, 'Say hello to June. She's one of my dancing ladies.'

Emily made us both smile as she stood in the doorway, taking us in, like a shepherd.

'I've been traipsing these fells since I was as wee as you,' June said. Emily didn't answer because children don't, not shy ones like Emily.

I looked behind June to see if anybody was accompanying her. There were other walkers and some dogs, but nobody who seemed to be taking an interest in the three of us.

'Are you here on your own?'

'Yes.' Her voice was put-on patient.

'How did you get here?'

'I got the bus and I'll get the bus back.'

'How far did you go?'

'Up to the ridge.'

Beyond us, towards Glasgow, the fields were soft, and the trees newly green. Hazy sun made the clouds gold, as if sunset was upon them already.

'Do you have a phone?'

'Stop it, Liz. Look after that child there, not me.' She was ferociously endearing.

Emily played in the hut, venturing in and out of its dark insides to bury grass and hide stones.

'She looks like you,' June said.

'If you saw her dad you wouldn't say that. But thanks.'

June put her hand to her forehead and squinted. She gestured towards a cluster of houses. 'That wee hamlet there was where my Aunty Betty lived. When we were weans my mum used to send us up the road to help her. I used to watch the farmer collect the sheep from up in the hills and bring them down for shearing. I used to help my uncle chop firewood. And I used to sit on the back of the truck and drive out to Twechar to pick the tatties. I see it all from my window still. What I would do if they took that view away from me.' The lines in her face were thick as potato drills, her hair as blown about and wild-looking as the grass at our feet.

Emily threw a stick out of the dark hut.

'That's a good house you've got there,' June said into the darkness. Another stick scudded from the doorway and Emily's face looked out and ducked in again.

'Does anybody know you've come out today?'

'It's not a lock-up I live in. It's sheltered housing. We come and go as we please.'

'But what if?—'

'What if I got lost and perished out here?'

I shook my head and chose not to speak. June closed her mouth and raised an eyebrow as if she'd won.

Emily walked out of the hut holding a worm on a stick. It was a thin, young worm, pink and sinewy like the underside of a tongue.

'Go find a home for it,' I said to her.

'I want to keep it.'

'You can't take it home.'

'I want to play with it.'

'Are you a ballet dancer like your mummy?' June said. 'She's a good dancer, your mum.'

Emily stood close to my legs and put an arm around me.

'Keep that worm away from me,' I said. Emily took her arm from my legs and went off again with her worm and her stick. I watched her tread over mounds of grass as tall as her knees, holding her stick straight out. If June hadn't been there, I know I would have felt a frisson of stress, I would have braced myself for trouble over the worm – a tantrum or a lengthy whine – but I felt sheltered from all that because of June's company.

'It was you, wasn't it?' June said. 'It was you who left her in the car.'

I turned to see her small firm face. There was no point denying what was true.

'How did you know?'

'English girl with a small daughter. It had to be you.'

'Who told you?'

'Gossip goes round a place like this.'

'Oh, God.'

'I wouldn't worry. My Aunty Betty left me outside a pub for three hours and I turned out all right.'

I shook my head. June continued and I stopped listening, imagining the gossip, the half-truths and the untruths.

'She was what you call a functioning alcoholic and the

urge must have come upon her. She left me outside in my pram, had a few drinks, went home and forgot all about me.'

Emily came towards us with the worm still on her stick.

'What happened to you?' I said to June.

'Someone pushed me in my pram to the police.'

'What happened to your Aunty Betty?'

'Not a lot. My mother battered her.'

'Nobody called social services?'

'Nobody called social services. But she wasn't my mother. I didn't have to live with her.'

'Mummy, look.'

Emily wanted me to look, really look, at the worm. 'It's like a noodle,' she said.

'Don't eat it.'

She laughed and said, 'That's disgusting.'

'You're doing fine with that lassie.'

I sighed. 'Thanks. This is a good moment.' I wished my mum could have seen us. For so long she'd witnessed me struggling and I was sure she resented us deep in her sherry nights. 'Keep taking your small steps, keep taking your medicine,' she used to say to me. She wanted my recovery to keep pace with her desires, which included Alan, and I was too slow. She would have looked at us today and seen that we were doing okay.

'You've come a long way to be on your own,' June said, tilting her chin in a superior way as if expecting a bad reaction from me or a remark she might have made herself had anyone commented on her own life circumstances.

'I know,' is all I said.

'If you need anything you know where I am,' she said, closing her mouth and clenching her teeth in a way I was becoming used to.

It felt right. Or at least it didn't feel wrong. 'I do need some help.'

'Go on.'

'Could you come to court with me and sit with Emily while I give evidence?' Emily took off her coat and dropped it on the ground. 'I can't risk leaving her at nursery in case it overruns.' I picked up her coat and folded it over my arm.

'That's a bit more than I bargained for,' she said. 'But I did offer. You don't know when it will be?'

'Within two weeks.'

'I'm not busy.'

I told her about the trial of the man who broke into my car and how I had no one to look after Emily.

'Of course I can,' June said. 'But I'm not standing up in court.'

'You might have to if they put me on trial.'

She shook her head. 'You'll be all right.'

'Thank you,' I said.

Three seagulls flew above us, wide wingspans, white and gold.

'I'll give you a lift home,' I said. 'Are you ready to go?'

We walked comfortably down the hill, June nimble, seemingly unafraid of falling like my other dancers at the sheltered housing. Emily ran on and I worried she would crash onto the road in front of the traffic.

'Emily, stop!' I shrieked down the hill and hurt my throat.

'You've got some gub on you,' June said.

'You should have heard her dad.'

Emily waited for us, like a good girl, and I told her I was pleased with her. I was.

'I hope he's paying you maintenance,' June said, after I'd told Emily to look left and right before we crossed the curving road.

'Oh no,' I said. 'No. You've got it wrong.'

No cars came but I couldn't move.

'Can I have my Freddo, Mummy?' Emily pulled at my arm, wanting me to cross the road.

'I'm sorry, I've spoken out of turn.' June looked back the way we'd come and I thought she might take off up the hillside.

'Robbie…' I said, and I let Emily tug my hand and walk me across the road. 'Robbie… do you want to know what happened to him?'

To her credit I saw nothing but patience in her face, none of the fear or awkwardness that people can show when they're about to hear a god-awful story they aren't expecting. I gave Emily the Freddo I'd promised her, put a plastic bag on top of her wet car seat and shut the door. Then, high in the hills above Lennoxtown, with the sun a pink glow behind the rainclouds to the west, while Emily kicked her legs against the driver's seat and ate her Freddo, I told June about the part of my life that had drifted into the black and left us washed up here.

In July we flew to London where I had my audition. I got the Lido, Robbie got on his physiotherapy course, we made our plans and changed them again when we found out I was pregnant. All I could think of was how we might sail again one day, either with a child who would live with us in our cabin, or later, when our baby was grown and independent and we were free to go back as a couple. I knew a magician and his assistant, a singer and guitar player duo. It was done, husband and wife teams.

So Emily was an intrusion before she was even born, but I would be lying if I said that I wasn't anticipating her, if I didn't secretly hope for a girl, if I didn't think that me, Robbie and our baby would be a formidable three. I tucked away the dream of the Lido. Such opportunities would come again. I was strong then, physically and mentally. And naive.

We found a one-bed flat to rent in Leytonstone on the Central Line, because we could just about afford it and it wasn't far from my mum. We didn't like it at first; the tube, the city, the waiting room in Whipps Cross Hospital with people not on holiday and not enjoying themselves. It was hard not to think about Paris.

I got a little teaching in a dancing school. Robbie worked in a gym while he waited for the new term at university. They offered him some hours while he was studying too. It wasn't a lot of money and we knew we'd be skint for a few years while he finished his training. I would be on statutory maternity pay. I'd paid my national insurance, thank God, my mum had seen to that. She does things properly.

We visited Robbie's gran in Lennoxtown and had our final – and only – holiday together. I liked his gran. She had Robbie's throaty laugh. I liked Robbie better. Almost every day of our holiday he ran somewhere. He was the fittest he'd ever been. He took me to the sides of lochs and the bottom of Munros and I'd watch him spring away from me. He confessed he was frightened one day. In a B&B in Oban he pushed his breakfast plate away and leaned on his elbows, hitting his head softly with his fists. For two reasons, he told me. One, he was worried about money. He would work full time eventually; the NHS would take him on as a physio, he'd choose a specialism, he would enjoy his work when it came. Two, he was worried about me and my dancing. 'You've stopped in your prime,' he told me. 'You should be in Paris right now. I'm worried you won't be yourself without your dancing.'

'Not a lot we can do about that now,' I said. 'Don't worry about it, babe. Life will work itself out.' I wasn't worried. Not at all. I was becoming more and more like him. He was good for me.

Emily was born with difficulty. They kept her in special care for days. We didn't know any differently so we just went with it. When we got her home we managed. We did. We found some kind of crazy routine, albeit under siege with her colic and my hormones, but my mum helped, and when Robbie went back to university after a week I managed to get her over the doorstep in her pram, out into the glare of each day.

I told Robbie I missed him in the days after Emily's birth, days that to me felt hot and thunderous, containing nothing of the soft contentedness I had imagined. He said, 'I'm still here, you know,' but he knew what I meant. And I felt no searing, binding love that books and relatives had told me I would feel for Emily. It crept in, later, in a way, not in a way to knock me over or anything but it was there, it really was, I'm sure it was. Is.

Then in the hours between feeds early one morning in April Robbie's heart stopped beating. He died. I found him in the morning lying still next to me. Before I realised, I told him to get Emily. 'I've just fed her,' I said. 'She can't be hungry. What time is it? Can you get her? Let me sleep.' But Emily's mewls turned urgent and my breasts were full and tingling so I got her myself and was feeding her and grumbling at him when I realised he was too still. The baby screamed on her back while I tried to do CPR. The noise, the stillness. The paramedics came but there was nothing they could do. At hospital they said it was sudden death syndrome. It happens to athletes and footballers, perfectly fit men who suddenly die. To think, we had been terrified of Emily dying in her sleep yet Robbie was the one I should have worried about. Emily was three weeks and three days old. I was broken. Destroyed. Utterly undone.

I had counselling. I fed and clothed and kept Emily safe from harm but I felt harmful. I was a danger then. It was a dangerous time. I found it hard to sleep and hard to wake and I drank and took pills. My mum helped. She said she knew grief too.

Four years on I wanted to come off my tablets. Was I better? No. But I'd carried on. When Aidan telephoned to tell me he needed my help I decided that Emily and I could do with an adventure, one her daddy would have approved of. A new start. A chance for us to return to where Robbie was born and to say goodbye. To be near him, as well, of course.

Un grand jeté, the biggest of leaps. We packed our bags and drove to Lennoxtown, against my mum's advice. She said I should leave Emily with her, but a bit of me worried that if I left her I'd never want her back, and my mum needed a break from both of us, honestly, she was just too stubborn to say.

I told June most of this as I watched Emily kick the driver's seat and lick chocolate off her Freddo wrapper. She had chocolate around her mouth. I wanted to open the door and wipe it off her.

'That's some story.' June stood with her arms crossed over her body.

'On days like this, especially on days like this, I feel so bad for him that he's not here. He misses it. I need him. She needs him. And he misses it all.'

I looked at Emily who licked her finger and drew shapes on the window.

'It's not fair.'

'No, it's not fair,' June said.

'I can't get over him. It's too big.'

'Thank God you've got Emily.'

I wiped a rogue tear. 'I don't usually feel sorry for myself. I just get on with things.'

'I can tell you do.'

Emily tapped on the window and showed me her licked-clean wrapper. I heard her muffled voice. 'Can I have another one?'

I opened the door and wiped the chocolate off her face with my thumb. I gave her another Freddo because what was the harm, she was alive and she wanted another Freddo.

'That woman who was in the news, who wanted to use her dead husband's sperm, I get that,' I said when I shut the door. 'She wanted a part of him back, a part of them back. But she was wrong. The child won't be him. It will be unlike him and unlike her and all she'll want to do is hide in her grief but the child will demand her, this child that doesn't even *know* the man she can't live without. Can you imagine that, Emily doesn't even know Robbie.' I swiped at another tear and shut my mouth.

'You've had one of life's worst shocks,' June said.

I thought of Robbie holding my hand, making my tea, sitting at our table and eating next to me, cleaning his teeth, kissing my mouth, throwing socks into the washing basket, washing his face, clipping his nails, kissing my mouth, running up the sides of Munros, kissing my mouth, dead in bed beside me.

'You'd have liked him,' I said to June. 'Everybody did.'

She nodded.

I looked at the clouds. 'I'm not sure I'm doing right by Emily,' I said.

'Of course you are.' She swatted away my self-pity. 'Have you told your mother any of this? That you miss him this much? Because you should.'

'She knows but I'm not sure she understands. She met someone else soon after my dad died. I don't think she felt this kind of grief.'

June removed her gloves and put them in her pocket.

'I'm sure she did. In her way.'

We watched Emily through the window. She looked at us as she licked her second Freddo wrapper and I could see a sugary glint in her eyes.

June said nothing more. She turned away and looked up the hill. 'They have to keep coming back to fix this path. So many people come stomping up and down here. Look at them, still coming.'

It was true. As if all of Glasgow had come out of the rain-soaked streets on this one half-sunny day and got out to walk in single file up the rocky path and down again. They should have noticed the gathering clouds.

'Come on, let's go home,' I said.

June took a tissue from a pack of hankies, gave it to me and blew her nose with another. 'I don't want you to drive out of your way,' she said.

'I'm already in trouble for abandoning my child, I can't abandon you—'

'—A helpless old lady.'

'That's not how I'd describe you, no.'

I found a pop music station for Emily, turned the volume up and drove us down the Crow Road, and I was glad I had June in the car because rain came on suddenly and the wipers worked hard to keep the downpour from the windscreen.

I felt a release as strong and sudden as the rain. Telling someone about Robbie, about my connection to Lennoxtown, made me feel a part of the place in a strange kind of way.

'Did you know him?' I dared to ask.

She tilted her chin. 'Ah, I knew all the weans in this village, if not by name then by sight.'

'I thought you'd know him. What was he like as a boy?'

'Oh, I have stories for all the weans in Campsie.'

She said no more and that irked me, slightly, but we drove on, through the now diminishing rain.

'Don't get out,' June said when we pulled into the sheltered housing. 'The bairn's sleeping.'

She was. Mouth open and head leaning against her booster seat, one hand on her leg, the other hand curled around the stick I didn't know she'd smuggled into the car and, hanging from the smuggled stick, gently writhing, her worm.

Part Two

I.

We took the bus as June suggested, early in the morning, with the sky full of pastels and Emily so tired she was placid. We three sat quietly on our two seats, June and I in our fine denier hosiery and Emily on my lap, tapping her heels against my shins. The bus joined the motorway's slow lit parade towards Glasgow. We barely moved, for a mile at least, and Emily fidgeted, breathing on the window and drawing faces in the condensation. From the bus station we walked downhill, past shuttered shops, crossing roads, crossing the river and I thought we were bound to be late. I tugged on Emily's arm to keep her from walking too slowly. Finally, when the pastel was gone from the morning and the traffic was inelegant and unlit, June said, 'There it is across there. It's not changed.'

The concrete court loomed and we took its steps quickly. Inside, staff scanned our bodies and our bags. Emily opened up her fabric bag sombrely and showed the security guard her Peppa Pig colouring book and felt tip pens.

'Children aren't allowed in court,' an official said.

'She'll be with me,' June said. 'We're accompanying her.' She nodded towards me.

'Children aren't allowed in the witness waiting rooms.'

I looked at June, helpless.

'I need a wee,' Emily said.

'She must be allowed in the toilets,' June said, and we followed the wave of the official's arm. 'There's a cafeteria in the basement,' the official called after us.

I went in the cubicle with Emily and helped with her leggings and pants. 'What's that?' she asked and pointed to the sanitary bin.

'It's for ladies. For rubbish. Don't touch,' I said, just as she was about to open the lid.

'What's that?' She pointed to a sign about domestic abuse.

'It's for women who need help.'

'Help for what?'

'Sometimes life gets difficult. Are you done?' I passed her the toilet roll and she wiped herself but stayed on the toilet.

'Are you done, Emily?'

She said nothing and I watched her face redden. I leaned against the wall of the cubicle and waited for her to poo. She sat forwards on the toilet seat, gripping the sides of the bowl with her hands. 'What's that?' she said, pointing to the toilet roll dispenser and her voice was so strained with effort that she made me laugh. She laughed because I laughed.

'What's that?' she said again with the same strain in her voice.

'I'll wait for you in the foyer,' June called over the blast of the hand dryer.

'Bye, June!' Emily said in her new voice.

I was aware of a shade of shared hysteria.

We agreed that June would take Emily to the cafeteria and I would wait in the witness room. If they were going for a walk, June would text me and I would text her when I was finished in the court.

'I hope she behaves for you,' I said.

'You will, won't you?'

Emily's face was tired and trusting. I kissed her forehead. June held her hand.

'Why aren't you coming with us?' Emily said.

'I can't. I have to stand up and say something serious.'

'Where? What about?'

'Grown ups' things.'

'He's already in custody isn't he? He'll be done first,' said June.

'I don't know.'

'Your mummy won't be long.' June patted Emily's clasped fingers with her spare hand. 'I know how courts work,' she said to me and she was as tough as I'd ever seen her.

'I wish you were coming with me,' I said.

'It's no big deal. This is about him, not you. Just answer their questions and we'll get a hot chocolate when it's over.'

'Can I get a hot chocolate?'

'Yes. Say goodbye to your mummy. And don't let anyone upset you,' she said to me with a point of her finger.

I found the crowded witness waiting room which is where I saw the three from the car park. We forgot ourselves and smiled a hello and in the way that humans do, or humans like me do, I found myself walking towards them. I sat down. The man wore a suit and a tie and told me there was a soft drinks vending machine in the waiting room but I'd have to get a tea or coffee from the cafeteria downstairs. The women held paper cups into which they blew.

'Where's your daughter?' one of the women asked.

'Outside in the car,' I said, and laughed, I couldn't help myself – but they didn't laugh so I stood up and got a Coke.

'How is your daughter? That's what I meant,' the woman said when I came back. 'Not where is your daughter.'

'She's fine, thank you,' I said. 'A friend is looking after her.'

'Oh.'

The women sipped their drinks. The man looked hard at me. 'We shouldn't have too long to wait. They do the custody cases first.'

'Yes. My friend said that.'

I listened to the sounds of footsteps from outside the door and wondered how Emily and June were. Other witnesses texted or talked or popped out, smelling of smoke or fresh air when they returned and giving us something new to hang our thoughts on. Several witnesses were let go by officials in suits and told they would be sent another date to return to court. They looked at us as they left as if we were the lucky ones because we got to stay and get it over with.

'Does anyone want my paper?' the man asked and held it out to me. I took it. He leaned in. 'We're not supposed to confer,' he said. 'But I'll tell you this. Just watch out, he's a slippery bastard.'

I nodded. I turned the pages of the man's *Metro*.

'Are you settling in to Campsie?' one of the women asked – the one who'd told the police about Emily.

I looked at her mild face with her soft scarf about her neck and truly didn't know how to answer.

'We were trying to work out who you were,' the man said to me. I closed the paper.

'Oh yes.'

'You've never been in court before?'

'Never.'

'My husband thinks you might be related to Audrey Watt,' the woman with the scarf said. 'She was our friend.'

'I'm living in her flat.'

'We know. Why is that then?'

'Leave her be,' the other woman said.

'I'm doing a favour for Aidan.'

'Her grandson. Why? Do you know him?'

'Leave her be.'

'Robbie,' I said. 'I knew Robbie.'

The man raised his chin. 'Ah.'

At that moment the door to the waiting room opened and a court official appeared. We fell silent. The official left. We stayed silent.

Robbie was never silent while waiting for my antenatal appointments, watching midwives approach with paperwork and calling for other women and not me. He needed to fling his energy somewhere and the waiting room was too hot, too cramped, too boring. The barely audible chat from the television on the wall pissed him off. Waiting pissed him off. If I was having a scan there was nothing he could do but if he was accompanying me to my injection for my rhesus negative blood, he became frustrated. 'All you need is a jag in your arse, I'll do it for you,' he said. Twice. Because I needed two injections on two separate occasions to stop my daughter's blood from antagonising mine.

Cooped up in the packed waiting rooms with toddlers making demands of their big-bellied mothers he liked to make up quizzes, challenges, things to occupy him. 'Ask me anything about any team in the Scottish Premiership,' he would say. And I would say I knew nothing about any team in the Scottish Premiership.

'You must have heard of Celtic? You must have heard of Rangers.'

'I've heard of them.'

'How many teams in the Scottish leagues can you name beginning with A?'

'I can't name any.'

'Yes you can. I'll help you. Aber…'

'Aberdeen,' I would say.

'Aye, that's one. Well done. Here's another. Albion Rovers. Can you think of any?'

'No.'

'Okay, my go. Auchinleck Talbot.'

'Why do they all have two word names?'

'Annan. That doesn't. That's junior league. Alloa Athletic.'

'That's two words.'

'That's where I had my—'

'That's where you had your first trial.' I gripped his thigh.

'There's another one. There must be another one.'

Even his eyelashes were restless. He was vital, vibrant, topped up. So much better, so much more than me.

'Ayr United!'

It passed the time.

It was nearly half past eleven before the court official came to get me. The woman with the scarf tried to pat my arm as I stood up. I grabbed my coat and bag.

'The procurator fiscal will ask you questions first,' the official said as he walked me to the courtroom. I felt suddenly sick with nerves. I thought of Emily leaning forwards holding on to the sides of the toilet. I hoped she'd washed her hands thoroughly.

'The defence lawyer may want to question you too.'

'What will I do with my bag?'

'Take it in with you.'

'When do I go in?'

'You're going in right now.' He was young. Red hair. Chapped lips.

'How long will it take?'

'I don't know.' He had a kind voice but he knew when to stop talking and looked down at his shoes.

The courtroom was smaller than I'd imagined. No jury. A judge, some lawyers. I didn't know who was who. I had to swear that I would tell the truth and felt utterly alone when I did so. My voice reminded me of the way I'd sounded in the meeting with the social worker and the nursery people, only quieter. There wasn't a soul I recognised. A woman and a teenage girl sat at the back with empty seats around them. That's where my mum would have sat, where Robbie would have sat, where June could have sat if she wasn't taking care of Emily. The man, the accused, caught my eye and looked away. He wore a T-shirt and jeans.

'Where do you reside, Miss Morley?' The procurator fiscal spoke.

I told her Audrey's address.

'Do you own a Ford car?' She gave the registration number in a pleasant, formal voice.

'Yes. It's my mum's.'

'Did you park the car in the Co-op car park on Main Street, Lennoxtown?'

'Yes.'

'Did you lock the car?'

'Yes.'

'What state was the car in when you left it?'

'What do you mean?'

'Was there any damage to the car?'

'No. No damage. No broken window.' This was simple enough. I felt my shoulders relax.

'Was there a child in the car?' Her voice was breezy, light, casual.

'Yes,' I said, trying to keep my voice as light as hers. The policeman had told me there might be mention of Emily, but I didn't expect it from her.

'Where did you go?'

'Into the Co-op.'

'How long were you gone for?'

'Only five minutes. If that. I just went in for milk and fish fingers and a few other things.'

'Thank you. Did you leave your child alone in the car?'

She nodded for me to answer. The judge looked at me. The defendant's lawyer looked at me too.

'Yes,' I said.

'Why?' Why? Why was this woman asking me? She was the prosecutor.

'Because she was sleeping. She had tonsillitis. She was sick.'

'She was asleep when you left her?'

'Yes.'

'And what state was your child in when you returned to the car?'

'She was asleep.'

'And what state was your car in when you returned?'

'The window was smashed. Cracked.'

'Cracked or smashed?'

'Cracked.'

'Which window?'

'The one on the passenger's side. The front passenger window.'

'Was anything stolen?'

'No. I think he was disturbed before he could take my phone.' I looked at the accused man and he caught my eye again. His face looked pale.

The procurator fiscal nodded at me. 'Thank you. That's all.' She sat down.

I took what felt like my first breath in minutes. The lights were yellow in the courtroom, the wood gleamed. A clerk shuffled in her seat. Somebody sneezed. The defence lawyer stood up.

'Just a few questions please.' He cleared his throat. His black gown swished. 'Why did you park your car in the Co-op car park?'

'I needed to get some shopping.'

'What age is your child?'

'Four.'

'And you left her alone in the car?'

'Yes.'

'Why?'

How many teams can you name in the Scottish leagues beginning with A?

My fucking mind. I stayed silent. I stared at the lawyer.

'Why did you leave her alone in your car?'

'Because she was sleeping.'

'Just to clarify, you left a child of four alone in a car?'

I looked at the prosecutor fiscal. 'Yes.'

'Had you checked the status of the queues at the checkout before you left her alone in the car?'

'I'm sorry?'

'Had you checked the status of the queues at the checkout before you left her alone in the car?'

'No.'

Ayr United! Robbie's voice was in my head again, his fist was punching the waiting room air. I must have smiled.

'You seem to think that's amusing.'

'No.'

'No.'

The thief and I glanced at each other. I saw him look at his lawyer with interest.

'How far from the entrance did you park?'

'I couldn't get a space close to the entrance.'

'So you were far from the entrance?'

'Not too far.'

'But you weren't close to the entrance?'

'No.'

'Can you be sure you were only away for five minutes?'

'Pretty sure.'

'Did you have some means of telling the time?'

Ayr United, Aberdeen, Albion Rovers. Auchinleck Talbot. Annan. Alloa Athletic. Go away Robbie.

'I'm sorry?'

'Did you have a watch, a phone, some means of telling the time?'

'No. I left my phone in the car, which is why it got broken into.'

'My client disagrees with your interpretation. I'll come to that. But please clarify; you could have been longer than five minutes in the Co-op? You had no accurate way of knowing?'

'Possibly. But probably not.'

'Possibly, probably. We know for sure that you left a sick child alone in a car as far away from the entrance to the store as you possibly could have. Can you tell me what state your child was in when you returned to her?'

'She was asleep.'

'Are you sure?'

'Yes.'

'My client tells me she was extremely distressed.'

I shot a look at the man, the client, and he met my eyes. Bold. I heard nothing but the buzz of a ceiling light.

'I don't understand,' I said.

'My client tells me your daughter was extremely distressed and he smashed the window in order to free her.'

'She wasn't distressed. She was asleep.'

'Are you sure she wasn't crying?'

'Yes, I'm sure she wasn't crying.' I think I shouted.

'She was screaming according to my client.'

'No.'

'Could you have heard her crying from inside the Co-op?'

'I'm not answering that.'

'You have to answer. You're on oath.'

'Probably not.'

'You probably could not have heard her crying?'

'No, I probably could not.'

'So she could well have been crying. Or screaming. You have no way of knowing how long she was crying for because you wouldn't have heard her in the shop.'

'She wasn't crying, she was asleep.'

'You were gone for at least five minutes. In that time she could have been crying, couldn't she, and you'd never have known?'

I shook my head.

'Can you answer the question? She could have been crying and you wouldn't have heard her from the shop?'

'Yes, but—'

'My client asserts that he attempted to free a distressed and hysterical child, one whose mother admits was suffering from tonsillitis, from a locked car. It was his intention to free the distressed child and alert the appropriate authorities. Is that not why he attempted to break into the car?'

'No.' I shook my head.

'You chose a spot as far away from the entrance to the shop as was possible, you were away for five minutes, most likely more, and your child was suffering inside a locked car. My client did what he felt to be morally correct. He smashed the window of your car in order to free a distressed child.'

The lawyer let the slight echo do its work. The judge looked at me. The accused man looked at me. The lawyer looked at the judge.

'I have no further questions.'

I waited until I was dismissed then stepped down from the witness box, picked up my coat and bag and let the court official escort me out.

'He lied,' I said to the official who looked at his shoes.

I took the lift to the foyer where guards and staff stood at ease. There was no wall to lean against or pillar to hide behind. The floor was shiny and I wondered how many times a person had come fresh from court and puked on its glistening tiles.

Outside, I saw them before they saw me. June stood on the concrete steps while Emily played. She ran along the length of them, going as far from June as the steps would allow then returning to her. When I called her name Emily charged up the steps towards me and June looked at me with sympathy. I heaved up tears and had to stay bent doubled for a time with Emily's hand pat-patting my back.

He got a fine and community service. The judge didn't believe him and none of the other witnesses' accounts corroborated his story. The young policeman gave me another courtesy call to tell me the verdict and said the man narrowly avoided jail. For the thief, it had been worth the lie. For me, the lie had sliced me open. I was glad no one had been there to see it. The policeman told me there were no plans to charge me with Abandonment. The social worker telephoned too. When she said, 'You and Emily are making good progress. Keep up whatever you're doing,' I considered it a good day. I've had worse.

2.

The estate agent returned to value the flat on a day that was fine, at last. The sun was on the hills, exposing every crevice and crease. We'd been surprised by the crocuses in the narrow beds alongside the path and although the grass needed cutting the front garden looked pretty. Perky and full of promise, the estate agent praised it, as well as the plastering and the paintwork Paul had done and the vases of tulips I'd put around the house. He made me feel good which is how he sold houses, I suppose.

'What will you do when you sell?' he asked, and his phone buzzed in his jacket pocket.

'We'll find somewhere else to live,' I said, as if that would be easy.

'I'll sell your flat for you, no bother. So you'd better work out what you're doing.' He almost reminded me of Robbie, I almost liked his manner.

Later, we saw a man in a van park outside the flat. I helped Emily carry a chair to the window and we watched him pull a For Sale sign from the back of the van and clip it to the gatepost.

'There you are, Emily,' I said. 'Our work here is done.'

'Can we get a cat?' She had a way of surprising me.

'We could get a cat. Yes. Not yet. But soon.'

I wondered where we would go once the flat was sold.

We would need somewhere with a cat flap. We would need somewhere a cat could come home to, somewhere permanent. The idea felt nice.

The man waved at us watching him through the window and we waved back. Maybe the sunlight made people more friendly. Even in the Co-op the cashiers passed the time of day with me now. They spoke to Emily first and because she was too shy to reply I replied for her, with one hand on her head, patting it for my own reassurance. 'Still cold, but,' they would say, and I would agree, but it almost wasn't cold today.

The man drove away in his van and the street settled. A blackbird made a nest in the hedge and we watched it dart in and out of the leaves.

'You are the best mummy in the world,' Emily said.

Surprised again. I suppose you open a box for those moments and put them in, like the blackbird, adding as they come.

'And you are the best daughter,' I said and I put my arm around her narrow shoulders.

'I love you too much,' she said.

That was almost too much.

'You can't love somebody too much, can you?'

I kissed her forehead, put my cheek against hers and felt the enormous responsibility I had for her. It was good, sometimes, to be reminded of your great responsibilities, but most of the time it was easier, less daunting, to let it happen, to let the profoundness be. When Robbie died, I lost the ability to feel and the truth is I envied her all that love. Mine was hard to grab: a blackbird's wing on a quick turn.

Emily licked a finger. I watched her squeak a smile onto the smeary window and realised I'd forgotten to clean it, and that was a thing all the house-selling websites advised: clean windows. So Emily stood on the chair and cleaned the bottom half of the windows while I cleaned the top. There was pink plaster dust along with the dirt. We showed each other our grubby pieces of kitchen roll and Emily screwed her face into a snarl as she cleaned as hard as she could. A teenager on a bike rode by and stared up at us. We waved.

'Some more spray?' I said and let Emily squeeze the Windolene against the glass.

'Bam,' she said as she sprayed.

'Bam, bam,' I said.

'Bam. My daddy was a bam.'

'Pardon?' I stopped wiping but Emily wiped on, her elbow a point at my body. 'Emily what did you say about your daddy?' She rarely spoke about her dad. I was the one who talked of him.

'He was a bam.'

'No he wasn't.'

'Yes he was. Lilly said he was.'

'Who's Lilly? I took her kitchen roll from her and she tried to grab the Windolene but I held that away from her too. 'He was a what, Emily? What did Lilly say he was? Who is this Lilly?'

'She goes to my nursery.'

'And what did she call him?'

'A bam.'

'What's a bam?' I knew what a bam was. Robbie used to call me a bam when I tap danced on the bedcovers and tangled my feet in the duvet, but he called the boys at the end of our street who asked us to buy alcohol bams too, boys at the violent edge of adolescence.

'Why did she say he was a bam?'

'I don't know.'

'I'll do the rest of the windows,' I said and I asked her to go and play somewhere else. She didn't want to. 'Put the telly on then.'

Sara would have said my parenting was wrong, that I punished Emily for telling me what she did, but honestly, it was all I could do to stay standing on my chair with my face pressed against the glass watching my breath cloud the pane, while my head buzzed, and not smash the glass right there and then. People here talked of Robbie? The teenager on his bike passed by our house again and I think I frightened him. He looked back at me several times before leaning forwards and pedalling hard. Control yourself, I told myself, got off the chair, put the kitchen roll in the bin, then went to find Emily.

That night I phoned Aidan. I told him the For Sale sign was up and pictures of the house were on the internet. I listened for sounds of Australia. He was driving with his phone on speaker, and there was a muffled rush of engine and passing traffic.

'What are you going to do?' he asked.

'Can we stay in the house until you sell it? I'm not quite sure where we'll go next.'

'Are you not going back to London?'

'I don't know. Did Robbie live anywhere else? Maybe we could follow his life.'

Aidan didn't laugh. 'Stay until it sells. It might take a while. Isn't your mum missing you?'

I said nothing and listened again for Australia.

'I'm nearly at my work now,' Aidan said.

I couldn't help myself.

'Why didn't Robbie like Lennoxtown?'

A pause. 'No one likes where they were brought up.'

'Why not?'

'Did you ever ask him?'

'I'm asking you, Aidan.'

He coughed. He started to speak a couple of times but he didn't finish any sentences. It was hard to hear.

'Someone called him a bam,' I said.

He laughed now and said, 'We all know what he was like.'

'But it was one of Emily's friends at nursery. A child. Why would she say that? Her parents must think he was a bam. Does everyone think that?'

'You're reading too much into it.' His voice became clear and the background noise disappeared. 'I'm not sure Lennoxtown is the place for you, Liz. You should move on, pal.'

'Maybe bam means nothing at all.'

'Exactly. I'm at work now. I have to go.'

He was no help to me. The only thing he said when I asked him to tell me one thing – one thing – about their childhood in Lennoxtown was that Robbie was gullible, despite his tendency to show off. Gullible. We're all gullible, even me. Well, I must be.

I tried to forget it. I had many people to let through the door. The flat attracted interest and there were regular viewings. It was hard to keep it clean and tidy, especially when Paul came to see me in the evenings and instead of tidying, we slept together or talked or watched TV. I began to look forward to his visits. I got used to them. I got used to the jaunty patter of the estate agent too and got panicked when he said someone had made an offer. He told me he would introduce a closing date, on which day people would put in a bid, and I would take the highest offer. Or Aidan would. We'll get you a good price, he told me. Too soon, I told him. You'd better make your plans, he told me.

3.

When I arrived for our next class, my dancers were polite and pleased to see me but again not inclined to dance, preferring instead to talk about another woman who'd had a fall and was found, by Ruth, in her bathroom, conscious but with a fractured ankle. They sighed and shook their heads. Charlie wore his dressing gown, Senga and Agnes sipped milk from teacups, Alice sat, as she always did, poised and interested, and John folded his newspaper into a square but didn't bend his head to do the crossword. 'Her trampolining days are well and truly over,' he said.

'Did she used to be a trampolinist?'

'I just meant… she won't be good for much anymore.' He put down his square of newspaper.

Eve came from the kitchen with a pint glass.

'Where's June?' I said.

'Not here,' Eve said.

'Does anyone know if she's coming today?' I hadn't seen her since the day of the court case.

Nobody knew. Eve wasn't worried. She slipped off her shoes and told me that June wandered off from time to time, that she often disappeared then returned, saying she'd been on a bus trip to Perth or an overnight stay to an Ayrshire caravan.

'When did you last see her?'

'You don't see anyone unless they're in the lounge on purpose.'

'Is she all right?'

'Who knows with June.' Eve cleaned her glasses.

I asked them to wait five minutes while I ran along the carpeted corridors and knocked on June's door. I could hear a television from the adjacent flat but nothing from inside June's.

'June! You know I charge double if you don't attend my class.'

Nothing.

'He got community service. Emily wants to go to the Campsies with you again.'

Nothing.

I knocked a final time.

Nothing.

'Ruth will have a key,' Senga said when I returned. 'But she won't use it yet.'

'Perhaps she just doesn't want to do your dance class,' Eve said, and I couldn't argue with that.

'I think if you fall,' Agnes said, 'you can say goodbye to your life. That's why I won't ever go out when it's icy. Even if the pavements are gritted.'

'It would be the end of me, right enough,' Eve said.

'I have a button now,' Charlie said, and felt inside his dressing gown, pulling on a lanyard around his neck.

'Stop it, all of you!' I pushed the last chair into the middle of the room to make the barre. 'Enough. Come and dance.'

They moved quietly to the chairs and only when they were settled and I was helping Charlie with his frame did Eve say, 'You're awful bossy.'

'You're awful gloomy,' I said.

We danced. We did our barre work and then borrowed techniques from the contact improvisation I'd learned at college. Fuck it. They couldn't roll on the floor but they could respond to a finger's press or a palm's graze.

'Use your partner's touch to set your own body off,' I said. 'How do you react if someone touches your hip with their elbow, say?'

'Give them a slap!' Eve made them laugh.

'Take it seriously. You'll see. Be careful with each other.'

Senga sat her mother in a chair and although she did most of the big movements – spinning away when Agnes stretched a hand to push against her shoulder, then making her body wide in response to her mother's outstretched arms – the two of them moved well together. I called the others over to watch. 'Change your levels, if you can,' I said. So Senga crouched by Agnes and responded catlike to the bending of her mother's legs and the flexing of her toes. Then she lay her body across Agnes's knees and her mother curved her spine to meet her daughter's back and the two breathed and that's where I stopped them.

'I liked that,' Eve said.

She partnered John and their movements were stronger. In a stranger, slower version of a couple's jive they turned back against back, flank to flank, palm to palm, hands gripping elbows and sliding down forearms. She curled a shoulder under his armpit, he twirled her shoulders with his two hands. They were playful. I liked their flat feet and the bend of their legs.

Charlie and Alice did a delicate dance with their fingertips and they changed their facial expressions each time their fingers met. Of all of the dancers it was Charlie and Alice who most understood that to move according to how you are touched creates a spark and generates, drama, tension, interest, beauty.

'Good dancing,' I said.

'It's not really what I had in mind when I came to this class,' Eve said when they were finished, chests heaving, mouths relaxed into smiles.

'It wasn't what I had in mind either.' I passed around a box of feathers. On one of the ships I met a dancer who wanted to be a movement therapist when she settled down and she'd told me about feathers.

'Take one,' I said, and asked them to caress their faces, arms, necks and chests, to enjoy the feather's softness. 'Circle it over your foreheads, your cheeks, your chins,' I said, and I came between them, smoothing my feather down noses and over eyelids and ears. Charlie smiled as I found patches of skin that weren't covered by his beard.

'I feel like a child again,' he said.

'Good. Don't stop.'

I saw that John had tears that turned the feather's edges to wet clumps. Eyes watered for many reasons. Then I saw June in the doorway, staring in. She looked fierce. She carried a plastic bag in each hand. When I beckoned her into the room she didn't come so I went to her, carrying the box of feathers, all colours.

'I've missed you,' I said. It was true, I meant it. I held out the box of feathers for her to take one. She ignored them.

'I was hoping you'd have a couple of new ones today,' she said.

'I was hoping you'd be here.'

'You need to publicise it more. You won't be getting enough for your petrol.'

'Are you okay, June?'

'It's a bit on the pretentious side. I think that puts some people off. Maybe you need to play some old music like you did before and let us clap along.'

I turned back to the class and saw that the dancers were still working with their feathers but they were chatting now, their concentration gone.

'He got community service and a fine,' I whispered. 'The judge knew he was lying. He's done it before.'

'Have you told your mother about the trouble you've been in?'

The music stopped and I returned to my dancers who stood in squares of sunlight on the pink carpet and shielded their eyes. I told them what to practise for the following week's class.

June went to the kitchenette. I heard the sound of her filling the kettle.

'Do you want your feathers back?' Charlie said. 'Or can we keep them?'

'You can keep yours if you like,' I said.

'No!' June shouted from the kitchen. 'The girl doesn't make enough money as it is. You can't go taking her dancing things. All feathers back in the box.'

I noticed Eve shaking her head and Charlie smiling. They asked me to stay for tea and biscuits from a tin that Alice had won in a church tombola. John excused himself and read his paper. As we talked, Charlie held out a hand and said, 'Excuse me for interrupting but I want to say this while I have the urge.' We looked at him. 'I am getting immense joy from these classes. I look forward to them. And I want to thank our lovely teacher, Elizabeth. Can I call you Elizabeth?'

Nobody scoffed or shut him up.

'Well, I look forward to them too,' I said. 'I really do.'

Alice spoke then, slowly and gently. She told us she'd been on a cruise ship with her husband for their fiftieth wedding anniversary. 'I keep thinking about those dancers we saw and then looking at you, Liz, and yes, I can see it. I can see you up there on the stage twirling away, quite the thing.'

'That's where I met my partner,' I said.

'Was he a dancer too?'

'He worked in the gym. He did the sports.'

'What a couple. My husband's gone now.'

'Mine's gone too.'

I heard quiet gasps and saw June nod her head as if to say it is what it is.

We talked briefly about loneliness, admitting we felt it keenly from time to time. And then the conversation turned to trivia and other things. But the warmth of Charlie's words and Alice's words stayed with me.

June asked me to come into the kitchen to help with the next round of tea. While the kettle boiled she said quickly and matter-of-factly that she needed a quiet word with me.

'My son's coming to visit.'

'That's nice.'

'No, it isn't.'

She put four tea bags into the pot then seemed to struggle with the weight of the kettle.

'I can do it,' she said when I offered to help. 'I don't know why he wants to visit me. I haven't seen him in seven years. But he says he's coming and so he will.'

'Is he coming here?'

'No. I've suggested the town. Glasgow. I don't have the details.'

'Why haven't you seen him?'

'Ach, it suited us both.' She stirred the water then put the lid on the teapot. 'I wondered if… you remind me of my own self. I think we're similar. We've both got the street smarts.'

I smiled at her words.

'Shall I come with you? When you meet him? We'll help each other with our trials.'

She shook her head at my joke. 'If you would, I'd like that please.' She took the milk from the fridge and poured it into a jug. 'I'm sorry about your loss. I really am. I've been thinking about you and I think you're brave. Standing up in court and getting grilled like that. And doing what you did with that lot in there today, shaking them up. I was watching through the doorway. I think that's nothing short of a miracle.'

'Thank you.'

'Shaking them up in a good way, mind,' she said.

'Not so their teeth fall out.'

'Wait till it happens to you.'

We carried the tea things through to the lounge.

'Just don't stay too long here, it won't be good for you,' she said to me as we walked, and at the time I wasn't sure if she was referring to the lounge in the sheltered housing or Lennoxtown itself. She meant Lennoxtown of course.

4.

We ate outside. Good God. Warmth grazed my skin the way the cloud shadow passed over the hills: a delicate touch. I could smell barbecue smoke and hear our neighbours talk. I caught the clink of their cutlery and the shouts of their children. I could see into their windows from Audrey's paved garden. Emily was like a pup, stopping to listen each time she heard a voice. And when she heard the regular sound of a child bouncing on a trampoline she stood on a paving stone and jumped. 'This is my trampoline,' she said. I watched her feet in her thin-soled shoes crash down onto the concrete.

'Would you like a trampoline in the new house?'

'What new house?'

'I don't know, but we'll get you a trampoline.'

I jumped with her and she liked that. That's how Paul found us. We were holding hands and jumping on Emily's trampoline. He'd heard us from the front door. We waved. Emily became shy.

'Can I use your bathroom?'

'Go ahead.' I threw him the keys.

I jumped some more with Emily then sat down and raised my head towards the evening sun. I could almost smell the grass from the fells, they were so close. Paul returned with a pint glass of water. He wore plaster-spattered tracksuit bottoms. The hairs on his arms were spotted with plaster too.

He drank the water in one go and patted Emily's head. I stood and we hugged and it felt good to hug him. Emily put her arms around my legs.

'This evening's got a lively feel to it,' I said when we sat down. It had. There was laughter from other gardens. I had company. Emily turned circles on the paving stones on a trike I'd got her from a charity shop. I pushed a plate of oven chips towards Paul and said, 'Finish them if you're hungry.'

He squirted some ketchup onto the side of the plate and ate.

'Sold your house yet?' he said.

'Why did you come here first, straight from work? Haven't you got a home to go to?'

'Not anymore.' He put a chip in his mouth. 'I'm starving. And full of lust.' He put a hand through his hair and said, 'Sorry, I shouldn't have said that out loud.'

He made me laugh and Emily came to see why I was laughing. I watched him eat and Emily climbed onto my lap.

'Behave,' I said.

'I am behaving,' Emily said.

'Not you, him.'

'I haven't got a home to go to anyway. I'm still at my mum's.' I could see it now. The man was displaced. He pushed the plate away from him and rubbed his face. Then he leaned to smooth some hair behind my ear and I leaned my head into his hand.

Emily tapped my arm and showed me what was in her clenched fist. 'I found it. Can I keep it?'

It was a pebble.

'It's beautiful isn't it?'

It was beautiful, perfectly smooth. She put it in her mouth.

'Take that out! Honestly!'

She took it out of her mouth and pretended to put it up her nose. I batted her hand away. 'I like these bits,' she said and touched her finger to the marbling that ran through the pebble. I noticed that her fingernails needed cutting.

Paul said, 'She wants me to start building a wall around her front garden. A nice neat brick wall. And I don't want to. So I came to see you.'

'Who wants the brick wall?'

'Georgia.' He shrugged his shoulders.

'Does she want you back?'

'She says she's seeing someone else.'

'Do you still get to see your daughter?'

'All the time. My mum's only a few doors away. She's probably round there now getting her dinner.'

I caught the guilt in his eyes.

'Are you going to build the wall?'

He looked towards Emily then the chips. 'Probably. I just want to keep everyone happy. You know how it is.'

I tried to work out if I minded Paul's complexities and concluded that I might mind. I knew they'd split up. But I also knew they shared a daughter and that fact was like a stake in the ground. Georgia must have been sure of herself to leave a man like Paul, to hurt a man like Paul.

'I'm going to put it in my special box,' Emily said.

She got off my lap and went to the bottom of the garden.

'What are you going to do when the house sells?' he said.

'You're the third man that's asked me that.'

'So what are you going to do?'

'I thought it would take longer than this. There were two second viewings today. I don't know. Where shall I go?'

He took my hand and we kissed suddenly and fully. We fumbled with our chairs, scraping them closer over the paving stones until our knees were touching. Emily shouted at me. 'I can't find it!'

'Have another look!'

Paul smiled and we sat back in our chairs. I noticed specks of plaster on his cheek.

And then I had to ask. 'Bam. Why would anyone call Robbie a bam?'

'Your man?'

I told him what Emily had heard at nursery. I said it made me feel anxious. I said it was a strange thing for Emily to hear about her dad. It was a strange thing for me to hear too.

'I've been called a bampot a hundred times, I wouldn't worry,' Paul said. 'But I'll ask around for you. Georgia might know. She might have known his family.'

I looked at the square paving stone where Emily had imagined her trampoline. Paul took his phone from his jacket pocket and checked the screen. He put his phone away.

'I want to see you more,' he said.

'Come anytime,' I said. I meant it.

'I better say hello to my kid.'

He kissed me on my forehead, right at the spot behind which my thoughts jangled. 'Come anytime,' I said again and Paul closed the gate behind him. He was respite, that man. I felt the sun on my arms again.

Emily came back carrying a shortbread tin with thistles on the lid. After the trouble with the clock I'd let her keep anything of Audrey's she wanted to. She called them her precious things and liked to show them to me. I'd seen them before but it was good to have Emily close to me, to marvel, as she was calm, at the tiny size of this girl whose presence was enormous, who held my very being to ransom, who made such relentless demands on my mind and body. She was so small and she was mine. I felt it, suddenly, that I loved her, a peck of love. I kissed her head.

A thimble, a pair of clip-on earrings, a coaster made of slate with a felt back.

'Be careful with that one,' she said.

Two photographs of Robbie and his brother, sitting side by side in school uniform, smiling at us. His mother had them so close in age. I looked for signs of Emily in Robbie and Aidan and I found them. It was nice.

Emily's fingers scrabbled at a piece of paper at the bottom of the tin.

'What does this say, Mummy?'

It was a newspaper cutting I hadn't seen before, not very big, about half the size of the coaster.

'What does it say?'

'It says, it says, it says, "Emily, this is another ticket to the park with the swings and the slide. Please bring your mum and eat your Freddo when you get there."'

Emily ran to her paving stone and jumped up and down, holding the newspaper to her chest. It didn't say that, of course. It said the trial of Robert Watt and Michael McDermott had gone into a third day. There were angry scenes from relatives in the courtroom. A representative from the school refused to comment. There was no date on the newspaper cutting, not even the paper's name. I thought perhaps Robert might have been Robbie's father's name, but his father's name was Andrew. There were no uncles called Robert or Robbie. He'd rarely spoken of his childhood other than to say it was poor and boring, football was the only thing he loved, and he couldn't wait to leave Lennoxtown.

As soon as Emily put the cutting down I picked it up and reread it to see if there was anything else to glean but the words were as I'd read them. The trial of Robert Watt and Michael McDermott had gone into a third day.

'Show me my name, Mummy,' Emily said, crashing in to me, nearly knocking the plate of chips from the table.

I couldn't find a word that looked like Emily. No capital E. Nothing.

'Where am I?' she said, grabbing the cutting. 'Where's my name?'

I pretended the R of Robert was an E. She believed me.

I spent the rest of the evening and the whole of the next morning wondering what Robbie could have done. I took it out on Emily. She wouldn't stop fiddling with a rubber ball when she was supposed to be eating the sandwich I'd made. But before that, I'd had to lift her to the toilet and wait with her while she peed. She always lied and said she didn't need the toilet when she did even though she fidgeted on her seat or pressed her heel into her bum. It was obvious. So she'd finally done a wee and was sitting at the table but then she wouldn't stop playing with the ball so I took it off her. And put it on a shelf. When it rolled from the shelf and bounced high on the lino floor she dived off her chair to grab it and I lunged for it too and she hurt her head on the cupboard door because she'd hurled herself at the ball. She began to cry, rolling on the floor, kicking out and holding her head. I knew she wasn't hurt badly. I knew she was roaring because she loved the sound of her roars. It made me angry and sad and I'm sure she was angry and sad too but she wouldn't let me near her and she wouldn't stop crying. As she kicked out she kicked my thighs and when I went to pick her up she punched my arms with both her fists which made me yank her up by her armpits. I pushed her onto her chair and held her struggling body down. She kept screaming so I put one hand over her mouth and held it there. My hand was so much bigger than her face it could have covered her nose as well. She screamed on but she was pinned down by my hand on her thin thighs and finally her rage was stopped by my hand over her mouth. I held her like that for a few seconds, not many, until her eyes became frightened and I was suddenly aware of my strength. She had noise and rage but I had force and power. I hated her and I hated myself. I could have killed us both.

'I want my granny,' she said when I took my hand from her mouth. 'Why are we here?'

I sent her away from me, kicked the wall and looked around for something to break.

The telephone rang. I hoped it was my mum but it was the family worker.

'Sorry if this is a bad time. How are you getting on?' she asked.

'Fine,' I said. 'Absolutely fine.'

'We're looking forward to seeing you tomorrow.'

'You know what, I can't come. We're busy.'

'Well, that's a shame.'

'Yeah.'

I didn't have to go. It wasn't the law. Emily and I would find our own way out of our trouble. We'd go swimming and get a McDonald's. We'd invite Caroline and her kids to the park. Or we'd ask Paul round to eat chips outside. The family worker could leave us be.

She first smiled at eight weeks. That's two weeks after they say a baby might smile but I don't blame her for holding back because I will have looked at her with my ragged face and she will have thought: Can this woman really be my mother? Now Emily rarely smiles at me or even looks at me. It's always *I want, I want, I want.*

Before she smiled we had Robbie's funeral. His family came: a muted, round-shouldered collection, who barely moved from the corner of the function room we found. There were two ancient uncles and an aunt, dead now, and his brother, back from Australia and near silent with cold and grief. We squeezed hands and they shook their heads. His gran wasn't there. She sent a card. Many of our friends were at sea and couldn't come so the congregation was small. I didn't have anything black and smart that fitted me so I wore my maternity clothes. My mum sat next to me and we put Emily in her car seat on the floor in front of us. Occasionally one of us leaned forwards to rock her. When she woke and cried my mum took her outside. I no longer heard the words of the vicar just the desperate wails of my baby. My milk came and I was worried it would seep through my breast pads. I kept looking down to check my chest or behind me to see my mum pacing in the lobby and it distracted me from Robbie. Or it kept me from losing myself completely. In the end my mum brought Emily in to me and I stayed sitting to feed her while our small congregation stood to sing The Lord is my Shepherd. The trial of Robert Watt? Robbie? What the fuck?

5.

A few days later, after Paul had left to put his daughter to bed, Ruth telephoned. She said, 'June's not been in to do Harry's sheets.'

I thought, Good for June. She's not his maid.

'She usually leaves a note if she can't do it.'

'He can work a washing machine, can't he?'

I had a sink full of dishes. Emily was walking with both feet in one pyjama leg.

'Have you heard from her?' Ruth asked me.

I told her I'd seen her at the end of my last dance class and that she'd asked me to come with her when she met her son.

'Oh.' Ruth's voice scuffed a low note. 'I didn't know her son was bothering her.'

Emily took off her pyjama bottoms and climbed onto the sofa. She didn't like me to speak on the telephone, to people in the street, or to anyone, really. When she thought the conversation had gone on for too long she would tug at me, demand me, shout at me and try to take my attention. I don't blame her. These people were nothing to Emily and I am her mother. But it was annoying.

As I listened to Ruth, Emily stood on the arm of the sofa with bent legs, wiggling her bum close to my head. I held one of her outstretched arms. Ruth told me that June had been missing for four days. She'd neglected the sheets and she'd also missed a residents' meeting. This was not the first time she had gone away without warning.

'My partner's on the fells looking for her right now.'

That shook me. 'You're worried, aren't you?'

'My instincts are usually right.'

I saw twilight through the gap in the curtains. The streetlights were lit. There was nothing to be seen of the Campsies, only their dense dark bulk.

'Call me if you hear anything,' Ruth said. 'She can get quite agitated.'

'And if she doesn't come home?'

'I'll call the police if she's not here by nine.'

When I hung up, Emily jumped nimbly and fiercely into my arms, her legs bending to form a diamond in the air. *Pas de chat*. One of the first ballet steps I learned where I felt as if I was properly dancing, not training or strengthening or preparing, but dancing. Cat Step. I caught Emily and cuddled her and we made our way to the bathroom to clean her teeth.

'What's the matter, Mummy?' she asked me.

'June, the lady we went to court with and we climbed the big hill with, do you remember her? You had a Freddo. We took her home. We're a bit worried about her.'

'Why?'

'She might be lost.'

'Has somebody died?'

'I don't know. I actually don't know.'

'I like June.'

'Does she remind you of Granny?'

'No.'

I was watching television when I heard a tap on the front door. I expected it to be Paul back to see me, but it wasn't. It was June.

'Surprise,' she said and she made me laugh because the way she spoke was so ordinary, so charmless and deadpan. There's nothing wrong with you, I thought, but I was wrong about that.

'I'm not going to stay long because I know you have your hands full.'

'She's asleep. Come in. Have you told Ruth you're okay?'

'Ruth knows I'm always okay.' She looked full at me. 'And here you are in Donald and Audrey Watt's house. You look quite the part.'

'Are you coming in, June?'

She came through the doorway and brought the night air in with her.

'Where have you been?'

I held out my hands for her coat but she kept it on. She took off her gloves and put them in her pockets. I let her go up the stairs before me.

'These stairs were always steep,' she said.

'Do you want a drink?'

'I'm only here for a wee look.'

'I can give you a tour.'

She nodded. 'Aye.'

I'd only been half serious but she was keen. She looked around her at the hall, even though there was little to see.

I flicked on the light, pointed to the room where Emily slept and put a finger to my lips. 'She'll be sorry to miss you,' I said. June nodded and walked slowly down the hall, letting her fingers trail along the painted wall. The fresh paint smell lingered. She stood at the door to the room at the back where Emily and I had the sofa and television.

'This is the living room, obviously,' I said. 'They're saying the new people could knock through from the kitchen and make a lounge-diner thing. Apparently there used to be a door there anyway.'

'Yes,' June said and she walked straight into the room as if it was hers, touched the curtains and looked at a pile of Audrey's bric-a-brac.

'Do you want anything?' I asked. 'It's going on Gumtree or to the charity shop.'

'Oh no.'

She turned to me and folded her arms. I noticed traces of mud on her pale coat sleeves and thought perhaps she'd been back to the Campsies and traipsed through the dark and the dirt.

'I expected him to go for someone sweeter. No offence, Liz, but you have a way about you.'

'What?' I was so surprised I didn't know that she was talking about me.

She shook her head and although she spoke kindly, what she said was unkind. 'His gran wouldn't have liked you.'

'Are you talking about Robbie?'

'Aye, I'm talking about Robbie.'

'She did like me! Do you want to see this flat or not?' I think I showed uncharacteristic restraint because I remembered Ruth had said she was agitated.

We went into the kitchen and I was pleased I'd managed to do the dishes. Pots lay upturned on tea towels. June leaned in to look at some of Emily's artwork that I'd stuck to the fridge.

'I need to talk to you about Robbie,' I said. 'You worked at the primary school. You remember him don't you?'

'We weren't cooks,' she said. 'I did him a boiled egg once or twice. The hob's different. They must have got a new cooker.'

I presumed she was still talking about Robbie. I flicked the kettle on and put two tea bags in two mugs.

'You go on and have a look around,' I said. 'I'm making us tea. You don't have to drink it.'

While she was out of the room I texted Ruth. *She's here with me. Safe. Can't talk. Will call.*

June was in the spare room when I returned to her, the one that Paul had completely re-plastered and painted cream.

'He called that the good room. We didn't go in there much. He was going to order a table and chairs.'

If June had looked closely she'd have seen the marks in the carpet from where the table legs had rested for years. It seemed so long that the men from the Salvation Army had taken away most of Audrey's furniture. We shut the door on the room.

'Do you want your tea now or shall we have it when we sit down?'

'Later, hen.' She'd softened. 'I can see us here,' she said and her hands were folded tight against her body. 'It's that real to me.'

She looked up at the ceiling in the hall, the freshly-plastered ceiling under which Paul had worked on his stilts. 'That's nice,' she said of the lampshade I'd bought from Home Bargains. 'It was a bare bulb when we were here.' She gazed at the walls and the floor. 'I cleaned this place from top to toe. I made it sparkle. There used to be a fire in that room.' She gestured back into the good room. 'I cleaned the grate until it sparkled. It was floorboards and tiles in the kitchen. The lino is new, the carpet is new. But it has the same feel.'

I didn't understand why she knew the flat so well. I carried the cups of tea and showed her the bathroom that according to the estate agent was in need of updating. I showed her the cupboard in which the two boxes for sea mail to Australia were stacked. June's eyes were less confident. Her mouth was closed and it was me who spoke, me who pointed out the original cornicing and dado rails in the living room, me who showed her the wallpaper on one wall that had come up nicely when I cleaned it with sugar soap.

'This room,' she said as she pushed my bedroom door open.

I worried that Emily might have been in my bed already and would wake up with our noise but I couldn't stop June. She was going through the rooms so keenly. My bed was empty but unmade. My towel had fallen from the radiator. Our clothes were on the floor. June stepped inside and closed the wardrobe door. She picked up the fallen towel and folded it. I saw her shoulders relax. I pulled the bedcovers back towards the pillows. She put the towel on a chair and looked out of the window just as the estate agent had done.

'There's a nice view from the window isn't there?' I said.

'Yes, I suppose there is.'

I laid Emily's slipper socks on top of her dressing gown and bent to pick up leggings, cardigan and top, discarded the night before and left all day.

'But I found the silence so good for sleep. Do you? Is it still silent in this room?'

'Yes.'

'We stayed in here a few times. I truly thought this would be my home.'

She stood in the brightly lit, messy room, as if she didn't know where to put herself, turning to look about her, hands clenched in fists at her sides.

'I was a foolish girl, Liz. I don't blame him. I don't even begrudge Audrey anything. But I wish it had never happened. I wish it had never happened.'

She smiled briefly and with the smile came tears which she wiped with her fists. We sat on the end of my bed and looked at the windowpane with the night behind it and our reflections silver and gold upon it.

'I'm sorry for what I said about you and Robbie. I see why you got on well. I see why he needed a strong head.'

'Thank you.'

'A long time ago I did a foolish thing,' she said. She wiped her eyes again. 'It's not like me to greet.'

'Drink your tea for a bit.'

'I'll have to use your toilet before I go.'

We drank our tea in silence. June drank hers in gulps as if it was water and I took her cup and put it on the floor beside my feet and held my mug with two hands, waiting. June blew her nose. Then she gave me one of her direct stares and said, 'You. You coming to Lennoxtown has set it all off.'

She straightened her back, like a ballerina, and sat with her hands in her lap. 'I knocked on the door of this house with my bucket and mop fifty-nine years ago. Donald was alone. His fiancée, Robbie's gran, had taken ill and was in Stobhill, up the road. It was a freezing time, just after Christmas. He'd got a flat from the council and they hadn't moved into it yet. She didn't even know about it. It was supposed to be a surprise for after they married. It was a big deal in those days to buy a house.'

'It still is.'

'It still is. So that's why they got theirs from the council. They must have bought it in the eighties when everyone bought their houses.' She nodded and said, 'Aye, but the pipes burst because they'd not been used during the big freeze and the flat flooded. It was a damp flat anyway but that flood ruined it. And because he was on his own and had his fiancée to contend with up in the hospital, and his job to carry on with, my mother sent me and my cousin to help with the clear-up once the council had fixed the pipes. We were girls without children and only ourselves to look after. I was killing time before nursing college. It was a close-knit village and older women like my mother were inclined to put younger women to work.

'I can't mind what she was in the hospital for originally. It was serious but not life threatening. It might have been a cyst. I think she needed monitoring. And then it got worse. She got some infection or other and needed round the clock care.

'Straight away we hit it off. We talked about the government, the football, the pictures. He was interested in my nursing. He said he had childhood dreams of being a doctor but the bank swallowed him up. We had a lot in common and I have never, before or since, liked anyone so much. I liked him through and through. It was love. On both sides. Without a doubt.'

She looked at me then and nodded her head. I nodded too.

'We finished the clean-up in two or three days and he moved into the flat. He asked to keep me on as a cleaner which I agreed to. It was supposed to be once a week but I came every day when he was back from his work or the hospital. I know this flat intimately.

'I expected when Audrey was better that he would let her down in a kind way. I expected that I would move into the flat, so I looked after it tenderly. I was angry with myself, with us, for not meeting sooner. We lived in the same village. We had done all our lives. He was nine years older than me and when he told me of the night he and Audrey had spoken at a dance, I cursed myself for not going, for being somewhere else. Because I could have met him there. Properly. Things would have fallen into place in a more simple way. I can't recall what I was doing instead. I was probably with Jim.

'My mother twigged that I was up to something and when she asked I came straight out with it. If you've had a tough life you know what feels right and you don't mess about. I knew we'd cause some pain for that lassie up there in the hospital. She'd have the shock of being jilted but she'd get over it and then we'd all move on with our lives. I had the full support of my mother.

'Audrey got better and she came home to her parents and as the days went on I expected he'd tell her. He said he wanted her to get fully better so she had the strength to cope with her loss. His one reservation, he confessed, was that they hadn't waited until they were married. After they became engaged they slept together once or twice, that's what he said to me anyway, and now he was dropping her. It didn't sit well with him. It didn't sit well with me. I was sick jealous.

'And so because of that I wanted what she'd had. This is where I should have had a word with myself. Donald was adamant that he didn't want to impose himself on me, to compromise me. No he wasn't. He was delighted. He resisted for all of five minutes and then we too were at it like a newly married couple, as if it was the most natural thing in the world.

'It must have been three weeks since she was out of hospital and she was up and about and telling him she wanted to see the new flat he'd finally told her about. I said to him he couldn't bring her to the flat. If he did that a line would be crossed. So he said, give me a day, and I'll take her for a walk and tell her. And then an awful thing happened. Her mother took ill very suddenly, she nearly died, and Audrey asked to bring forward their wedding so that her mother could be alive for it. He should have said no there and then. There would have been the pain, as I said, and worse pain now, and the humiliation and the disgrace, but everyone would have got over it. Life is long.

'But the wedding preparations continued and he married her in Campsie Parish Church. The only thing he couldn't, shouldn't, oughtn't have done, he did, and it meant that us, our plans, our lives together were ruined.'

June stopped talking and looked at her hands.

'I should have gone away and boarded at nursing college but I didn't. I married Jim. I gave up my course. And I don't know whether my son is Jim's or Donald's. I like to think he's Donald's but he's always looked too much like me to be sure and I suspect he's Jim's. What I do know is that I have never stopped thinking about Donald and I have lived my whole life in jealousy.'

There was a sigh from Emily's room and we both looked towards the door to see if she would come in, half asleep, but she didn't. I stood and drew the curtains and turned to June. Her face had regained its fatalistic set and when she wiped her tears she frowned and looked about the room and I expected her to say something sharp or bossy like it wouldn't kill you to tidy up once in a while.

Instead she stood up slowly. I tried to take her elbow but she shrugged me off.

'I would have had our bed on this wall and at the foot of the bed I wanted one of those blanket chests. An ottoman. I wanted a dressing table with a mirror. I do believe that would have happened if her mother hadn't fallen ill. He never liked her anyway. He shouldn't have gone through with it.'

'Does anyone else know? Does your son? Is that why you don't—'

'Oh no. My mother took my secret to her grave. I couldn't even tell the priest so I stopped going to mass. It was a mixed union anyway. Who knows how that would have gone.'

She bent down to pick up her empty cup.

'I'll get it,' I said.

She seemed worn out, spent. It must have pained June to keep her secret, to see Donald in the street and not rush to him. Her body must have responded with pain, it surely must have put a strain on her heart, her head. It made me glad of Robbie and what we had. It's a cliché and I'm not afraid to say it: we were halves of each other, we knew each other completely.

I touched her arm. 'Maybe you'll feel better now you've told someone. Now that you've been back in the flat. It's quite a story.'

'It gets worse than that.'

'Does it? Do you want to tell me?'

'No, that's that,' she said and stepped in front of me, out of the door towards the living room.

'Your wee one's a good sleeper,' she said as she went.

'Yes.'

I asked her if she wanted another cup of tea. Then, because we seemed to be passing stories between us and sharing a little of our lives I said, 'I found out Robbie was in a trial. Quite serious, I think. You'll know what happened, won't you? He never told me. It doesn't fit with him, you know?'

June pulled her gloves from her pocket and said, 'It's too late and I'm too tired for that.' She took time over her gloves and I thought she might relent and speak after all. But she didn't.

'Sit down. Do you want me to call you a cab?'

'The bus is no bother.' That familiar defiance in her face.

The on-off blue light of an emergency vehicle lit up the room. I walked to the window and saw two policemen coming up the path. I thought they were coming for me but when I opened the door they said 'June?' and looked past me at June who was holding tight to the banister and walking down the stairs.

'Yes,' she said.

'Do you want a run home? We'll take you up the road.'

'Why?'

'We were having a wee look for you,' one said to her, 'and now we've found you we don't want to lose you again.'

They talked to her as if she was a child. 'That's Ruth, that is,' June said and she went grudgingly with the policemen into their car for a lift home. June was right. When I telephoned Ruth after June had gone, she told me she'd called the police at eight-thirty instead of nine, not being able to bear the wait and the not-knowing and fearing the sharp wind and erratic spring temperatures. Even though she called the police to say June was safe, the search was already on, police time was committed, and these things have a habit of carrying on until their conclusion so they offered to collect her from my flat.

'How was she?' Ruth asked.

I didn't know how to answer. 'Agitated,' I said.

It occurred to me that June hadn't used the toilet before she left and I hoped she wasn't uncomfortable on her ride home.

6.

At the next dance class June chaperoned two new dancers into the lounge and collected their money. She turned the radio off, pulled the curtains across the big windows to give the new and shy dancers privacy, then asked me how I was and told the class to hurry up and stand at the chairs, there would be plenty of time afterwards to chat.

Agnes and Senga had bought ballet shoes and wore them over tan pop socks and they were keen to come to the barre. Their feet were neat and elegant.

'Now I'm jealous!' June said and took orders from the others for shoes, saying she would buy some from the dancing shop when she next went into Kirkintilloch.

She tried harder in the class and I could see that she was developing as a dancer, they all were. It was easier for them to lift up through their spines and keep their shoulders down. Their movements were less jerky, their faces less strained. I tried them with a slow *pas de bourré* – two steps on their toes and a third step ending with a bend of their supporting knee and their pointed foot tucked behind their supporting ankle. They held on to their chairs with two hands. As long as they didn't over-balance and pull the chairs on top of them they would manage, I thought. They all did except for Charlie and Agnes. I told them to practise their *relevés* and *pliés*.

After the class June and I didn't speak about either of our losses. There was no need; our conversations seemed held like a pact between us and there was little point returning to them.

Only once, making tea in the kitchenette, she said to me, 'I considered buying Audrey's flat when she died. It hasn't sold yet has it?'

'Oh my God, are you nuts?' I said.

'But I couldn't afford it anyway, and yes, it would have me committed wouldn't it?'

'Stay here with your view, June.'

If I'd had any doubt before, her words showed me how much this man, Robbie's grandad, lived in her head. She'd never got over him or got rid of him. Whatever she'd needed to do to have a life beyond their brief and intense affair, she hadn't managed. We were similar in many ways. I told myself I ought to see Paul again soon.

I was keen to wonder about her son, but wary of asking. If it was true he was Robbie's grandad's son, he would be related to Emily. It would make him some sort of uncle. This revelation, this lucky nugget, was why I'd come to Lennoxtown, I realised, and I could go home satisfied after all. I'd leave with more knowledge than when I'd arrived and that would be the point of Lennoxtown.

Eve slapped the sole of Senga's ballet shoe on the table. She sniffed the leather. 'Takes me back to my daddy's cobbler's! Oh!'

'Sniffing shoes, I've seen it all now,' Agnes said, and Charlie asked to sniff the shoe too.

Alice watched quietly, her eyebrows raised, her lips mouthing unspoken sentences.

'What size are these?' Eve said. She held out her hand for the shoe and put it against her foot. 'Too small. I'll need a couple of sizes up, June.'

'Come with me,' June said.

'I don't want ribbons on mine,' John said.

'You don't get ribbons on these ones,' Senga said. 'You get elastic.'

'I want ribbons on mine,' Charlie said.

'I guess you could sew them on.'

'Who sewed your elastic on, Senga?'

'Me. Four shoes. I couldn't let my mum near a needle with her eyes.'

We turned to look at Agnes's blue eyes. She widened them for us, better to see. Their chat was nice. Still want your painting class, Eve? I thought.

June walked me to my car and I was surprised by the look of the Campsies. Only their top ridges were visible. The sides of them were covered by cloud that had dropped almost as low as the trees and houses at the bottom.

'The sun will fry it off,' June said.

'You're very optimistic about the sunshine,' I said.

She shook her head then bent to pick up a crisp packet and cigarette butt. When she returned from the bin she told me that even though no date had been set she could feel her meeting with her son gnawing at her stomach. 'He'll be after money,' she said. 'He's not interested in me. But it pains me all the same. I don't know why I'm telling you this. I shouldn't be.'

'You don't have to meet him,' I said.

'He's my son. It's hard to switch that off.' That stake in the ground again. 'I'm not afraid of him,' she said.

'Will you give him money?'

I was prying and she didn't like it. She asked about Emily and I said she was doing well, which she was, that day. 'Would you like to see her again?'

'Aye, I would,' she said.

Perhaps we would go to the swings, perhaps we would go to the Campsies and climb through the clouds.

'You just let me know. I don't have much on at the moment.'

'Nor do I.'

One thing I wanted to do was to put some flowers on Audrey and Donald's graves and Robbie's parents' too. Paul came. He waited in the Co-op car park while I jumped in for some daffodils.

'Do you know where they are?' he asked when we parked at the cemetery.

'I came here a few years ago,' I said. 'I should remember.' We walked through the rows of graves and read the headstones. A woman kneeled at one grave and dug with a trowel. There were miniature roses in plastic pots next to her. She looked up as we passed and Paul said hello.

'Here,' I said.

Someone had put flowers on Audrey's grave but they had no life left so I gathered them up and put the daffodils in their place. I put some daffodils down for Donald too. They shared a plot. Such a long time to keep a secret from his wife. Such a long time to miss someone, if he missed June at all. I suspected he didn't.

I looked for gravestones for Robbie's parents. I searched up and down the paths, remembering the time Robbie and I had come, but I couldn't find them.

'Maybe the headstones go in date order,' Paul said. 'When did they die?'

'He was fourteen when his dad died and twenty-two when his mum passed away.'

'Poor lad.' Paul shook his head.

We passed the woman tending the grave. She patted earth around a rose plant, pressing firmly, wearing thick gardening gloves.

'How's your mum?' the woman said to Paul when she looked up.

'Aye, she's grand.'

'Tell her I was asking after her.'

Paul raised a hand. He pushed his hat over his ears.

'Does Robbie have a gravestone?' he said.

I was unable to speak. Any words I wanted to say seemed to stop in my throat so I shook my head. We walked in silence to his car.

Robbie's ashes aren't scattered or buried. They're safe at my mum's and I'm happy for them to stay there.

7.

Emily's birthday was approaching. She would be five. Poor child. She asked me each bedtime, *How many sleeps?* and I counted down the days with her, trying to find a voice to match her eagerness. I dreaded and longed for her birthday. I wanted the day to come so I could plunge into the past, into memories of when the three of us were alive. Today five years ago, I would think, you were born and we three were alive and within a breath of each other for the first time ever. Today five years ago Robbie and I emerged shattered and near-broken from a brutal labour and you too Emily were damaged from the delivery and smuggled into special care but you were out and breathing and we three were alive. Today five years ago you were a day old and Robbie was at my side as I stood over your incubator, touching you through a hand hole in the side. Today five years ago we were on the ward and Robbie was watching me learn to breastfeed, or holding you in the crook of his arms like a poke of chips, he said, and passing you to my mum. Today we were home with the curtains closed. Robbie was taking pictures of my milk-filled tits, I was smearing cream on my stinging nipples and he was walking with you on his shoulder patting your back for burps and trying to settle you as you wrestled with colic. We were sleep deprived, my body was fizzing with hormones that made me manic and overwhelmed but we were alive and together.

Today five years ago the midwife came to check my stitches. Today five years ago we put you in the car seat and drove to register your birth and the street was alive with people who didn't know us or realise that our time was running out. Today I told you I missed you. Today we had our last day, with little sleep the night before other than a stretch between three and six, and we walked, I think, to the shops and back and Robbie got his university books out and I slept whenever you slept so our last day wasn't full, it was patchy, with me desperate to close my eyes and get away from it all for half an hour, whatever it took to rid myself of the tiredness. Then, today five years ago you died. I would plunge, wanting to be alone to grieve, and every day onwards would be me and Emily, no longer a three, only a two.

After he died I used to wonder as I went to sleep if I would wake in the morning. I would feel acute fear for Emily who might be left with no parents. But sleep came so quickly and heavily, from exhaustion, from the tablets I took, that I had no time to worry before I was out. And then I would be hurled into consciousness by a snuffle or a cry from Emily. I would wonder how I never heard Robbie that night, if he struggled before his heart stopped. It sickened me that I could let him die next to me in my bed and not hear it or feel it or stop it.

We got through those weeks each year, Emily and I, and we would get through them again. I don't know if it gets easier. It's not seeming so.

It took a rendition of 'Five Currant Buns in a Baker's Shop' to pull me up from underwater. Emily was learning songs at nursery to perform in front of parents and grandparents a week after her birthday, during that murky sad time I was dreading. A Scottish song called 'Allyballybee', another one called 'Three Craws'. Keep singing, Emily, I said, and she sang her nursery rhymes for me, her voice holding a sweet tune, taking on a Scottish accent, just like her dad's.

One day I emptied the vase in which I'd stuffed notes and pound coins from the sale of Audrey's things and took the lot. It was nothing compared to the tens of thousands Aidan would get for her house, and the cost of converting it to dollars would halve it so it was dead money, really, useless. I considered it mine, without a qualm.

I rang June and said to her, 'Jump on the bus to Glasgow with us.'

'I'm not dressed.' Her voice was as stroppy as mine.

'Get dressed then. I've come into some money. I'm taking us to the food court.'

I'd wanted to take Emily out of nursery but she'd insisted on going in because she needed to practise her songs. 'All right, we'll go after nursery,' I said and, as promised, I was waiting for her, on time, with snacks and a carton of juice and I walked her to the bus stop and we sat on the bottom deck on the left-hand side looking out of the window for June to get on a few stops later. When we found her waiting at the bus stop I banged on the window to get her attention. She looked at us as if we were her weans and shook her head.

Emily sat on my lap and we made room for June to sit next to us. She offered Emily a mint and Emily hesitated because she'd never had a mint before.

'You can have it but don't choke,' I said, so Emily sucked the mint. She took it out of her mouth from time to time to check on it.

'How was nursery?' June asked.

'Good,' Emily said. She widened her eyes as she sucked her sweet.

'June, I've got the money from Audrey's things. Over a hundred quid. Come and we'll get you some perfume or something. It's on Audrey. There's justice in there somewhere.'

She didn't appreciate my words. We passed through the well-to-do streets of Lenzie and then along the roads of forest and fields and when we reached the roundabout for the motorway to Glasgow Emily dropped her mint. She cried out and tried to slide off my legs to pick it up from the floor. 'Here,' June said and gave her another one.

'She's a lot like Robbie,' June said. 'Not just because of the curls, but something about her mouth.'

'Gobby,' I said.

I showed June a picture of me and Robbie that I kept on my phone. The two of us standing side by side in the crew bar, our heads close, nearly touching.

'That's nice. He never grew much taller did he?'

'I've always been taller than him.'

That was all she said. No memories of him as a boy as I hoped she'd share. No insight into the newspaper clipping Emily had found. Perhaps she didn't know anything. Perhaps she was retired by then. I put my phone away and leaned back in my seat to look out of the window. I wondered if Robbie had made this same journey as a teenager with a tenner in his pocket for a McDonald's or a cinema ticket. The motorway merged with another motorway, two gas towers loomed and then almost as soon as we were past them the bus was indicating left towards the city.

'I used to come to the town for the dancing,' June said and while I was remembering her rebuttal on the first day I met her – I never took to dancing – she said, 'He wants to meet me in Glasgow. He's going to stay in a Travelodge.'

'Your son?'

'Yes.'

We were in the city now with the high glass college buildings either side of the road and the construction sites and cranes and traffic lights. Crowds of people crossed the junction where our bus had stopped. Emily put her fingers and face to the glass and looked out.

'Why isn't he staying in Lennoxtown?' I asked.

'He doesn't associate Lennoxtown with anything good anymore.'

'Why not?'

'And to be honest, I think I'll handle him better away from Campsie. Neutral territory. He might feel like less of my son, if you know what I mean.'

I didn't, but I put Emily's coat on her as the men and women in yellow jackets guided the bus into its stance at the terminus. I helped Emily off the bus – she jumped – and we turned to watch June's careful steps in her small leather shoes and then we were wandering through the shops like any family, Emily touching everything she saw and June refusing anything I offered to buy her with Audrey's money. She held Emily's hand and distracted her while I bought a doll that came with a carrycot and an extra set of clothes, for her birthday. That was helpful.

In the food court June let me buy her lunch. She asked for fish fingers and chips and a coffee, which I bought her happily and the three of us sat with our meals but Emily didn't want to eat. I'd given her too many snacks.

'This is your lunch,' I said. 'There's nothing else.'

'I've got a headache.'

'Just eat your nuggets then.'

'I'll eat one.'

'Eat one then.'

She took a tiny bite and put the nugget down. I had to look away. She was making me mad. I couldn't let it go. 'Have another bite.'

June put her hand over Emily's. 'You just take your time, pet,' she said.

'Are you afraid of your son?' I said.

'I've got a headache,' Emily said again.

June scowled. 'That's a personal question.' Then, 'I don't know if I like him anymore. You seem wound up, Liz.'

'Why not?'

'Mummy, my head is really sore.'

I put my hand on Emily's forehead and it was hot. I noticed her red cheeks and told her to drink some milkshake.

'If you don't want to see him just tell him not to come. You're a forthright woman.'

'I'll see how I feel nearer the time.'

Emily pushed her nuggets away from her and knocked over her milkshake. June caught it. I looked again at Emily's flushed face.

'Is your head still sore?' I asked.

'Yes.'

'How's your heart? Is it beating fast?' I felt her pulse. It seemed fast to me. This would not do.

I told June it was an emergency. We grabbed our bags, left our food on the table, and I carried Emily down the escalator to the street. I yelled at the first taxi I saw.

'A&E,' I said, not knowing how near or far the nearest hospital was.

'Is the wean okay?' the driver said.

'No, she's not.'

'Will I take her to the new hospital?'

I looked at June. She said, 'Aye.'

'Mummy, we're in a taxi,' Emily whispered. She sat as still as she's ever sat.

'How are you feeling?'

'Fine.'

It was my heart that was beating fast, my breath that was ragged, my head that had pins of panic all through it.

'Liz, I don't think there's much wrong with her,' June said as the taxi took us alongside the river through a city I'd barely seen.

'She could be very ill but you can't see it,' I said.

The taxi driver didn't charge me. June tried to give him money but he didn't take hers either. We raced from the taxi into the A&E waiting room and I shouted, 'Help! My daughter needs help!'

A triage nurse sat her down. 'What's the matter?'

'It's her heart. You need to check her heart. She's not well.'

The nurse was too slow. Over-kind. He talked to her, not me, and Emily answered him quietly. He put a plastic thimble over her thumb and hooked her up to a monitor. He checked her eyes and ears and took her temperature.

'Her dad died because of his heart,' I hissed into the nurse's ear, not wanting Emily to hear me. 'Sudden death.'

'How's her breathing been?' he asked.

'Bad.'

'How do you mean bad?'

'All over the place.'

'Has she described any pain?'

'Yes.'

'Where?'

'In her heart.'

Emily looked up at me.

'What about her skin?'

'Sweaty.'

'What colour?'

'Grey. Red.'

Emily looked at me again. She must have known I was lying but I couldn't stop myself.

The triage nurse took Emily's hands and held her fingers. He leaned towards her, bouncing her fingers up and down in his. He was about to speak.

'You need to check her out now. Get her an ECG. Get a cardiologist. Get her looked at.' I wasn't going to have him tell me to sit in a waiting room. 'Her dad,' I hissed again. 'This is an emergency. She might have his heart. We're not leaving.'

I know. I wasn't myself. And I was frightening Emily who sat still, swinging her legs underneath her chair.

'Liz, you need to calm down,' June said, and she put her palm to Emily's forehead. 'She looks all right to me. Are you better now, Emily?'

But I didn't stop until we'd passed through to the doors of the emergency ward and they'd hooked her up to a machine and sent a paediatric cardiologist to look at her. She said she could see no anomalies on Emily's ECG: 'Show me, show me the ECG.' I said. Her fingers traced the triangles on the printout, showing me everything was normal. They would send Emily an outpatient's appointment and she would come back for an echocardiogram. Belt and braces, the doctor said. I looked into her eyes and saw that she was attempting to reassure me. June nodded and said, 'See, she's fine.'

'Are you Gran?' the doctor said.

'No,' June said, but she took charge as if she was my mother or my grandmother. Again, I was glad of her.

It was June who noticed the doctor and a colleague talking outside the cubicle then going together to lean over a computer screen.

When she came back the doctor said, 'We'd like you to stay here for a little longer. I'm going to re-examine you,' and she removed Emily's leggings and inspected her legs, then rolled her on her side and lifted her top so the soft skin of her back was revealed. 'Shouldn't be much longer,' she said as she closed the curtain on her way out.

'I'm hungry,' Emily said.

'She was checking for bruises,' June whispered to me.

'They're getting a social worker aren't they?'

June stood up. 'Get her dressed, put her shoes on, and when I tell you, we'll go. This is an outrage.'

At June's word we burst from the cubicle and ran without looking back. We struggled with one door until Emily noticed the green push-button which released the lock and we didn't stop running until we reached the row of bus stops on the other side of the hospital. Emily thought it was a game.

'She didn't have any bruises,' I said and cradled Emily's head in my hands, pulling her body to my body. Emily looked up, exhilarated, breathing heavily in an exaggerated way. 'They saw that there were no bruises, didn't they?' I said again.

'Of course they did. But you'll be on a red flag or some such. We'd have been hours in there waiting for a duty social worker to let you go. No way.' She looked as if she was going to say something else but closed her mouth.

The electronic displays on the bus stops showed numbers of buses to places I'd never heard of. 'Where are we?'

'Govan.'

'Where's that?'

'South of the river.'

'How will we get home?'

'I need a wee,' Emily said.

There was nothing but roads and paving and landscaped grounds, nowhere to conceal a small child as she peed outside. I was afraid to return to the hospital but we went back because Emily would have wet herself, I know she would. I left June outside the door to the toilets and made sure that Emily sat on a toilet seat with no piss on it. When she was washing her hands in the wash room's ultra violet light I felt suddenly so tired of it all. I called Paul. 'Can you help me out?' I said.

'Has your plaster cracked?'

I couldn't play along. 'No. But we're miles from home.'

'Give me half an hour. Tell me where you are.'

Emily asked me to lift her up to the mirror so she could see her face in the strange light.

Perhaps it was the slowness of my walk when we came out of the toilets or the limp way I held Emily's hand, but June stepped towards me and put her arms around my shoulders and I bent my head to be embraced. Emily joined in too.

'I would get yourself out of Lennoxtown,' June said to me. 'You've done your bit. Go home now.'

I said nothing. We sat down outside to wait for Paul. God knows what detour he made to pick us up but he got to us within half an hour.

'What's wrong with her?' he asked when he'd strapped Emily into his daughter's car seat. June sat beside Emily in the back, a plastic ball and a McDonald's toy still in its wrapper at her feet.

'My heart,' Emily said.

'Your heart?'

'Mummy said it hurt, but it didn't.'

Paul turned round in his seat and I wished he would keep his eyes on the road.

'What's wrong with your heart?'

'Mummy thought it would be like Daddy's.'

'Oh.'

He looked at the road and drove on.

'I'm hungry. Is there something to eat?' Emily asked. She'd taken her shoes and socks off.

I had no snacks left. June gave her a mint.

'There's an orange in the glove box.'

'I don't want an orange.'

'Can I have it?' I said.

I peeled the orange and ripped the skin into tiny pieces as I told Paul about Robbie's heart and how his condition could be hereditary. I told him I feared for my daughter. June and Emily spoke quietly in the back seat. Their voices were soothing. Emily began to sing 'Five Currant Buns in a Baker's Shop'.

'You're an unlikely friendship,' Paul said to me.

'Me and June? We have an understanding, don't we June?' I called over my shoulder to her. It was more than an understanding. It was an affinity.

She didn't answer.

'You're not Michael McDermott's mum are you?' Paul said.

'I am, yes. You can drop me wherever's convenient. I'll pick up some shopping in Kirkintilloch.'

'I'll drop you to your door.'

'No, no. Drop me in Kirky if you please.'

We drove slowly and in silence: slowly, because the motorway lanes were clogged with traffic, in silence because Emily was near sleep, June had turned her head to look out of the window and I had nothing to say. Paul checked his rear-view mirror frequently and I think he was checking on June. When I looked at Emily, her mouth was pursed around another mint and I wanted to ask June to take it from her in case she choked but was afraid Emily would get angry. I watched the gas towers go by and felt my pulse. I think my heart was still racing.

Paul took the turn-off to Kirkintilloch and his car growled along the fast roads through the fields with the half-built new houses, the Campsies ahead of us yellow in the afternoon light. In Kirkintilloch June chucked Emily's cheek and said to her, 'Feel better soon,' and to me she said, 'Get an early night. That's some day you've had.' She set off with her turned out feet and swinging arms to goodness knows where.

'How old is June?' Emily asked, after she'd gone.

'I don't know, maybe seventy-five, I don't know.'

'She has lines all over her face.'

'She's had a long life. That's what happens.'

'I want another mint.'

'You'll have to wait till you see her again.'

'I want another mint!'

'Don't start, Emily.' She didn't.

Paul said, 'You know who she is, don't you?'

Emily kicked the back of my seat.

'Yes.' I thought he was talking about her brief affair with Robbie's grandad and was suddenly devastated for my private and fierce friend whose story must have been known by the whole village. 'She knew Robbie's family,' I said.

'She's Michael McDermott's mum.'

'Oh.'

'Your man Robbie, he used to knock about with Michael McDermott.'

Michael McDermott. I recognised the name now.

'Are you all right?'

I wasn't. 'They did something didn't they?' I said. 'Michael McDermott and Robbie. They were in trouble.'

'You'd have to ask someone who knew him.'

We drove through the fields, the Campsies lit up and dazzling, beautiful spring leaves on trees emboldened by the new sun. I pulled down the visor to shield my eyes.

'I thought you didn't know Robbie,' I said.

'I didn't. But Georgia did. She knew him.'

'Why didn't you tell me?'

He slowed as a van took a corner too fast.

'It's not really my business. Is Emily awake?'

'I think she's asleep,' I said and turned to check. She lay with her head against the car seat, her fists clenched in her lap. I stretched as far as I could stretch and took the last of the mint from her mouth and, because I had nowhere to put it, put it in my own mouth.

'They were at primary school together. He was a lot older than her.'

Paul told me that Georgia remembered him kicking a football in the playground and was aware of him as they grew up in the way that kids know who has come before them and who will go first into adulthood.

'She told me she felt sorry for him. But I didn't want to tell you that. He was your big love wasn't he? No one wants to hear that about their big love.'

He turned left onto the road into Lennoxtown.

'I'm quite tough you know,' I said.

'Still.'

He was decent, Paul, when I think of him now: ready to accommodate my life thus far and expecting I would do the same for him. He said, 'She was probably talking about his parents. He lost his anchor when his dad died. You would, wouldn't you?' I didn't say that Robbie shored himself to me and used to tell me plainly that apart from his brother, I was all he had. I was happy with that.

When Paul cut the engine and we parked outside Audrey's house the birdsong was loud. It was a pretty street in the sun.

'Shall I help you in with Emily?'

I turned to see her sleeping. 'Can you lift her straight upstairs to bed?'

Paul unbuckled Emily from her car seat then scooped her sleeping body into his arms.

'She's still hot isn't she?' I felt her forehead and walked in front of them to the door. 'What about the toilet?' I said to Paul. He paused, holding Emily. 'She did one at the hospital. She hasn't drunk since. I'll risk it,' I said, and he nodded.

I followed them up the stairs and went to the bathroom to find a clean towel to put under her bum in case she had an accident in the night. Paul was sweeping the duvet across her body when I went into her bedroom. We stood for a couple of seconds looking at her as she slept.

'That's a nice age, four,' Paul said.

'Nearly five,' I said, and felt a ripple of worry in my stomach and then it was gone, in much the same way I first felt her moving in my womb; a bubble of something that stopped no sooner than it came. I wondered if I should take my pills again. The ripples were becoming more frequent.

'What did Michael McDermott do?' I asked Paul.

'You should speak to your pal June about that.'

'But do you know what he did?'

'No.'

'Do you want to stay?'

'I'd better not. I should go and see Holly. But I'll come back.'

'Tonight?'

'If I'm allowed.'

'Yes please.' I presumed he was asking my permission, not anyone else's, so I answered that way.

8.

Before I could see June, I was housebound with Emily. She was flushed in her face not because of her heart but because her tonsillitis had flared up again. Even I, with a spoon on her tongue and only the natural light from the bathroom window, saw white spots at the back of her throat. We got more antibiotics and I kept her off nursery. I phoned the estate agent and cancelled a second viewing and we had two slow days where we didn't leave the house. We slept for hours at a time and watched CBeebies cuddled under a blanket on Audrey's sofa.

During one tentative hour after a sleep and a snack she regained some energy and began to leap around the living room. I heard cries from where I stood washing dishes in the kitchen. She'd sliced a stinging oval off the top of her big toe. It wasn't bleeding but the exposed skin was raw and she was appalled by the sight of it, crying harder each time she looked. I washed it and put on cream and a plaster. This act of care soothed her. She was brave. She asked to put a plaster on a dolly and I let her. I lay her back under the blanket and switched on the telly and she wanted me to lie next to her so I did, leaving the soapy water to cool around the dishes. It seems I knew how to help with Emily's physical pain – which is something.

Her scrape was in the exact same place my feet would bleed when I wore my pointe shoes. I still have shiny scars on the tops of my toes. The woman in the shop, a ballerina herself, told me my first pair of shoes would no doubt hurt but after that my feet would become used to them. She prescribed lambswool to pack between my toes and the stiff shoes. I tried it out in class, holding the barre and standing with my feet in first position. I did as the teacher said and pressed from my heels through the pads of my feet to my toes and when my weight was on my toes I pressed into the floor and lifted higher, pulling in through my pelvis and tucking in my stomach. It was easy; I was up, the shoes supporting my toes, my legs supporting my feet, my stomach supporting my legs. With the help of the barre I balanced, up there on my pointe shoes. I was strong.

But my feet bled and the tips of my tights were stained. I threw the bloodied lambswool away and packed more into my shoes. No plasters, the woman in the shop had told me. Your feet will harden. So I followed her instructions and coped without. It hurt. The second time I wore the shoes was hard. I knew my toes would bleed again and the pain would start immediately, the cuts not needing much to reopen and sting. I did it for several weeks but the pain took away the thrill of dancing en pointe.

When my teacher saw the blood she told me to wrap plasters around my toes and save myself the hurt. It was easier after that. I will never know if I would have been better to tough it out and wait for my feet to harden, even though I would never have been a true ballerina, it wasn't in me, so what would have been the point?

I showed Emily my scars and told her this story and said the next time we were on the fells we would seek out some lambswool and she could feel how soft it was. I expected she'd want to take it home with her and put it in her tin.

I looked at Emily and the life I was giving her in Lennoxtown and felt I was failing her. When I was four nearly five I was dancing in a church hall on a Saturday morning. I knew where I lived. I had a school. I had a stable life and it was an okay one. Emily, what did she have? Me. Her dad gone, her gran miles away. We lived in a house that belonged to a dead woman I'd barely known. We had no idea where she would go to school. I didn't even know where we would live in a month's time. Was that good enough?

It was Emily's stinging oval of skin that did it. I made a decision. My life was as it was, without Robbie, and I had to live it somewhere. So when the social worker called at the house to check on us and said, 'Have you thought any more about school?' I replied, 'Yes. I'm enrolling her here.'

That surprised her. I enjoyed her praise and pleasant words and felt like a pet. 'I'm delighted for you,' she said.

'We're doing really well. I have work. I'll try to get more. She's settled. We like it here.'

'Good for you.'

'I didn't need those parenting sessions after all.'

We paused to look at Emily who sat with one finger up her nostril, her eyes fixed on the television.

'Look, Liz, you appear to be doing well. But the hospital…
the doctor telephoned us. You need to be careful.'

Of course the hospital would have phoned Sara. 'Careful
about what?' I said. I knew I should try to be less difficult.

She checked to see if Emily was listening, which she was,
and then stood up and beckoned me to follow her. In the hall
with her handbag over her shoulder she spoke quietly. 'You're
in the system now. They'll be aware of you. I wouldn't take
her to A&E unless it's absolutely necessary.'

'Why?'

'Any injury she has will be treated differently. And with
extra due diligence.'

'In case they think I've harmed her?'

'In case they think you've harmed her.'

'What if she falls out of a tree and breaks her arm?'

'Don't let her fall out of a tree and break her arm.'

Sara told me she was speaking as she would to one of her
friends. This was a gentle warning. I took it.

'You're going in the right direction. Just be careful. Tell
Emily I said goodbye.'

When I closed the door behind her I understood that our
trip to A&E had been more about me than Emily. It was my
cry for help. No more of that, I told myself. Be virtuous, like
Robbie always was. Be more. Be less. Get yourself back on
your pills and even yourself out.

9.

The primary school headteacher took us into her office to fill out the forms. I don't know what she knew of us or how much she would find out. They tend to know a lot, teachers. But at that moment I tried to appear like any other parent with any other child.

'It's nearly your birthday,' she said to Emily. 'How old are you going to be?'

Emily said nothing. The head didn't seem to mind. 'Well, by my calculation,' she looked down at the form in front of her, 'you will be five in four days' time. Happy birthday for four days' time.'

Five years ago we were still a three; Emily in my womb, yes, but we were still together and still a three.

Emily peeked at the headteacher.

'Are you looking forward to school?'

Emily shook her head.

'Are you ready to learn and have fun?'

Emily pushed her forehead into my side.

'You're just in time. They're bringing the nursery in for a visit on Monday next week. She's missed the first one but that doesn't matter.' She spoke to Emily. 'You'll get a buddy. A big girl in primary seven will look after you when you start. How about that?'

Emily nodded and peeked again at the headteacher.

They'd told me at the nursery not to worry about reading and writing, not to teach her myself. Mark-making was all the children needed to do. And I'd taken them at their word. Emily knew nothing. She'd barely lifted a pencil with me next to her. Perhaps she was behind. They'll have noted that. The headteacher gave me a pack with important dates and school policies. She showed me the uniform list and told me there was a second-hand, nearly-new collection of clothing in the school office if I needed. I told her I would need it and she said to come in at any time and speak to the office staff. We passed brightly-coloured walls on the way out. We are a Rights Respecting School, one piece of artwork declared. Be the Best You Can Be said another. I saw Emily looking around her at her school and felt proud of us.

'You'll like it here,' I told her. 'This is the school your daddy went to.'

'He liked it here too,' she said, and they were the only words she spoke, her eyes as wide as her mouth had been shut tight.

10.

Her birthday came. I heard her voice scooping me out of sleep – 'Mummy I'm five!' – and opened my eyes to find her leaning over me. She patted my head. 'You're nice and hot, Mummy.' Her mouth was wide and smiling.

'Happy birthday, my big girl.' I pulled her in for a hot cuddle.

There was nothing I could do about Robbie. He wasn't there. He didn't know he was going to miss every birthday his daughter ever had.

'Can I have Coco Pops for breakfast?'

'Yes. Do you want your presents?'

'Yes!'

She loved her baby in its carrycot. We changed its clothes and gave it a bottle and she put it on her shoulder to burp it. 'Your daddy used to do that to you,' I said. 'You liked your legs tucked right up to your tummy, like this.' I showed her on her dolly.

'Could my daddy hold me in one hand?'

'Probably. He used to say you were like a poke of chips.'

'Can I have my Coco Pops?'

'Yes.'

She poured Coco Pops over the side of her bowl.

'Oh no!'

'It's okay, no harm done.' We swept them into our hands and dropped them into her bowl.

'What do you want to do today?'

'Is it a nursery day?'

'No.'

'Can I have a birthday cake?'

'Of course you can have a birthday cake.'

'Can we make one?'

'I can't make cakes, kid.'

'Can we buy one?'

'Yes. And we'll buy some candles too.'

She got excited about the candles, said, 'Mummy I love you so much,' then wriggled next to me.

'Go to the toilet,' I said. 'I love you too.' I got up with her and waited while she peed, as she liked me to do, handing her the toilet roll and helping her with the soap. Perhaps now that she was five I should stop handing her the toilet roll, but it was so hard to get her to go on the toilet and once I was there, it was quicker and easier for me to help her along. That wasn't neglect? That wasn't ambivalence?

The day was getting itself together so when she asked if she could use her ticket to the playground I said yes and we took a chance and left our coats behind and walked to the park. We did like that playground in the dip between the land and the hills, with the graveyard around the corner and all that silence.

'Push me higher.'

'Five years old, baby girl,' I said and my voice seemed to carry way up the steep fell sides. 'Do you want me to teach you how to swing?'

'No. When I'm six. Higher.'

We called out with each push, enjoying the sounds we flung into the day, her birthday. I felt my heart work a little harder.

My mum rang and sang down the phone to her.

'Granny, do you want to come to my concert?' Emily asked and my mum said she didn't know about a concert but told her that the postman would be bringing her a parcel. Of course Emily wanted to go straight home and wait for the postman.

'I could have come up,' my mum said to me. 'I nearly booked a ticket. I was just waiting for you to ask.'

'Aren't you enjoying the peace?'

'You are my child and my grandchild.'

'But you want to go to Spain with Alan. You're saving up your leave.'

'There is more than one kind of love, Liz. Do we need to talk, you and me?'

Emily climbed the steps up the side of a slide.

'What did you think of Robbie, honestly, Mum?' I said.

'It's that time of year for you, isn't it?'

'Yes it is. But what did you think of him? There was no side to him was there?'

'No. Why?'

'I'm hearing half-stories. Strange little things. He was straight up wasn't he?'

'Of course he was. He was one of life's good ones. And he made my daughter very happy.'

That was all I needed to hear. My mum's voice and her plain truths. Emily slid down the silver slide and then ran towards me holding her bottom. I thought she'd peed herself but the slide was wet and her leggings were damp. I felt the backs of her legs and wiped drops of water from her arms and elbows.

'You'll be fine, birthday girl.'

I gestured for her to keep playing, her leggings would be okay, and I watched her climb a ladder and stand on the frame above it.

'When are you coming back?' my mum said. 'Any offers on the flat?'

'We might stay a bit longer.'

'How much longer?'

'I don't know. I haven't decided yet.'

I didn't tell her I'd enrolled Emily in the primary school in Lennoxtown.

'Come and visit,' I said. 'Bring Alan if you want.'

Emily returned and pulled at my arm. 'Mummy, come on the see-saw with me.'

'I'm talking to your gran,' I said, but then, 'It's her birthday. I'd better play, I'd better go.'

The good feeling stayed between us as we walked home hand in hand. She skipped, actually skipped, as she held my hand, and I skipped with her for a few steps and when the wind blew at us from behind we ran as if it was pushing us down the street.

*

On the cruise ships I felt the best I could ever feel. Miami, New Orleans, St Kitts, Lisbon, Barcelona, Casablanca, Rome. I bought handbags and shoes with currencies I kept in envelopes in my cabin drawer. There was money left over. Robbie and I were in love and I danced almost every day. We would bow at the end of a show and stand in line, side on, one leg in front of the other, and clap the band, and I would feel the feathers shaking on my headdress and the sweat cooling on my back. The cooling sweat would make me tingle and I felt elated. I didn't need pills then. In the daytime I would meet holidaymakers who had seen me dance the night before and they would say great show and tell me I was talented and I would wish them a happy vacation. I was dazzled. Dazzling. Robbie caught that. He got that bit of me. I got that bit of him that dazzled too. I'm glad. He would have liked to have seen me holding hands and skipping with our daughter.

My mum was the only person we spoke to on her birthday. I could have phoned Caroline and invited her and her kids to the playground but I felt shy and doubtful that she'd come. I didn't think Emily would want that anyway. In the afternoon when we were watching television, before I cooked her fish fingers, I told Emily I was sorry there was nobody else to spend her birthday with but she said she didn't mind and for the whole day she didn't act as if she minded so I supposed and hoped she'd had a good day.

*

The house sold on its closing date as the estate agent had promised. The new owners asked for a move-in date of six weeks' time which left me six weeks to find a home. I was optimistic. The hills were even more enticing now that the sun shone on them. Emily had a place at school. I had my dance class and Ruth was talking about finding funding for more classes in other complexes. Proper money, not five pounds in pint glasses. I put my name on the council's housing list. Paul came with me to look at a flat to rent on a short-term let. 'I've always wanted a walk-in shower,' he said and I thought, Why not? Things were possible.

And then *fondu*. To melt.

I use the term *fondu* even though a harder strike of a word might be more apt. In ballet to *fondu* is to release, to surrender, to melt. It's a thoughtful, soft, controlled movement. However, think of the act of melting. Whatever was there becomes altered, misshapen, destroyed even. Think of butter or wax. I've never known melted butter or wax, once hardened, to resemble anything like it was before. So *fondu* in my mind is to alter irreparably.

II.

It began with a conversation on the street. Emily and I had rummaged through the school's box of second-hand uniform and taken a couple of polo shirts, a skirt, two cardigans and a pinafore. We were on the street outside, zipping our coats and pulling our hoods over our heads when we saw Paul. He was with Georgia, his daughter's mum. They walked quickly, possibly because rain had come on heavily. She was checking her phone. He looked straight at us. I saw the comical change in his face from surprise to cocksureness – that primal flicker of *I've had both these women* – then fear. There's a man who hasn't told his ex about me, I thought. Yet I didn't care. I was secure enough with what we had and it made me want to tease him. I wondered if Emily, shy Emily, would speak to him and make his predicament worse, the fool. I rested my hands on her head and held her to me as they approached. When I sensed Georgia's hostility I was glad of Emily and kept her, protective, in front of me.

'How's the plastering?' Paul said.

'Good, thank you. No cracks yet.'

'We've been called in to Holly's school,' he said and took a hand from his pocket to gesture at the building next to us.

Emily pulled at my arm, really yanked it. 'We've been dropping some forms into the school,' I said.

I saw a flash of something in his eyes – warmth, pleasure – and it warmed me too. My decision to stay in Lennoxtown felt justified. I had a lover in Paul and a friend in June. Emily would grow up in her father's village.

Emily said, 'That's my school.'

'It sure is.' I put my hands on her shoulders and wished I could tell Paul about another flat viewing I'd arranged. This one had no bath though. I kept quiet. I could feel Georgia studying me.

'I did some work for Liz. Remember the Watts?' he said to Georgia.

She nodded. 'We need to go, Paul.' She looked past me at the school and then spoke to me. 'We have an appointment.'

She was so much younger than me, and Paul too, but I could see tired circles under her eyes.

A gust of wind pushed rain at us. I felt light.

'Paul said you might know my daughter's dad's family. Robbie Watt. He was born here. Do you remember him?' I said.

She pulled her coat tight to herself. 'He was a fair bit older than me. He hung about with my big brother.'

'Yes.'

'They both had trials for Alloa. Then Falkirk.'

'Yes.' I smiled. 'Does your brother still play?'

'What?'

'Does he still play?' Was it my accent she couldn't understand?

'Aye, only amateur. He works in IT now.'

I heard the school bell ring. It must have been lunchtime. Or playtime.

'You know Robbie died.'

'Yes.'

'So, anything you can tell me about him, I'd love to hear. To complete the picture.' I sounded too formal as if he wasn't mine. Emily tugged on my arm again but I wasn't finished. Something about Georgia's hardness made me feel hard too. 'You don't know why anybody would feel sorry for him?' I said. They were her words.

Georgia looked at Paul who was looking at me and she must have caught kindness in his gaze. She turned to me sharply. 'Paul's done a lot of work for a lot of women. I can't keep up.' She paused. 'You could feel sorry for Robbie Watt but there are other emotions you could feel too. You'd have to ask his victims. There are a lot of them in Campsie. This rain!'

Paul wiped rain from his cheek. 'Let's go.'

Georgia pulled an umbrella from her handbag and the rain cracked onto it. 'We'll be walking round Campsie, just like now, and suddenly I'll be saying hello to some woman I've never met before and because it's the polite thing to do I'll talk away. But afterwards I'll feel like a bit of an idiot.'

Her phone buzzed and she checked it. I glanced at Paul who made the tiniest of apologies with his eyes.

She put her phone away. 'Have you got a boyfriend? Seeing anyone? Or are you just seeing my boyfriend? That's what I'm going to ask you women from now on.'

'Georgia, we better go.'

'No, she's asked me a question about Robbie.' I noticed the freckles on her cheekbones, heard the tug in her voice. 'But will she like what I tell her?'

'What do you mean by victims?' I said. 'Emily, stand still.' I took it out on Emily. I always did.

'Cut it out, Georgia.'

'Well, first there were the prescriptions they used to fill for the old people, he'll have told you about that?'

'No.'

'The jellies.'

'The what?' My turn not to hear.

'The jellies.'

'No.'

'Georgia, she doesn't know anything.'

I looked at the Campsies and saw nothing but cloud. Paul said to me, 'They worked together, Michael McDermott and your Robbie. Michael had a gardening business.'

I nodded.

'My brother stopped hanging about with him then. They exploited Michael McDermott's clients essentially. All the old folks,' Georgia said. 'They took their prescriptions to the chemist – their pills for this, that and the other. And the good tablets, the sleeping tablets, the diazepam, the jellies, they kept a few back for themselves.'

'No they didn't.'

'I'm surprised he didn't tell you.'

'I don't believe you.'

Paul looked distressed now. 'It's hearsay.'

'It's not. It all came out in court. Maybe he really did have more to do with it than he let on if he didn't tell you a thing.'

Emily stepped onto the road and splashed in water that poured towards a drain. I pulled her to the pavement.

'Can I have a flip?' she asked Paul.

'You're too muddy. No flips,' I said.

'I don't mind.'

Almost in slow motion, with Georgia and me watching, Paul held Emily's hands and she climbed her wet shoes up his legs and onto the edge of his jacket. She pushed her feet off his body and he helped her flip her legs through her hanging arms and land back on the ground.

'Again!' she said.

His jacket was muddied.

'No, Emily.' I should have gone away with her right then. 'That's enough.'

Georgia continued, rain hitting her umbrella and dripping from the silver ends of its spokes. 'I won't tell you about the high school. Somehow, kids at the high school ended up getting hold of all these prescription drugs. Someone sold them to them. There was a tragedy. I won't tell you what happened. Robbie had nothing to do with it, so he said. They both left Lennoxtown after that. Michael McDermott ended up in the jail. My brother went to university. Come on Paul, we have to go.'

'Can I have another flip?'

'No.'

'No.'

'I don't mind.'

Oh God, they did another flip with Emily struggling to walk her feet up Paul's legs and then hanging upside down, her wet hair and her hood falling. I had to put my hand on her back and push her down so she could land. Of course she loved it.

'We're making another go of it, by the way,' Georgia said to me. 'So get rid of any notions you have about my partner.'

Paul's horrified eyes told me otherwise but I realised I didn't know him well enough to know what was truth and what wasn't.

We stood in the hard rain and watched them walk through the school playground to the office door. Emily put her hand in mine. Back to a two.

'Who were they talking about? Was it Daddy?' she said.

'No. Definitely not Daddy.'

That woman was lying. She was jealous and lying and I didn't believe a word of what she'd said. Yet I did. And because of that, I felt sick. June. I had to speak with her. *Oh, I have stories for all the boys and girls in Campsie.* At what point did she realise that I was Robbie's, that Robbie was mine? During which dance class? During which conversation? And why didn't she tell me that Robbie worked with her son, the son she didn't want to see, the son she needed an escort to meet?

I can't remember what Emily and I did for the rest of that afternoon. It probably kept raining so I suppose I let her watch television. I honestly was as far away from my life with Emily as one of those big-bellied seagulls that soared above us, their wings white against the grey. Why the seagulls came so far inland and what they were doing in Lennoxtown I didn't know.

12.

I should have cancelled the class when June didn't come. Or they could have run it themselves. We did the same things each week, that's what ballet was: *repetition, repetition, repetition.* But there they were, willing and waiting at their barres, feet in first position, hands soft at their thighs. I left them in the lounge as I'd done before and banged on June's door. Her neighbour stood in his doorway watching me.

'I couldn't tell if it was me you were wanting,' he said. His television sounded loud through his open door.

'Have you seen her? Has she done your sheets?'

'Not yet,' he said. He wore slippers and checked pyjamas.

'Do you know where she is?'

'No idea. She takes herself off.'

'Tell her I'm looking for her, will you?'

'Are you the dancing girl?'

'Yes.'

'It'll be a week before I see her because I only see her when she does my sheets.'

'It's time you did your own sheets.'

A burst of television laughter came from inside his flat. A woman in a uniform smiled down the corridor, told June's neighbour it was nice to see him up and about, took him by the arm and escorted him inside.

'She's not home,' I said to my dancers.

'Up to her old tricks again,' Eve said. 'But she got our ballet shoes.'

I looked at their feet. Eve and Alice now as well as Senga and Agnes wore ballet shoes. Eve also wore a ballet cardigan, crossed at her chest and tied at the back.

'No teasing,' she said to John.

John pointed to his feet and said, 'Same applies to you.' He and Charlie stood in ballet shoes too.

'Did she buy any for herself?' I said.

'Oh yes,' said Eve. 'And a cardigan.'

'Where is she then?'

'Up to her old tricks.'

'Did she say anything about me?' Perhaps she was avoiding me; she didn't want me to ask about her son and Robbie. But she owed me that, surely? She owed me nothing.

'I've only seen her in passing. Can we start this ballet class please?' Eve stood in first position.

We got through the *pliés* in first and second. We did backbends and forward bends and side bends with accompanying *port de bras* and I felt a heat in my stomach that hadn't been there before. A kind of hot grip which I ignored. We began John's favourite, *rond de jambe*, and I told them they were improving.

'My granddaughters came to visit on the weekend,' Charlie said. 'And I showed them a *plié*. They said my turnout was good.'

'Your turnout is good.'

Eve passed comment on the women who came once to the class and never returned. Senga said Eve had reminded her: she and Agnes couldn't attend the following week. They began their gentle chat, Charlie saying he missed his grandchildren's wee voices, John saying they sounded like buffalo charging along the corridor above his. Only Alice was silent. But it didn't matter. I was thinking of June.

I told them to turn to their chairs and stand in first position, holding on with both hands. I asked them to press through the soles of their feet, lifting their weight onto their toes, ending heads high, stomachs pulled in, in a *relevé*, just as I had done as a teenager, only I had gone onto the bleeding tips of my pointe shoes.

'Tell me,' I said to the sides of their concentrating faces. 'Tell me about June. And her son, Michael McDermott. What's the story there?'

'She's away to meet him… when is it? I can't mind,' John said.

Eve flicked a sharp look at him and then at me. Nobody said a word. I watched their heels rise and fall to the piano music I played: *Swan Lake*.

'Chins up everyone. Don't look down. She's your friend, Eve. You must have talked about your children?'

'Shush, I'm trying to dance,' Eve said.

Dancing had never stopped her talking before.

'Anyone else? Charlie? You're from here. Do you remember June's son?'

Up they rose and down they lowered.

'I don't like to talk about a person's private life,' Charlie said.

'You talk about everyone else's.'

Eve flicked me another look and I saw Charlie's chin go down. 'Heads up. Eyes up,' I shouted. 'John, when is she meeting him?'

'I can't mind,' he shouted back.

They danced on. I tried again when they were in second position.

'Let's talk about my private life then. You must remember Robbie Watt. My partner. He's from Campsie. He knew June's son. Eve? Charlie? You've lived here all your lives. Who else has lived here all their life? What do you remember of Robbie?'

Silence. Just the piano's 'Pas de trois'. I noticed Agnes and Alice struggling with their balance. 'Drop your shoulders and squeeze your tummies in,' I told them. 'Bring your feet closer together if you need to.'

I'd never known the room so quiet. All of them danced with a focus I hadn't seen before. Guarded. Secretive. Protective.

'When you've done a *relevé* sink into a *plié* but be careful of your balance, don't lean forwards or backwards, keep that straight line from the crown of your head through your shoulder blades and down your back.'

'A plumb line,' John said.

They could talk when they wanted to. I gave up.

I asked them nothing at all when they danced their *chassés* in the centre of the room or at their barres if they weren't steady. I watched them bend their knees and transfer their weight from one foot to another, in front, behind, second – *en avant, en arrière, à la seconde.* Ruth looked into the lounge just as they danced a *chassé en avant* and breathed their arms into a luxurious *arabesque.* Their focus was exquisite – because they were determined not to speak of June, that's why.

'Magic,' Ruth said and gave me a thumbs up. 'Catch me at the end. We need to talk about funding.' She came back into the lounge with her camera and took a photograph. Just as well because that was our last class, not that any of us knew that then.

'Do you have your feathers?' Senga asked. 'We love the feathers, don't we, Mum?'

I passed them round but apart from Senga and her mother, nobody played with the abandon or the expression they'd had previously.

Charlie dropped his feather and I picked it up.

'Please,' I whispered near his ear. 'June's your old friend. What went on with June's son and my Robbie?'

'Don't abuse Charlie's good nature,' Eve said to me. She waggled her feather.

'Actually, I never discuss people's private lives,' Charlie said carefully as I stroked his feather on his forehead and nose. 'I practise discretion.'

'Someone then!' I threw the feather pathetically then stooped to pick it up. 'June's not here. Tell me while she's not here.'

'That's exactly why we're not telling you. She's not here to speak for herself,' Eve said.

'So you do know!'

'I remember Robbie.' Alice spoke and stunned us. 'He was a lovely boy. One older brother. His parents died young. I knew his grandparents, Audrey and Donald.' She looked at me, her mouth a smile, her feather flat in her hand.

'You knew Robbie?'

'Yes,' she said. 'Did you?'

'He was my partner. He's my daughter's dad. Remember, we met on the cruise ship.'

'I went on a cruise with my husband. He's not here anymore.' The feather trembled in her hand.

'I'm sorry for your loss.'

It was unethical to press a woman on the edge of dementia but I did, and as I walked her to one of the tables with the fabric flowers and told her to sit down next to me, she was already talking. Why would I stop her?

'Robbie was a footballer wasn't he? That's right, he did all the trials. I think Falkirk were after him.'

'Alice,' Eve said. 'Alice, watch what you say, hen.' She collected in the feathers. The others came to our table and the music played on.

'Robbie was a lovely boy, wasn't he? He was the footballer,' Alice said.

'What about Michael McDermott, Alice? June's son. Do you remember him? They worked together.'

'Liz,' Eve warned.

'June's boy worked over on the Carrick farm for years. Fifteen, twenty maybe. They took him on at sixteen which was a blessing for June because until then he'd smoked and drank and carried on and scared the life out of her.'

'Were you her friend?'

'Perhaps not her friend. Everyone knew everyone in Campsie though.'

'Alice,' Eve said gently as she sat down next to her. 'I'm June's friend.'

'I know that, dear.' Alice was lucid and fluent. 'He worked on the farm for years. He lived with his mum. June's husband, what was his name, he left her a long time ago.'

'This is not your story to tell, Alice,' Eve said.

'Then he became a gardener, didn't he? He did our garden. Him and Robbie Watt, the footballer. That was so nice of him to give the boy a job. His dad died so suddenly. I used to see them working in the gardens together. Or I would hear their lawnmowers and wait for the smell of the cut grass. It was nice. Did anybody make tea?' Alice looked up.

Eve patted her hand. 'It's coming, pet. Senga, I can't leave this. Can you?'

Senga stood and Agnes tried to stand too. 'I'll give you a hand.'

'No, you won't, Mum.'

'I'm not incapable.' The table rocked.

'Sit down, Mum.'

Agnes sat and sighed.

Alice turned to smile at all the faces looking at her. She shrugged and asked again for tea.

John spoke now. 'You'll know all this though, won't you? That your man was a good footballer.' So he knew Robbie too.

'I knew he was a good footballer, yes.'

'Why don't you leave it at that, eh? He was a good footballer.'

'No.'

Alice continued to speak as if she hadn't heard us. 'Now, we had the police at our door one afternoon. They knocked on all the doors on our street. But we had nothing to tell them. We were healthy then. I think my husband had been to the doctor's only twice in his adult life before he took ill.'

John shook his paper. 'I have a crossword clue Alice that I need some help with.'

'The police asked you about prescriptions? Because Michael McDermott was taking people's medication was he?' I said.

'That's right. He was filling their prescriptions at the chemist. And then he was opening the bottles and taking five, ten, I don't know how many, but keeping some back for himself. But we didn't have any tablets because we were healthy. We didn't have anything to say to the police.'

'She doesn't need to know any more. It wasn't Robbie that was doing it anyway,' Eve said.

'Keep going, Alice,' I said.

Charlie shook his head.

'Where was I?'

'The prescription drugs,' I said. 'What happened next? He started selling them to the kids did he?'

'Oh yes, so he did.'

'That's enough!' Eve stood up and bumped in to Senga who was carrying a teapot and mugs.

Alice talked quietly on. 'Robbie was just out of school, or maybe he was still in school, I can't mind, but the police believed they were selling those pills to the schoolchildren up at the high school for months.'

'Someone make her stop!'

'Alice, dear,' Agnes said. 'Stop the memories, Alice, dear.'

'Keep going, Alice, keep talking.'

'John, make her stop.'

'That's enough, Liz, you're upsetting everyone.' John stood up.

'Then that poor schoolboy died. That's what stopped it. He took some of those pills and mixed them with drink and he died. He was only thirteen. It all came out soon after.'

'What schoolboy?' I said.

'One of the children. He'd bought the pills off Michael McDermott and Robbie Watt. The police were at our door several times. They even searched our garden in case they'd hidden anything there. Yes, the boy died.'

Eve shouted again. 'Alice, stop talking. I swear to God I will batter you Liz if you don't shut up. You are abusing this woman. She's not in her right mind and she's saying things she oughtn't. June McDermott is my friend. She's a private person. She is a private person.'

'She has no right to be a private person when it concerns my partner. Keep talking Alice.' I wouldn't stop.

But Alice began to cry. 'He had measles as a boy but that was all. And he was healthy for decades. Decades. We didn't know he was so ill until it was too late to operate.'

Senga and Agnes leaned into her, offering her napkins and tea.

'Young Robbie Watt died of a heart attack didn't he? Some said he got what he deserved.' Alice let herself be consoled by Agnes and Senga, Charlie shook his head and I had to turn my back on her.

Eve tried to drag one of the ballet barre chairs back to the table. I stood next to her and put my hands on the chair.

'See! I told you not to go there,' she said.

'You tell me what you know.'

'Haven't you heard it all?'

'I want to know everything about Robbie. What the fuck was he doing with Michael McDermott?'

'No need for swearing,' John said. He stood between us.

'He was groomed!' Eve said. 'That's what you call it now. That's what they said happened to Robbie. He was groomed by Michael. He got him doing all his dirty work. June was saying only the other day that she believes Robbie was innocent.'

She acted caught. I saw her look at John. And yes, she was caught, because that pretence at the ballet barre about not knowing anything, keeping quiet and dancing hard, was blatant deceit.

'Why didn't anybody tell me?'

'I think June would have, eventually,' Charlie said.

'What happened?' I asked. 'What happened to Robbie and Michael? They got caught.'

John spoke now. 'Well, the whole village knew before the police did – officially anyway. The boy who died, his uncle dealt with it the way some men deal with things and I think the whole village and the whole police force turned a blind eye. He gave Michael McDermott an old fashioned doing. And as is the way with another type of man, Michael went straight to his mammy with his bloodied face and didn't want his mammy to patch him up, he wanted her to pay for it. There's a certain type of man that hits a woman and June's son, to her shame, is one of those.'

'Which is why she won't talk about it,' Eve said.

John spoke again. 'Robbie was there and got between Michael and his mother and ended up getting a beating. He didn't need to follow him into June's house because he'd have had the measure of Michael by then. He'd have known what to expect. There must be madness in you to hit your mother.'

'Unforgiveable,' Eve said. 'She was right to abandon him.'

'What happened to Robbie?'

'The police arrested the two of them. It went to court. Michael got the jail. Robbie was let off. He pleaded coercion. Grooming. Blackmail, whatever. He laid it all on Michael.'

'He never told me,' I said.

'Do you wonder why not?' Eve said.

Then there were footsteps. Ruth stood in the doorway, alarmed. 'I heard shouting,' she said. 'Eve? Is everything all right? Why is Alice crying?'

I saw them sitting around the table, watched Ruth kneel beside Alice, and felt that hot grip in my stomach again. There was a rushing sound in my ears and I could hear every beat my heart made. *Petits battements*. My heart made a sound, honestly, and it hurt as it beat, as if it had swelled too large, dangerously large. I stood still, amazed yet terrified by the physical thumps and jumps inside me. Then I found it hard to breathe, hard even to slip a feather of breath into my lungs and I wanted to escape but was afraid to move because I thought, at any moment, I would fall. My heart thudded viciously on. I sat on the floor, waiting for it to pass, but it didn't stop and my breathing was hard and the noise in my ears sent my head underwater. I leaned my head between my knees and shouted out that I was ill, that my heart was breaking down, and asked someone to help me, help me. I think it was Eve who called the ambulance. Ruth made me lie on my side and found a cushion for my head. My heart was still racing, *battement, battement.* I remember seeing the clean leather ballet shoes of my dancers.

Ruth accompanied me to hospital in the back of the ambulance. I was tired after the great crashes in my chest and I was frightened. My arms had a heaviness to them, the fire in my stomach still hurt. Nurses put pads on my chest, took blood and monitored me. It was Ruth who remembered Emily and stopped me from racing out of the hospital to get her.

'Can you ask anyone to pick her up for you? One of the mums?'

I could only think of Paul. She found Paul's number in my phone and called him, nodding her head as she listened and telling me afterwards that he would collect Emily and take her back to his mum's house and feed her if necessary.

'She likes fish fingers,' I said. 'I'll need to call the nursery.'

'I'm sure they've got fish fingers. We can call them now.'

I lay on my back and looked at the ceiling tiles.

My diagnosis? Panic. People think it's a heart attack, the young doctor told me. It can present as a heart attack. In your case it's not a heart attack, it's panic. An attack of panic. Rest, sleep, avoid stress, see your GP. We'll just wait for the bloods to come back.

Ruth excused herself. I pulled the hospital sheet to my chin and thought of Robbie stealing diazepam from prescription bottles, selling pills for coins to schoolchildren. The cause of a boy's death. No. Robbie was better than me. He always was. He didn't do it. No way. The running, the tenderness, the care, the love of life. He didn't do it. He would have been a better parent to Emily. We should have swapped places. He didn't do it and he should have been alive.

The young doctor whipped back the curtain and the nurse told me to look after myself. Ruth drove me to Paul's mother's house and Paul took me and Emily home. He stayed with me for an hour, helped find Emily's pyjamas, suggested I put mine on too and the three of us sat on Audrey's sofa and watched one of Emily's programmes. My body had that rinsed feeling you get when you're utterly spent, physically and emotionally, done with everything. I was grateful for Paul's arm around my shoulder no matter whose partner Georgia said he was.

13.

If Robbie had been alive I'd have confronted him with his secret, fierce and forceful, in a corner of the house while Emily played with a toy or watched television. *Ecarté.* I'd have thrown open his past and dealt with it immediately. But he wasn't alive so I couldn't do that and it made me agitated. I couldn't even butter bread without getting distracted or nicking my finger with the knife or crying or snapping at Emily. She was excited about her trip to the primary school. I told her to hurry up and get dressed.

'I might be too shy to say hello to my buddy,' she said.

'Nonsense. Be brave, be a big girl, tell me all about it when I pick you up.'

She went into nursery with no fuss, put her outdoor shoes on the cloakroom shelf, hung up her coat and gave me the most beautiful hug. I didn't deserve that girl.

A technique we used in performance, especially of contemporary dance, was to listen for our fellow dancers' breaths and take that sound as a cue to move. If we were lying on the floor or standing with our backs to each other it was often our only way of keeping in sync. When I explained the technique to Robbie he acted as if I'd revealed the workings of a magic trick.

I walked home, breathing carefully, like we did at the start of a class, trying not to obsess over the words Alice had said –

the death of a boy – no teaching that day, nothing to do but search on the internet for flats and jobs. Sara phoned. Her voice was serious from the start.

'Where are you, Liz?'

'Outside my flat.'

I picked up some rubbish blown in from the pavement. I noticed they'd changed our sign from FOR SALE to SOLD @ CLOSING.

'Something else has come up.'

'What?'

'Rather than me launch in, can I ask how you and Emily are? Have you found somewhere to live? How is Emily feeling about school?'

'She's meeting her buddy today. I'd rather you launched in.'

I felt in my pocket for my door keys. I heard her take a breath. 'We've had a report from a member of the public about an incident between you and your daughter.'

'Where? What incident.'

'In the home.'

'When?'

'Within the last month. Can you think what I may be referring to?'

'No.'

I put my key in the front door, opened it and stood in the hall. There was a smear of dirt on the new paint.

'Okay,' Sara said. 'I'll tell you what the concern is. We

had a phone call related to somebody who did some work in your house.'

'Paul. He did some plastering. And decorating.'

I felt sick. It was inconceivable that Paul could have harmed Emily. I never left him alone with her. He mostly came when she was in bed. He went to the toilet sometimes, but he was gone for two, three minutes at most. What could you do in two or three minutes? Did he take pictures?

'What has Emily said? Because I don't... I think... I don't know how he could. Paul wouldn't. We're seeing each other. But there's no way...'

Had a neighbour seen him coming into the house? Had Emily said something at nursery? That's how these things came out wasn't it? Odd revelations to teachers, inappropriate knowledge. I climbed the stairs.

'It's not Paul we're concerned about. It's something he witnessed when he was here, in your home.'

Now the fear increased. I tried hard to think what he could have witnessed.

'We've had a report that we're obliged to follow up.'

'What report?'

'We have a report concerning a punishment for Emily involving nakedness. There is also a report that you hit her, although I have to stress that the caller didn't witness any hitting, it was just a verbal note from something Emily had said.'

'What did Emily say?'

'She said "You hit me mummy."' *Battu.* Beaten.

'She didn't. I didn't. And what punishment? What are you talking about?'

'The child was distressed. And the caller was concerned enough to contact us. We have to follow it up. Given your history.'

The night of the bath, when I dragged her out, ages ago, she was talking about that. Paul wouldn't have called social services. Surely not. The fight was awful, it was horrific, I was so, so angry but it was done with an hour later. We made up. I'll never do it again.

'Can I ask who phoned you? Am I allowed to know that?'

'Yes. We were telephoned by a Georgia Murray. She's happy for me to disclose her name.'

'Georgia Murray.'

'She is the partner of Paul Bain who is the person who related the concern to her.'

'I know who she is.'

'She then passed it on to us.'

I shook my head. Georgia must have phoned social services out of spite. But Paul had been concerned enough to tell her in the first place. I tried to remember what had happened. Emily was screaming because I'd put her in time out. She threw her own towel away. I didn't take it from her. It was an inconvenience when Paul came to the door. He saw Emily naked and crying. Yet he'd come back and fucked me. He can't have thought I was doing anything too bad.

'I know what you're talking about now,' I said.

'Would you like to tell me about it?'

'I can see where someone might think… she wouldn't have been in time out for that long had the doorbell not gone… she threw her towel away… but I absolutely didn't hit her. I didn't. I never have. She was awful. She was hitting me and kicking me and scratching me. But I didn't hit her.'

I wanted to. I did want to hit her and I was probably rough with her, I'll own that. But I was more likely to have hit myself than her.

'She was naked and shivering?' The social worker spoke as if quoting someone's words.

'I don't know if she was shivering. I put her in time out and then the doorbell rang.'

From the living room window I saw a man who could have been Charlie, as old as Charlie, bent over his frame, walking slowly along the pavement, wearing a black coat and a green scarf. It wasn't Charlie. Sara asked me to describe the hours and minutes before the incident and she asked me to describe my relationship with Paul.

'I'm going to have to go away and think about this,' she said. 'I may have to get some colleagues involved. I'll certainly have to interview you again. And I would like to speak with Emily. I'll do this at her nursery. You work with older people don't you?'

'Yes.'

'I would advise you to tell your employers. You work with vulnerable people. Your employer has to protect them too.'

She said she would be in touch. When she'd hung up I was aware of my heart whacking itself against my breastbone and in the silence of Audrey's flat I heard my breath coming out ragged and loud.

Ruth was eating cereal when I opened the door to her office without knocking. I've always preferred to barrel into a situation, to dance on in an audition, to fight for my place in the front row or the call-back group. It's one of the things Robbie liked about me.

'Funding!' she said, put down her spoon and wiped the corners of her mouth. 'I didn't get any breakfast.'

'I need to speak to you.'

'Good.' She read from a form. 'What is your methodology Liz? What is the artistic excellence you bring to your classes and how will they decrease isolation?'

'It doesn't matter now.'

'You're not quitting are you?' Her face looked concerned. The phone rang and she told me she had to get it. She dealt with the caller quickly. It was the bottled water company. 'Just the one tub please. And one empty to take away.'

She ate a mouthful of her cereal.

'I have to tell you something,' I said. 'It's to do with social services.'

'Yes?'

'They're investigating me. It's nothing to do with old people. It's a personal matter. To do with my daughter. It's not what you're thinking. I haven't done anything bad. I haven't. But they're investigating me because it's come off the back of something else that happened when I'd just moved here. I didn't have to tell you.'

'Liz, with all due respect, I can't get a grasp of what you're saying. Obviously I have to put my manager hat on. I have to think about what you're saying in relation to the residents.'

'Please don't judge me,' I said.

'Is it regarding your daughter?'

'Yes.'

'Is it something you've done or someone else has done?'

'Something I've done.'

I told her. The way it came out I would have investigated myself. Ruth told me she'd heard a rumour about something in the Co-op car park. 'I obviously haven't shared that around,' she said.

'Nor have I.'

She looked puzzled and opened her mouth as if to speak and then appeared to stop herself.

I wondered what the social workers were considering. Was it neglect or was it cruelty? I couldn't get the picture of Emily out of my head, shivering and naked on the stairs.

'I think I know what's best for now,' Ruth said. 'You must be thinking the same.'

'The trouble is,' I said. 'My classes are my income. I rely on the money. If I stop the classes—'

'You have to stop the classes.'

She pushed her bowl aside, took off her glasses and rubbed her eyes. 'I wish you hadn't told me this. What a complete nightmare. I could come in and supervise the class myself, we could get around it that way, but I haven't got the time.'

'Is that one way round it?'

'It is one way. Because you can't be alone with them anymore. But it's not ideal time-wise. And also if you're under investigation for, you know, and I know about it, if anything came out, later on, well it doesn't look good does it? If I've kept you on just because we like you. Look at some of the people in the news recently.'

The phone rang again and she held her hand on the receiver for many rings while she told me she wouldn't tell any of the residents. She would say I'd gone for personal reasons. I stood up.

'Wait, I'll need to escort you out.'

The phone rang on.

'I'm going to find June.'

'No, you can't be in the building unsupervised. She's not here anyway.'

'Where's she gone? I can't be in the building?'

'Not anymore. We have procedures that'll have to kick in now. I don't know where she's gone but I saw her leave.'

'When? How long ago?'

'It's not for me to say, Liz.'

'She's my friend!'

The phone stopped ringing. Ruth stood up and smoothed her skirt.

'Come on, pet, let's get you out of here.' She promised to be honest and fair and tell social services if they asked that she personally didn't have any concerns and she stood in the doorway and watched me leave.

Fuck them all: the social workers, Ruth, June, Paul, Georgia, this whole village. If anyone wanted to ask me about my daughter, let them fucking ask me. If anyone wanted to tell me my dead partner was a drug-dealing thieving bampot let them tell me and see what I did to them. Liars! Come and judge me, come and tell me why I'm not welcome here, why our luck is so bad in this gloomy, cloud-covered village. I was pure raging, as Robbie used to say. Not a friend. Not a soul to go to.

I saw John smoking beside a tree fresh with blossom and new leaves. 'Go and get June for me, will you?' I said to him.

He looked at his feet as if to wonder why he wasn't wearing his ballet shoes.

'There's no class today. I need to speak to June. Go get her for me. Please,' I said.

'She's away,' he said. 'Two minutes ago. She's away to meet her son.'

I started to run.

'Liz!' John called after me. 'I think your man was innocent. I think he was forced onto the wrong tracks. We were saying that after you'd gone—'

'Too late now, John.'

'Good to see you on your feet.'

I ran up the road and looked towards the bus stop. There she was, June, her small figure in her pale coat, carrying a handbag and a pink gift bag. The bus approached the stop as I was running to get there and I felt a surge of something – adrenalin, panic, I'm not sure.

'June!'

She turned when I shouted but looked away from me and stepped onto the bus.

'June, I need to talk to you.'

There were other people at the bus stop and I had to wait for them to get on.

'Where are you going?' the driver said to me as I tried to barge my way past.

'Nowhere. I need to speak to someone.'

'You need a ticket if you want on the bus.'

'June, where are you going?'

She shouted at me from inside the bus, her voice louder and better than mine. 'Glasgow!'

I paid by my card, there was money in my account for now, took my ticket and found June.

'Where are you going?'

She didn't answer me.

'Are you going to see your son?'

'He wanted to meet me in Glasgow.'

'I thought I was coming with you.'

'I don't think that's suitable now.'

'Oh, it's very suitable,' I said. 'I have much to say to him.'

The bus went through the housing scheme, stopping to give way to cars when the road was narrow. June seemed annoyed with me, gathered up her coat and patted it onto her legs, put her arms over her handbag.

'I don't want you to come,' she said.

'It's gone beyond you now,' I said. 'I'm representing Robbie. I have some questions for Michael McDermott.'

'I want to see him on my own.'

'This is my only chance.'

'You're bullying me.'

'I'll bully him.'

I loosened the zip on my jacket. It was hot on the bus.

'You look as if you're about to commit murder,' June said.

'I will if you want me to.'

'Calm yourself.'

The driver cleaned his windscreen at the traffic lights and I watched the wipers swipe the dirt and water in a great arc across the glass. More people got on the bus. June waved at a woman. I thought the woman may have come to sit near us so I shook my head and glared at her and she sat elsewhere. God, I was awful.

'I heard from my social worker today,' I said to June.

'What did she want?'

I told June I'd been reported, that I'd lost my job, that Paul had betrayed me.

'Your generation do some stupid things,' she said to me. 'Time out. What a waste of time.'

Two women with a pram came on the bus. One pressed her foot on the pram's brake and they both sat down.

'We're coming into Lenzie now. You know it doesn't stop when it's on the motorway.'

'I'm not getting off.'

We drove through the fields and crossed the roundabouts.

'He's been in jail again, hasn't he?' This struck me as we turned onto the motorway: the gifts in the bag, the years they hadn't seen each other, his history. 'What did he do?'

She sighed and shook her head. 'Fraud. It was a low security prison but they told him if he does anything again he'll be put away for longer. He has a thing. A compulsion. My daughter-in-law kept in touch with me. She sent letters and photos.'

'I know about the prescriptions. I know about the boy who died.'

'I heard. Alice decided to speak for once.'

'I know what he did to Robbie. And to you. Why are you even seeing him?'

I saw that a tear cut a path along her cheek to her jaw. I watched her wipe it away with her fist.

'I've been enjoying your company, Liz, that's all,' she said. 'I didn't want you to find out. And your wee Emily. How is she?'

'She's starting school in August.'

'Where?'

'Here.'

'Here?'

'Yes. Campsie.'

June raised her eyebrows. 'I wouldn't recommend it for a girl like you. But there are worse places to bring your children up, I suppose.'

We both knew the truth and the lie in what she'd said.

'Please don't change the subject, June.'

She took a slow breath in and I heard it come out through her nose.

'You know he was a nice wee boy. His teachers loved him. He wanted a brother or a sister but his father left me quite early on. He met someone else. I think he suspected all along. You know, don't you, when someone is half-hearted about you. So there's one of Michael's excuses right there. No father. I'm sorry Liz, I know your wee girl has no father, but she'll use it against you, even though it wasn't your fault.'

All I did was sniff and shake my head. Emily has more to use against me now and it has nothing to do with Robbie.

June swiped at another tear. 'My heart broke for Robbie. He was a gullible boy. His own father had just died and he got taken advantage of. I was devastated when he took off. I couldn't look his mother or his grandad in the face again. I told Michael to disappear. Well, he had to disappear. They jailed him.'

'So I hear.'

She looked at me and her face was plain. She clasped her hands together and held them in her lap. I couldn't tell her it was all right. I couldn't bear to think of Robbie being hurt. Of someone's fists coming into contact with his face. The shame. The talk. These things stay with a person. No wonder he didn't want to come back to Lennoxtown.

June spoke. 'It's both kept me going – that encounter in my kitchen – and given me reason to give up on everything. A son who hit his own mother, who took medicine from pensioners, who dealt drugs to schoolchildren and a young boy who put his body between me and the blows. Funny, how a moment can hold both things. I didn't deserve it. But it's kept me alive until now.'

Funny how a moment can hold both things. I sat with June in silence, listening to her weep, knowing that a single word of mine might console her. And part of me wanted to console her because she'd been my friend. But I couldn't.

At the bus station I stepped aside to let her out of her seat and I followed her off the bus, walking next to her or behind her through the crowded streets to the place she'd arranged to meet her son.

He began by offering to drive her home, squeezing first her hands then her arms. 'How did you get here? Did you get a return? Bin it, Mum.' He spoke quickly. He looked at June – then me – then June – then settled on me. Perhaps he was waiting for an introduction. He didn't get one.

June said, 'Son, the bus station is across the road. The bus takes me to my door. Sit yourself down.' She didn't seem cowed or scared, she was her usual self. I'd never heard her speak any differently to anyone else but I'd expected her to be more hesitant with him. He didn't sit down.

'I'd like to see your flat,' he said.

'There's nothing to see.'

'I know where it is. I looked it up on Google Maps.'

'Speak English, Son.'

And they laughed. I saw affection. I saw their similar chins, their identical face shapes. His hair was blonde and the same texture as her grey. He was hers, there was no denying. He must have used the gym in prison because he was lean. June handed him the gift bag and he put it on the floor next to his chair.

'Presents for the children,' she said. 'And chocolates for you and Julie.'

'You didn't need to, Ma.'

'It's a while since I've seen you all.'

I pictured Robbie and this man mowing lawns and tidying the gardens of all those neat white-walled houses and flats. Robbie, barely out of boyhood. Michael, so much older, he could have been Robbie's uncle. I looked at Michael's eager face and tried to imagine him skimming diazepam from bottles.

He must have felt me staring at him. 'Who are you?' he said to me.

'She's not staying,' June said. 'She used to teach me dance.'

June and I hadn't spoken since we'd got off the bus.

'Dancing?'

I nodded.

'I've never met a dancer.'

We stood by the table we'd found him at.

'I didn't know you did dancing, Mum.'

'Aye. There's a lot to catch up on.'

That galvanised him. He rubbed his hands together, pulled the chairs away from the table and told us to sit down. He asked if I had time for a drink before I went on my way and without looking at June I said yes and asked for a coffee. He seemed surprised at my accent.

'You sound like my wife,' he said.

'Do I?' I said.

He took his wallet from his pocket, hung his jacket over the back of one of the chairs and walked to the counter. I was irritated at June for being besotted with him, for showing none of the guard she should have shown, for not pushing her finger into his chest and telling him that the boy who hit his own mother should not be allowed anywhere near her, should never be allowed back. Instead she leaned towards me and said, 'Please don't start anything. I haven't seen him in seven years,' as if it was me who had the problem.

There he was, returning with our drinks on a tray, smiling and full of business.

'One for you, Mum, and one for you – what's your name?'

'Liz.'

He set down the coffees and sat down himself, grabbing two sticks of sugar and tearing the ends off.

'What brought you to these parts, Liz?'

'My partner died. So I moved back to the village where he was born.'

'What village is that?'

'Lennoxtown.'

I was wondering if he would work it out, somehow, that I was Robbie's, that Robbie was mine, but apart from a moment of recognition – Lennoxtown was where he was from – he treated me as if I was just a normal woman.

'I'm sorry about your partner,' he said, and he actually seemed kind.

A bus passed by the window and an elderly woman with a walking stick struggled in the doorway. Michael bounded towards the door. It was as if he was atoning for everything he'd ever done, and as he held the door open for the woman with her stick I caught him looking at his mum.

'It won't do you any good going over it,' June said to me.

'It will,' I said, and I was sorry that I would cause her anguish, and I'm still sorry for what she heard, but he needed to be told and I needed to say it.

'Pictures, Mum,' he said when he came back. He pulled an envelope from his coat pocket and took out some photos. 'That's their most recent school photo.'

'Very nice.'

'That's Chloe's prom last year.' His children stood on the doorstep of a house. The girl wore a dress. Her brother, younger, in a tracksuit, held a book in his hands.

'She's at college now. And Adam's in year nine at school.'

'Clever weans. Can I have that one? I've got the school one.' She pushed it across the table to her son. 'Julie sent it.'

'I forgot Julie would have sent you things.' He didn't seem to know what to do with it so he passed it to me.

'Good-looking children,' I said. 'I like their curls.'

That animated him. He held his own sandy hair between a finger and a thumb and said, 'God knows where they get it from.'

Robbie's brother has curls. So does Emily.

He put the photograph in his coat pocket and we sipped our drinks.

After June put her cup on its saucer and wiped her lips with a napkin she said in a steady way, 'What are you here for?'

Michael seemed embarrassed. He rested his wrists on the table's edge. He laughed, looked at me and then his mum.

'She's here,' he said, meaning me. 'I feel a bit stupid talking in front of her.'

I said nothing but watched him lean in towards his mum. He wasn't looking at me anymore. In a quiet voice he said, 'Leave it for now, eh?'

'No,' June said, her voice strong and loud. That's better, June, I thought.

The woman behind the counter shouted 'Toasted cheese and ham!' and Michael looked away from his mum.

'Shall we get some food?'

'No,' June said.

The woman carried the sandwich to a man who sat by the window.

'I take it you want money,' June said.

He squeezed the table edge, looked at me again then said, 'Yes.'

'That wasn't so hard.'

'I do want money but I want to apologise first.'

'For what?'

'For the whole lot. I'm sorry.'

For all that she'd said to me, I sensed that June had forgiven him years ago.

'I had counselling in the jail. They were really good. I had to face up to everything.' He glanced over at me again.

I spoke now. 'What did you go to jail for?'

There was a small beat before he spoke. I watched him turn his head from June to me.

'Tax fraud.'

I nodded. 'What do you mean by tax fraud?'

'I told a few lies on the tax return. We were quite a big outfit so they were quite big lies.'

He looked at me plainly and I carried on. 'It's not your first crime is it? Did anyone come to harm this time?'

He didn't like that. 'Fraud is a victimless crime. I was

greedy. Not bad.' I saw the underside of his tongue as he spoke. His diction was good.

'We can come to a loan arrangement,' June said. 'I've got an amount put aside for the children when they're twenty-one and I'm not touching that. But if you want a small loan I'll come to an arrangement with you.'

She should have said no. She should have told him he had a fucking cheek even being in the same space as her.

'Do you have a thing about money?' I said to him, goading him.

'Who even are you by the way?'

'You're about to leave, aren't you, Liz?'

'Robbie Watt was my partner. Do you remember him? Because you say fraud is a victimless crime but you've had victims before, haven't you?'

He leaned back in his seat and if I was to be kind I'd say he had distress and remorse in his face, but I'm not kind and I never wanted to be kind. He shat it, as Robbie would have said.

'Your mum was one of your victims wasn't she?' A worry about saying that lasted for about a second in my head. 'And Robbie was a victim too. And those old people you deceived, they were victims weren't they? And what about the schoolchildren whose lives you fucked up? What about the boy who overdosed on your stolen pills?'

'You don't know what you're talking about.'

June looked worried and I didn't like to see my strong and

stubborn friend take a tissue from her handbag and hold it in both hands as if waiting for tears, but it didn't stop me. I had to attack him, I had to.

'You've made a lifetime of thieving and bullying,' I said.

I was pleased, finally, to see anger in his face, to see it change from benign to hostile.

'Your thing isn't about money is it? It's about deceit and manipulation and power and you can't control yourself. Is that what your counsellor told you? Did you tell your counsellor you beat up your own mother? Did you tell her you beat up a teenager? You weak man coming all the way up here to swindle your mother out of her money.'

I wasn't afraid of him. I leaned towards him. I met his finger pointing at my face and I stared full at him when he said, 'Robbie was every bit as involved as I was. He loved taking the kids' tenners and spending them on his weed and his birds.'

'No.'

'Aye. He knew what he was doing. His eyes fucking lit up when he talked about dealing at the school. I said no!'

'You manipulated him.'

'Oh no. He got a whiff of the money and the power and he fucking went for it.'

'You groomed him. You ruined his childhood. He could never go back.'

'Nope. He groomed himself. He was all about expanding the business, getting some younger lads to work for us.'

June touched her son on the arm and said, 'That's enough now, Michael.'

'He's dead now, so you can't ask him, but believe me, he was every bit as involved as I was. And that's why I hit him. Because I knew he'd play the innocent little shite if we ever got caught. And that's exactly what he did. It's true isn't it, Mum? The police made him lie to stitch me up.'

'There might be some truth in that, aye.'

He did something strange then. He lunged towards June and put his arms around her neck.

'Forgive me, Mum,' he said. 'Forgive me. I did a terrible thing. I should never have hurt you. I can't get it out of my head. I'll go to my grave regretting what I did to you. I've had the counselling. I'm saying sorry. I'm sorry. I'm really sorry.'

'It's all right, Son,' she said and held him close.

He turned his head from her bosom and looked at me. 'I'm telling you, from the moment he came to work for me, that boy was slippery. And you can stay away from my mother.'

June sat there with her boy in her arms, patting him lightly, her face stiff yet jubilant. There was nothing else to say. Fuck them. I left them to their embrace and walked out of the cafe and across the road, back to the bus station, back to Lennoxtown.

I think cars are dangerous things that break down and cost too much money to run but when I closed the door and sat inside my own, parked up outside the sheltered housing, I was glad of it to cry in. I felt relieved to be away from that pair, cuddling in the cafe like nothing had ever happened, and I was happy to put my weight onto the steering wheel and feel myself get cold in that cold car. I should have known that June, for all her tough talk, felt the lack of her son like I felt the lack of Robbie. She would want him near her, to feel the heat off his skin: her own boy. She would welcome her body's sudden exhale, its release of stress and hate and its surge of stupid gulping tenderness.

If Robbie was with me in my car, wouldn't I question him about what Michael had said, wouldn't I demand he prove to me his actions were those of a senseless, grieving, gullible, foolish boy and only that, nothing worse, nothing pathological, nothing criminal? And when he told me what I wanted to hear wouldn't I believe him?

But he wasn't there and he couldn't tell me anything and in that cold car it cracked – the accumulation of his stories and my stories and our brief life. *Fêlure*. To crack. You don't crack in ballet like you jump or stretch or leap. There is no such thing, no such term.

I was driving to the nursery to pick up Emily and do God knows what when my phone rang. I pulled over. It was Sara. She wanted to meet with Emily and me that afternoon.

'Will you be home? Do you have a next of kin who could be there too?'

'No,' I said. 'This is all so unnecessary.'

'We'll do what we did before,' she said.

'Waste our time,' I said. 'In that case we might be home, we might not be.'

'It's a bit more serious now,' she said. 'I would advise you to be home.'

Of course. I was accused of something dangerous. It was an issue of child protection. An accusation made by a woman I'd met once on a street whose ex I'd quite enjoyed shagging.

I knew where she lived. I remember Paul telling me how easy it was to see his daughter even though he'd moved back to his mum's. He could see her jumping on her trampoline from his old bedroom window, the houses were that close. I told myself I would drive by to see if she was home. I wondered if his car was parked outside the house, if he was building that wall she wanted. Maybe I'd put my head at her window and stare inside to give her a fright. I'd tell her she was a cliché. The jealous, jilted ex. The stupid girl. The stupid pair.

That's when I turned off Main Street before I should have and went up a narrow road with cars parked on either side and found the house that was similar to Robbie's gran's except it was a whole house not a flat. I saw that it had a tidy lawn with a gravel border and a half-built wall and Paul's car was indeed parked outside.

My first thought was to shove my hand on my car horn, so I did that. I was going on instinct and impulse now like they trained us to do at dance college: go with your instincts, let one action move into another, keep the flow, retain the energy. The horn made a satisfying sound and I hit it again, holding my hand down. I saw Georgia's face at the side of a blind. I saw Paul's face at the upstairs window. I turned off the engine and got out of the car and stood at their gate.

'Paul!'

Nothing.

'I want to talk to you.'

Nothing. They were inside and gutless, away from their windows, in the sanctity of their sanctimonious house. People from other houses were at their windows now and I shouted again for Paul, for Georgia, for one of them to talk to me.

'It's a fucking lie, you know,' I yelled. 'Paul, do you even know what you've done?'

I picked up a piece of gravel and threw it at their front door.

'Paul!'

He appeared again at the upstairs window, opened it wide and stuck his head out.

'What are you playing at?'

'I've lost my job.'

'What?'

'Do you know what she's done?'

'Who?'

'Her.'

'Georgia?'

'She called social services on me.'

He seemed as if he genuinely didn't know what I was talking about. I saw the downstairs blinds twitch and it was all the encouragement I needed. I ran up their garden path and got my fist and thumped it against the window and then I stepped back to shout up to Paul.

'Calm down, Liz.' He leaned out of the window.

'I can't. She's accused me. And you told her. I did nothing wrong, Paul. I've lost my job.'

'I didn't know, honestly.'

'But you told her. Who do you think I am?'

'It'll blow over.'

'It won't blow over. It's social services.'

'Wait a minute, I'm coming out.' He closed the window but I heard shouting. I heard Georgia saying, No, you won't go out, and then there was nothing and I was standing waiting, with my heart thudding and my head roaring. I didn't know what to do next but then Georgia was standing at the downstairs window again, pulling up the blind and opening the window. She stuck her arm out of the window and pointed at me and said, 'I was right to call social services.'

'No you weren't.'

'You left your daughter on her own in a car park where you couldn't see her.'

'What's it to you?'

'That's child cruelty.'

'No it's not.'

'You're a lazy mother.'

'No, I'm not.'

'Too lazy to take care of your own child.'

'That's not true.'

'Too lazy to get a boyfriend of your own.'

'He came to me.'

'You took him because he was there and you couldn't be arsed to look for your own man.'

'Bullshit.'

'He's my daughter's dad.'

'You kicked him out, love. You're the lazy one, the stupid one, acting like you've got all the time in the world with your on-off, on-off carry-on. You stupid, jealous, ignorant little girl.'

Oh God, and to think I was a feminist. To think I danced side by side with other girls who knew that if we were all good we all became brilliant. We shone and we tapped and we kicked in sync and stood in a line with our arms crossed around each other's waists and we turned slowly, kicking high like the Lido girl I could have been, dancing on a stage in Paris, and we did this night after night and here I was throwing insults with a girl I didn't care about over a man who'd let me down.

'You're not welcome here, and neither was your scumbag bastard boyfriend,' Georgia said and closed the window.

Despair made me pick up a stone and hurl it at their windows. It bounced off the glass, ineffectual, like everything I had tried to do in Lennoxtown. Useless. Bouncing off hardness. So I picked up more stones and threw harder. Fucking double-triple-glazing, hardened glass. Paul would have got a deal from one of his mates to put in the quality stuff.

From behind the window Georgia pointed a finger at me. I couldn't make out what she was saying so I picked up a brick and hurled it at the window but it was so bloody heavy it didn't even reach. It scared her though. She stepped away. Good. I found another brick and at last I smashed a window. It made a pleasing sound and the shattered glass had a satisfying look about it. I tried again with another brick but missed. Again and again and again I tried to smash the windows. I kicked over a pot of spring flowers and one of those miniature fir trees and only stopped when Paul came charging out of the front door and grabbed my whole body from behind and pinned my arms with his arms to my sides. It was a pose that without the force and the anger and viewed from a distance might be perceived as loving. That *pas de deux* again.

'Enough,' he said in my ear.

'You've wrecked me,' I said. 'I know I'm mad but I'm not bad like that.'

'I didn't know she was going to phone social services.'

'I think you did.'

A police car without its siren but with its blue lights flashing parked outside the house. Paul let go of his grip on me and I see this now as some sort of idiocy or cry for help or plain self destruction but I picked up another brick and held it high above my head. I could have crashed it down anywhere. I could have hurled it against the window, I could have hurled it at Paul, I could have smashed it onto my head, and that's what I wanted to do right then, I wanted to smash it down onto my own skull and be done with it.

'Put the brick down,' the policewoman said.

'Liz, put it down,' Paul said.

I could eat the fucking brick. I could swallow the brick and make it tear my insides so I bled and the new pain would take the place of the old pain that was inside me, every hour, every minute, every second of every day. I squeezed the brick hard, wanting to make my hand bleed. And then I threw it at the windows. Fucking smashed one again!

There was a terrible scream from inside the house and then cries – two cries – Georgia calling Paul's name over and over and a smaller cry, a wailing cry. Georgia came out of the house carrying Holly, their child, and Holly's face had blood on it, her head was cut, her mouth was wide with wailing pain. Oh my God, I wanted to run to that child and tell her I was sorry sorry sorry. But there was hysteria. There were bats in the air. Paul raced to Holly and took her from Georgia. Georgia flailed her arms and screamed at me, a horrible keening that she had no control over, I know she had no control over. The policeman ran to her side and made a call on his radio. Paul checked Holly's head. A neighbour jumped over the half-made wall and held out a tea towel which they used to wipe the blood from Holly's face.

I stood still, my hands at my sides, my fists no longer clenched.

'I presume you want to press charges?' the policewoman said.

'Yes we do,' said Georgia.

Paul said nothing.

'We'll need you to come with us,' the policewoman said. 'We are arresting you—'

It was then I realised. 'What time is it?'

Nobody moved.

'What time is it?'

Paul checked his watch. The police kept their eyes on me.

'It's five to twelve,' he said.

'I have to pick up my daughter from nursery.'

'We need to take you to the station first.'

'No. I have to pick her up.'

'We're not communicating very well, are we?' the policewoman said. 'You'll be coming with us.'

I turned to Paul. 'Please,' I begged him. 'Please can you get her?'

Georgia cut in. 'Don't you fucking dare.'

'Could your mum...?'

'It would be the least I could do,' he said to Georgia.

'No. It's the worst you could do.' She held her crying daughter close.

Resisting arrest. It was futile but I tried it. I ran away from them all, in the direction I was sure would lead me to the nursery, and I ran without looking back until I heard the policeman's heavy steps and felt his hands on me and after that I was as vicious as I could be. I kicked and screamed and punched and threw my body onto the ground, refusing to cooperate when he tried to stand me up. I hurt myself. I have strong legs so I expect I hurt the policeman too. In the end he restrained me and I let him lead me to the police car. We passed my car with its driver's door wide open, parked far from the kerb where I'd dumped it a few minutes earlier.

They drove me through Lennoxtown to the police station, away from Emily who had been on her visit to the primary school and would soon be waiting for me and wanting to tell me all about it. I was beyond myself. I pictured her standing with her coat and her outdoor shoes on, the name of her buddy held like a jewel on her tongue, the first thing she would tell me. The second thing she would tell me was that I was the last mummy again, always the last mummy.

I don't like to think about what happened next. Emily tells me the same small details each time I ask. She tells me that she waited until all the mummies and daddies had picked up all the boys and girls and when I didn't come they let her stay for lunch and when I still didn't come she stayed in the nursery for the afternoon and after that a lady came to pick her up. The lady had a playhouse in her garden and Emily played in that. I know very little else.

'What did she give you for tea?'

'I can't remember.'

'What was the lady like?'

'I can't remember. I missed you. Where were you? Why didn't you come for me?'

I asked her the same questions and she replied with the same questions of her own.

14.

At the police station they took my name and address and told me to empty my pockets. I gave them a twenty pence piece, my door keys and two hair slides that I'd clipped together after Emily had tugged them from her hair. Some hair was caught in the ends and I wanted to pull it from the slides and keep it. The policewoman took the slides from me. Maybe she thought I'd use them to dig bluntly at my veins or something.

I had no phone to give them because I'd left it in my car and I wondered if Paul would keep it safe for me. It was unlikely; he would be tending to Holly's cut face and placating her mother. I saw the futility and badness in what I'd done. I saw too the irony in leaving my phone in the car a second time.

'What about my daughter?' I asked.

'We've contacted social services and they've contacted the nursery,' one of the police told me.

'Who is going to pick her up?'

'Don't you have a relative who can get her?'

'Can you call Ruth from my work?' I asked. I even gave them June's name. They said they would pass the numbers on to my lawyer. I was to get a lawyer. I had a right to a lawyer.

'Is the little girl okay? The girl that got hurt?'

Oh, the contempt he showed me. 'The girl you hurled a brick at? She'll be in A&E just now.'

They charged me with assault, damage to property and resisting arrest, gave me a blue mat to lie on and took me to a cell.

I sat in the tiled room, a stink of urine coming from the toilet, and listened to voices from other cells. Through a high window I saw a rectangle of white sky. I had time to question Robbie. I wondered if he had known what Michael McDermott was doing. Had he received a tenner here and there for taking the old folks' prescriptions to the chemist and for keeping quiet while Michael snipped a line of tablets off a blister pack? Maybe Robbie and his friends were taking pills themselves so selling them was an easy next step. I remembered Robbie's refusal to speak about Lennoxtown and his reluctance to return. Perhaps you never really know a person. Perhaps I'd fallen for a man with a kink in his integrity, a penchant for stealing, concealing the truth and hoodwinking his lovers. Who knew I would throw bricks with intent to break glass, with intent to damage? Who knew I would hurt a small child in the process, causing her pain and making her bleed? Yet it was in me all the time. Those thoughts disturbed me. I thought I knew Robbie and he me. I thought I knew myself.

At one-thirty a policeman took me to an interview room. He told me I would be formally charged. First there were people who wanted to talk with me.

'What people?'

'You have a social worker.'

'Yes.'

'She's here.'

I was ashamed, but there she was, pulling back the chair and taking the lid off her cup of tea.

'I got one for you,' Sara said, 'but I couldn't remember how you took it.'

'Just milk.'

'I guessed right.'

The tea was too hot to drink. I watched the steam rise.

'There's a lot to unpick,' Sara said and she talked about the situation I found myself in because of the arrest and what had come before. 'These are two separate issues but they are connected obviously. And my job first and foremost is to safeguard Emily, to make sure she can be safely fed, clothed and nurtured.'

I listened as best as I could but the slowness of her note-taking was unbearable so I stood up and said, 'I need to get my daughter.'

Sara put her pen down.

'I've recommended that Emily be looked after for the time being. That certainly means tonight. And until I've spoken with other professionals—'

'What?'

'We need to assess your case and I can't do that until at least tomorrow.'

'No, what do you mean looked after?'

'We'll place her in emergency foster care.'

'No you won't.'

'Liz, we don't have much choice. You've been arrested and you're in custody. You have no next of kin.'

'She doesn't need foster care. She's not been abused.'

'Abuse comes in many forms.'

'How fucking dare you!' I was throwing stones. I was picking up bricks and hurling them.

'Cut out the swearing please. I will arrange a meeting to go over it all.'

'Do it now then. Instead of talking to me. Go and do your job.'

'Liz, sit down please.'

I didn't sit down. I stood by the wall and looked at the door and Sara at the table and realised that the world had closed in on me. We were detained, Emily and I.

'Where will she go?' This was ridiculous. I was her mother.

'She'll stay with a temporary foster carer.'

'Who?'

'We have a bank of very good foster carers. She'll be safe and well looked after.'

'Where?'

She wouldn't tell me and she was right not to because I would have gone straight there when I got out, without a doubt. I would have barged down the door or smashed the windows all over again.

'Is it likely,' I asked, 'is it likely they will keep Emily? Look at me. I'm not a risk. I won't stay. I'll go back to my mum's in London. We'll leave here and never come back. I'll go on my medication. I've not been myself.'

Even when Robbie was alive it was hard to find the immense love people had told me about. I think I may have had post-natal depression before he died. Maybe they would have got to it eventually but in the weeks and months after his death any depression I had merged with grief and I carried on like that. I do remember thinking one morning as I lifted her from her cot that if she did die in the night, I would feel her loss. So I must love her. I must. My feelings were messed up, I know that. I did not dare speak of them to the bereavement counsellor. I did not dare admit I possessed them before Robbie's heart gave out. I could not reveal them to the social worker in front of me. I think feelings are confusing. What was this I was feeling now? Was it love? Pain? Fear? Whatever it was, it hurt.

I tried one more time. 'Look at me,' I said. 'Please, look at me. Emily's okay with me. You needn't worry. Can you help me get out of here please?'

The look she gave me seemed genuine. She promised to work as quickly as she could and told me to be prepared for a meeting. 'Don't do anything stupid,' she said. 'We'll sort this out.'

'Will I be able to speak to her?'

'I'll try to make that happen.'

'Can I get her back tomorrow?'

'I want you to be reunited as soon as possible. Let's deal with tomorrow tomorrow.'

After she'd gone, the police told me a lawyer was available to talk to me. A man named Graham whose wristwatch clicked on the table when he leaned forward to speak. He told me I would stay overnight in the cell and be taken to court in Glasgow the next day. 'Is there anyone you want me to call?' I gave him my mum's number. 'Ask her to come to Lennoxtown,' I said. 'Tell her Emily is in care. Temporarily. She'll take it badly. Make sure she understands she has to come.' I imagined the lawyer in his rolled-up shirt sleeves repeating my message while my mum gasped out her shock and assailed him with questions.

I waited in the cell. Gold suffused the sky, as if the day was on the brink of tears, and the room brightened. The toilet and tiles shone and dust motes were gold when I moved my blanket. Then dullness came and there was nothing else to look at or do. I put the blanket over my shoulders. Despite my anguish I was bored. At one audition I spent six hours in a studio with dozens of girls and drank diet coke and eked out rice cakes so I wasn't too full that I couldn't dance but wasn't too weak either. During the endless day I promised myself if I got the job I would be a better person. I would be kinder to my mum and my dad too because he was alive then. I would give some of my wages to charity. I would be selfless. Funny how we cheat to get what we want. In the cell I made a selfish prayer to Emily. I will play with you whenever you want, I will take a bath with you whenever you want. I will listen, I will read, I will dance, I will treasure you if you come back. I never got the audition. The sky darkened. I lay on my blue mattress under my blanket, fucking starving, thinking of Emily, wiping my streaming eyes and nose with toilet roll, waiting for morning.

It came, along with breakfast. After that, the police took me to the Sheriff Court in Glasgow for a custody appearance. I knew the way. The court steps were occupied by other families, groups of two or three people smoking. No children. Emily would be awake now.

I waited in a cell with a woman who didn't speak. I was glad of the company however silent it was. A few minutes later another woman joined us. She wore a summer dress and sandals. We spoke briefly and then settled to quiet, looking up from time to time when one of us moved or coughed.

'I need a cigarette,' the new woman said. 'Jesus, I could murder a cigarette.'

The other woman sat with her head in her hands, her long ponytail nearly touching the floor, and complained that she needed to go to the toilet. 'I am actually going to wet myself,' she said. 'My bladder's fucked since having kids.' She stood up and banged on the door shouting with an urgency that was truthful. 'Come on to fuck; I'm bursting here!'

They finally let her go and she came back happier, redoing her ponytail. She smiled at me as she sat at her space on the bench.

'My pelvic floor's shot too,' I said and she looked at me as if she didn't know why I would say such a thing. 'Since having children,' I said. 'How old are yours?'

'Grown up now,' the woman said. 'Twenty-one and twenty-three. My youngest is at university. My oldest doesn't speak to me.' She stood up, took her hair out of its ponytail again and combed it with her fingers.

'That's my biggest fear,' the other woman said. She'd taken off her sandals. Her toenails were painted pink.

'What?'

'That my kids won't speak to me.'

We both stared at the woman. 'They live with their dad.'

The other woman dived in. 'Your choice or social work's?'

'Bit of both.'

'Do you see them?' I asked.

She nodded. 'I get them from school once a week and they have their tea with me. But they don't stay with me. They live with their dad and his mum.'

The woman with the ponytail held her jeans by the waistband and pulled them up, walking her legs on the spot. 'Bloody things are falling down.' She was thin. 'I wish they'd let me have a smoke.' She paced up and down the room and I watched her feet as she walked.

We were quiet. I expect the women heard the roaring of motorbikes from outside on the street because I did. I expect they heard footsteps and voices too.

'My daughter's in temporary foster care,' I said, not sure

what I would say next, if anything, but I felt like telling these women. It seemed appropriate.

'Since when?' the woman with the sandals asked.

'Since yesterday. She spent the night somewhere else.'

'Is this your first time detained?'

'Yes.'

'You'll be fine.'

I nodded. They didn't ask me why I was detained and I didn't ask them.

'Have yours ever…?'

'Been in foster care?'

The women shook their heads.

'It was a threat. But I always had someone who could watch them for me. I tell my daughter it could have been worse, she could have been taken off me, but she still wants nothing to do with me.'

'Have you not got anyone?' the woman with the sandals asked me.

'No.'

'Where's her dad?'

'Dead.'

'Where's your mum?'

'London.'

The woman with the ponytail smiled at me as if to say, 'Chin up,' and we waited again, in silence. And then the other woman nudged her sandals with her toes and spoke as if we'd never stopped talking, louder this time, more confident. 'It's easier to be a mother when I don't have them all the time.'

'Of course it is.' The woman with the ponytail hitched up her jeans.

'I'm serious. It actually suits me. I can do the nice stuff. I don't get so stressed out. They never behaved for me when I had them every day.'

'That's what they don't see. Especially my eldest. It was hard work bringing them up on my own. I tried my best.'

'Some people are better at being parents than others.' The woman nudged her sandals again.

'Some people are natural born mothers. Others aren't.'

'I'm not a natural born mother,' I said. 'I wish I was.'

The women shook their heads and seemed to dismiss my complaint.

'They're my life though. I don't know what I'd do without them.' The woman wiped dirt from the soles of her feet then bent to buckle her sandals.

'Same.' The other woman stopped her walking and leaned against the wall.

I wondered if I would be better without Emily and if she would be better without me. I really did consider it deeply. I concluded then that I wanted her. That doesn't mean she was better with me. But I wanted her. I said my selfish prayer again.

'Don't you find it hard to be on the straight and narrow now?' the woman with the ponytail said. 'When my kids were young and living with me that was the time in my life I tried my hardest to sort myself out. For them.'

'The hardest time for me was when I had them all day every day,' the other woman said. 'I was beside myself.'

'Whatever works,' the woman with the ponytail said, and she reminded me a little of me as she did a dance move to some absent music, a shake of the hips, a bounce of the knees, a click of the fingers, holding on to her jeans with one hand. Then she sat down and we waited. After an hour I was called from the cell and told I would be released on report. My court appearance would come another day. Today I was free to find my way back through the rain to Lennoxtown and to Emily.

15.

It was a relief to be outside in the fresh air and rain. Cars had their headlights on despite the daylight. A boy walked along the courtroom steps, holding a woman's hand. The woman looked like Caroline, my first friend from the library, but it wasn't her. And then I saw June. She stood on the steps wearing wellington boots and she held an umbrella. We didn't hug or anything like that.

'I was just on my way in to find you,' she said.

'How did you know I was here?'

'Ruth.'

'They released me.'

'Good.'

We walked towards the road.

'Where's your son?'

'I don't think we should talk about Michael.'

'Is he still in Glasgow?'

'We shouldn't talk about him.'

She was right; we shouldn't talk about him. I would never want to hear of any good she'd found in Michael in that cafe or any new defence of him. To me, he did a wrong to Robbie, an appalling wrong, and it was best to say no more.

At the roadside June hailed a black cab, opened the door and shook rain from her umbrella.

'What are you doing?' I said.

'Getting you home.'

'It's too expensive.'

'Not today.'

I watched the numbers rise on the meter all the way to Lennoxtown.

'Are you hungry?' June said as we came along Main Street.

'Yes.'

'Wait here please, driver.'

We bought a poke of chips each from the fish and chip shop. I held mine gently in the crook of my arm as the taxi took us to Robbie's gran's flat.

My car was parked outside. Paul must have driven it and posted the keys and my phone through the letter box because they were there on the floor when I opened the door. I had a voice message on my phone from a letting agent about a request I'd made to view a flat. There was a text message from Paul, sent the day before, saying *Holly will be OK. No stitches. Small graze. I'll see if I can convince G to drop the charges. Only because you're not in your right mind. But we're done. No contact please. Good luck, pal.*

I called Sara who told me she was due to discuss my case with colleagues. Emily would stay another night in care but the temporary order would most likely be lifted and I could have her back. There would be a thorough assessment to come – this wasn't over – but living with my mum would be seen as a good and necessary step. June took my chips from me and told me to take off my wet coat and shoes. She put the television on and we ate our chips on our laps in the living room.

'I'll need to pack,' I said. 'We're not staying.'

'Eat your chips first. Get your strength up.'

Sitting side by side she said she remembered eating chips out of newspaper in that very room over fifty years ago. 'Same old shite in the news now as there was then, I expect,' she said. After we'd eaten she helped me pack some of our things and said it felt fitting to be doing this in reverse so many years later. She put Emily's books into a plastic bag and said, 'I do regret dragging you into all this.'

'I wish you hadn't.'

'For what it's worth I know that boy would have turned out all right. He did turn out all right, didn't he?' She turned to face me. 'Did he ever talk about me? Robbie?'

I could have lied. It was like me to lie. But she'd have asked me what he said and I'd have had to make up more lies. So I told her no, he never did.

'Well, that's a surprise. Because he knew me well. And because he saw us once. Aye, he's always known. I knocked on the door when I knew Audrey was away. Robbie was coming along the street, swinging his boot bag. And his granda, him, opened the front door. He put his arms around me and held me tight. I think he was consoling me. I like to think he felt as much as I still did but I think it was just consolation he was giving me. You can't get over anything. You think you can. But you are who you are. He gave me a hankie and that just about broke me. After I'd wiped my eyes I saw your Robbie staring at me. At us. His wee schoolboy eyes. He'd seen everything and nothing. I said bye-bye to his granda and patted Robbie on the arm as I went by, and that was me. So Robbie knew and never said a word. I have no doubt. Which made what Michael did to him especially cruel.'

Yes.

'June, do I seem mentally unwell to you?' I asked her.

I caught her frown before she changed her face. She shook her head. 'They'll just be checking you won't harm the lassie. Which you won't.'

'They charged me with assault. I accidently hurt a child.'

I heard June's intake of breath. 'Ruth said.'

My lawyer had told me that the Crown could prosecute me even if Georgia dropped the charges. Which I knew she wouldn't.

'I didn't mean to hurt her. I really didn't.' I thought of Paul and Georgia wiping blood from Holly's forehead, giving hot milk and treats and comfort and feeling violent towards me. I thought of Emily spending two nights in a stranger's house.

'Do you think she slept? Will she be missing me? They'll have given her a toothbrush, won't they?'

'They take good care of the kids,' June said.

I cried into a pile of Emily's dirty clothes, felt June's hand on my back and remembered what a consolation it was to be soothed. I made my prayer again and told Emily I would soothe and cuddle and comfort whenever she wanted and whatever she did, however busy I was, however crazy I was. Then, because I knew it was the right thing to do, I asked June to leave. She need not burden me with her impenetrable sadness when my loss was in some corner of Lennoxtown in some room in a house where they changed the sheets whenever one child left and a new child arrived.

'It was nice knowing you, June.'

'It was nice knowing you too.'

'You were good to me.'

'I was. I hustled all those folk to your dance class.'

'I know it was you who made them come.'

'Goodbye, Liz.'

In the new silence, I heard Emily's voice loud in my head, crying like the seagulls so far from the coast.

At a few minutes past four in the afternoon my mum rang the bell. I took her suitcase from her and offered her chips, cold, but they could be microwaved.

'I'll take some. It's quite a journey.' She looked around her. 'So this is where you've been.'

The microwave pinged and we stood in the kitchen while she ate the chips and I made tea. I'd forgotten how tall she was. Like me.

'You look well,' I said.

'Thank you.'

'You don't need to say I look well. I know I don't.'

She appraised me like she's always done and I saw a bit of pity and a bit of love.

She said, 'I've made up your room for you. I can't give Emily her own room straight away but I expect she'll want to be in with you anyway.'

Emily.

'Has Alan moved in?'

'He put his guitars in the spare room. I don't know why I agreed to it. So now I have an excuse to tell him to put them in his son's garage or up in the loft. But Emily will get her room back. He knew what he was taking on.'

'We won't be there for long.'

'Be as long as you like.'

I shook my head. My mum raised her voice. 'Liz, I don't have the words you have and I haven't had the life you've had, but I mean it when I say I'll look after you.'

I thought about not saying it but I said it anyway: 'You were hard on me after Dad died.'

'Your dad had just died.'

'You got over him too quickly.'

'Well I think you're taking too long to get over Robbie.'

We stood in silence.

My mum took another chip then said, 'Come on, let's get you packed.'

16.

They said Emily could come home to me because my mum had promised to let us live with her. They were happy with that. They would speak to social services in London and if I didn't abide by what the London social services said, by God, I would be clamped down upon. The date of my court case would be sent to my mum's and I'd have to return for that, but finally my days in Lennoxtown were ending.

I collected Emily from a place they called the contact centre. It was a room in the social services offices with some chairs and children's toys. I waited alone in the room. I heard a gentle voice, saw a woman step inside and hold open the door then say, 'On you go.' Emily came in. She looked clean. She wore clothes I'd never seen and clutched a teddy I'd never seen. Somebody had brushed her hair and Emily had let whoever it was plait it neatly. It suited her.

'Hi darling,' I said.

Neither of us moved.

I held out my arms but Emily stayed where she was, by the door.

'Emily—' I said, but I didn't finish my sentence because I didn't know what else to say.

She looked around her at the toys in the room and she held her teddy by its arm. 'She gave me this one because I left mine at home.'

'It's nice. Does it have a name?'

'No.'

The woman at the door said, 'How about you come through into the room.'

Emily stepped inside and the woman closed the door. 'There,' she said.

'Have you got a hug for me, Emily?'

She came to me and I put my arms around her but she kept her arms at her sides. I couldn't reach my lips to her face so I had to kiss her hair. That was good enough for me.

'I got a sticker,' she said and turned in my arms to show me a yellow sticker that said Great Work.

'Who gave you that?'

'I can't remember.'

'Was it the lady you stayed with?'

'No.'

'Was it from nursery?'

'I got it from my school,' Emily said.

'Oh yes.' I remembered her visit to the primary school. There was a pain in my throat from trying not to cry.

'Where have you been?' Emily said.

'I had to go somewhere very suddenly. I'm sorry,' I said.

That wasn't a good enough answer but Emily accepted it. 'When are we going home?' she said.

I looked up at the woman and said, 'Now, I think.' The woman nodded and I stood up. But Emily seemed confused. She held tight to her teddy. I didn't know what the matter was, but the woman seemed to understand.

'You can take your teddy with you,' she said. 'You don't have to leave it behind.'

That cheered Emily. She showed me the red jumper it wore and asked me to take it off for her. Then she asked me to put it on again. So I did.

'Come on,' I said. 'I have a surprise for you. Your granny's here.'

'Is she coming to stay?'

No. She was coming to take us away.

17.

First we had to go to her concert at the nursery. It would have been too much to take her away without letting her sing the songs she'd hummed to herself when she played or walked or ate. So we stayed longer than I wanted.

She also had a cardiology appointment. My mum and I took Emily into Glasgow to the hospital. I drove this time, not wanting to relive the bus journey and the bus station or be reminded of June's son. There must have been something written in Emily's notes about my behaviour because they spoke slowly and treated me carefully and spent a lot of time talking to my mum to make sure she understood too. The doctor told us unequivocally that Emily's heart was no different to any other child's heart, but to be safe, they said, and given her father's death, she would need checks throughout her life. They told me they would write to Emily's GP. How we will ever see that letter or pass it on to a new GP in London I don't know. I should have asked for something in writing there and then. I'm annoyed I didn't because this is important.

Ruth accompanied me to say goodbye to my dancers in the sheltered housing. She sat at another table and did her paperwork. Senga and Agnes came to the lounge wearing their ballet shoes and I had to tell them that there was no class.

'We've got a new teacher next week,' Eve said, because she had asked a friend if she knew of a dancer and her friend had recommended a young woman, recently graduated from college, who was looking for experience. So that was that. Their lessons would continue.

They were all there – Charlie, John, Alice, Agnes, Senga, Eve – apart from June. They wished me luck and told me they were sad to see me go, that the classes wouldn't be the same no matter how good this new girl was.

'We'll miss your little dancing displays,' Eve said, and although I laughed, remembering the times I'd dropped to splits or tap danced across the floor for a laugh, I hoped they wouldn't ask me to do anything then. They didn't.

'I'm sorry about my other display,' I said, 'the other day.'

'The interrogation?' John asked.

'I was a bit much, wasn't I? Especially with Alice. I'm sorry Alice.'

'Don't worry, she'll have forgotten it already,' said Eve.

We looked at Alice who wagged a chastising finger at Eve but let us laugh. 'Losing yourself is devastating,' she said.

'We know, pet,' Eve said. 'I'm sorry. We know.'

I hugged them goodbye while Ruth watched me from her paperwork. I didn't go up to June's door and now I wish I had. Perhaps I'll write. Perhaps I'll see her when I go to court.

Emily chose a favourite dress and asked me to give her a cruise face. I put glitter on her cheeks and eyelids and brushed her hair. The rasping sound was satisfying as I mothered her curls into bunches.

'Sit at the front, Mummy,' she said. 'Don't be late.'

'I won't be.'

'Please don't be late because you're sometimes late.'

'I won't be late.'

I wasn't late because my mum was with me and we stayed out after dropping Emily at nursery. We were first in the queue. The children sat in a semi-circle on the carpet. I spotted Emily and she greeted me with waving hands. I gave her two slow thumbs up and she put her hands to her mouth and giggled. The headteacher welcomed us and then the children sang their songs. 'Five Speckled Frogs', 'Allyballybee', 'Three Craws', 'Five Currant Buns in a Baker's Shop'. One of the teachers put a tabard with a number two around Emily's neck and she acted the part of a currant bun who was taken away and eaten.

My kid is tough, I thought. She can learn songs and actions and perform them to strangers. She can sit cross-legged for thirty minutes and fidget no more and no less than the other kids. She can seek out my eyes and be reassured because I'm there. She can sing. It's not her voice shouting louder than any other child but I can see her lips moving and I know she's singing. She's enjoying it. My kid gets up and eats her breakfast and goes to nursery every morning and plays with other kids I don't know and talks with nursery staff I don't know and then she waits for me to pick her up to take her to a home she has made her home because I say it's home. As long as I'm there she's happy. She doesn't need much or want much but she needs me. She likes me. She believes me. My kid is tough. She has love and rage and sadness and a mother who is adrift with her loss.

I was thinking all this as I watched her concert. When it was over I clapped and clapped and then lifted her up and made sure I hugged her for as long as she wanted to be hugged. That was her last day of nursery. On the way out, I told her we would find another nursery in London and we would find another school. She cried.

I wanted us to see the Campsies for one last time so with my mum on a bus to Glasgow and our car packed with all our stuff I took her there. The wind battered our jackets as we crossed the car park. The recent rain had muddied the path up the hillside. Emily trod through puddles. We slipped at times and stopped when we found some grass we liked the look of.

'We'll do what daddy used to do when he was a little boy,' I said.

I didn't have a clue what he did as a boy. Robbie said he hated Lennoxtown, but I liked it. I liked the Campsie Fells and so did Emily. Even on damp and cloudy days the view was restless and striking.

I made something up. I said Robbie used to collect stones and pebbles and make nature pictures out of them. Emily had a happy time collecting stones and finding feathers, grass, flowers and twigs to put by her picture.

'There. Daddy would like your sculpture,' I said.

'My daddy was a fast runner,' she said.

'He was.'

'And this is a picture of him running. That's his legs, that's his arms, that's his feet.' She was pleased with her work.

I'd brought a candle and tried to light it but the flame went out.

'Bloody breeze,' I said. The grass around us turned circles in the wind's gusts.

I tried again but we were too exposed.

'Bloody breeze,' Emily said.

'Don't copy me.'

I put the candle and matches in my pocket.

'Did he die because of me, Mummy?' Her question took me by surprise.

'No, he didn't die because of you, Emily. Not at all. Not at all. No. He died because his heart got tired all of a sudden. It had ticked all its ticks. Nothing to do with you. Nothing, to do with you.'

I kneeled next to her and squeezed her tight to me.

'I love you, Mummy,' she said.

'I love you. We love you.'

The wind pushed our hair from our foreheads and necks.

'Why do you think it was because of you?' I said.

'Because I came and then Daddy had to go.'

'Sometimes bad things happen. Life is like that.'

'I wish I had a dad.'

'You do have a dad.'

'One who is alive.'

'What would you do with him?'

'Go roller skating. He was good at roller skating.'

He'd never spoken of roller skating. I'd never spoken of it. She must have added that to whatever image she'd made of him in her mind.

We hadn't talked about her night away from me and I wanted to say something. 'I'm sorry about the time you spent in that house with that lady. You must have wondered where I'd gone. I didn't stop thinking about you. I'm sorry.'

'That's okay, Mummy.'

'It's not okay. I did a bad thing,' I said.

'Like smoking?'

'Yes, like smoking.'

She looked horrified so I had to backtrack and say maybe not as bad as smoking. We are breeding a generation of zealots, I thought, but I also thought that Robbie would be pleased, he who had never smoked in his life, who drank in moderation, who advised me to cut down on the drink almost as soon as he met me.

'I thought you weren't coming back,' Emily said.

'Did you?'

'I cried.'

'I'm sorry.'

'That's okay.'

I stood up and hoisted her onto my shoulders and we stood for a while, staring out at the flat light on the fields and the grey sky, until she waggled her legs and I felt her heels against my chest.

'Let's go, Mummy,' she said.

'Bye, Campsies,' I said.

'My picture. Will it be here when we come back?'

'It might be. Possibly. Probably.'

Sometimes it's okay to lie.

I called it a road trip and we drove south, away from Lennoxtown. My mum used her return train ticket and said she would get home before us to put some tea in the oven.

Robbie liked me for my spirit and my flair. He liked me for my hard side, the brittle bit of me that could tell a person to fuck off or stand up to strangers. Robbie liked me for my guts and the way I practised and practised and got myself through the auditions and onto the cruise ships. He liked me for what I could have been. He liked me because I didn't mess about when I found him. It takes guts to do that. He liked me because we made Emily.

I don't know what he'd think of me now. I don't know what he'd say about me and Emily and how, five years in, we're still stumbling along, making mistakes and making up. I can only imagine. I don't know what he'd say if I confronted him about his past and the trouble he was in and the trouble he caused. Because I would have confronted him. Damn right I would. But there's no way of getting to him now. He's gone. He's a flash of silver on a seagull's belly. He's the yellow on the Campsie Fells. They really are yellow. I just wish the sun would shine on them more. When it does, they light up in gold as if they are made from the very sun itself, from the very essence of him, from the very essence of love.

Acknowledgements

I would like to thank the following people and organisations for their help with research: Catherine Armstrong, Tim Baker, Cove Park, Dance Factory, Helen Griffin, Maxine Hobson, Laurence Nicolson, Ronnie Mackintosh, Claricia Parinussa Kruithof, Carol Sallows, Anna Williams, and the staff and residents of Whitehill Court in Kirkintilloch including Margaret, Isabel, Joan and Ronald.

Thank you to my fellow writers for reading and commenting on extracts: Ailsa Crum, Emma Lennox, David Manderson, Emily Munro, Maureen Myant, Bert Thomson and Les Wood. Thanks also to the Campsie Writers' Group, especially Muriel Connell and Marion Donnachie.

Thank you to Amelia Collingwood, Nathan Connolly, and Jordan Taylor-Jones at Dead Ink Books. And thank you, of course, to Millie Hoskins.

Respect and thanks to the friends who have looked after my kids or helped me out at the school gates: Andrew, Clair, Gayle, Lynne, Lesley, Louise, Lucianne, Marissa, Peter and Sharon.

Love and thanks to Vic and Jan Irvine, Claire Hamilton, Alex Irvine, Jane Havemann, Vicky McCarthy, Gill Woods and Linda and Laurence Byrne. Even more love and thanks to Eddie, Arlene, Isla and Sadie Burns.

About the Author

Alison Irvine was born in London to Antipodean parents. She gained a distinction in her Masters in Creative Writing at Glasgow University and her first novel, *This Road is Red*, was shortlisted for the 2011 Saltire First Book of the Year Award. In addition to her fiction work, she writes creative non-fiction as part of the artist collective Recollective. She lives in Glasgow with her husband and three daughters.

About Dead Ink

Supported by Arts Council England, we're focussed on developing the careers of new and emerging authors.

Our readers form an integral part of our team. You don't simply buy a Dead Ink book, you invest in the authors and the books you love.

You can keep up to date with the latest Dead Ink events, workshops, releases and calls for submissions by signing up to our mailing list.

deadinkbooks.com